90 DAYS

CASSIE VERANO

BLACK
ODYSSEY
MEDIA

WWW.BLACKODYSSEY.NET

Published by
BLACK ODYSSEY MEDIA

www.blackodyssey.net
Email: info@blackodyssey.net

90 DAYS TO LOVE. Copyright © 2025 by CASSIE VERANO

Library of Congress Control Number: 2024916884

First Trade Paperback Printing: April 2025
ISBN: 978-1-957950-47-1
ISBN: 978-1-957950-48-8 (e-book)

Cover Design by Ashlee Nassar of Designs With Sass

10 9 8 7 6 5 4 3 2 1

Manufactured in the United States of America

Distributed by Kensington Publishing Corp.

Dear Reader,

I want to thank you immensely for supporting Black Odyssey Media and our ongoing efforts to spotlight the diverse narratives of blossoming and seasoned storytellers. With every manuscript we acquire, we believe that it took talent, discipline, and remarkable courage to construct that story, flesh out those characters, and prepare it for the world. Debut or seasoned, our authors are the real heroes and heroines in *OUR* story. For them, we are eternally grateful.

Whether you are new to Cassie Verano or Black Odyssey Media, we hope that you are here to stay. Our goal is to make a lasting impact in the publishing landscape, one step at a time and one book at a time. As always, we welcome your feedback and kindly ask that you leave a review. For upcoming releases, announcements, submission guidelines, etc., please be sure to visit our website at www.blackodyssey.net or scan the QR code below. And remember, no matter where you are in your journey, the best of both worlds begins now!

Joyfully,

Shawanda Williams

Shawanda "N'Tyse" Williams
Founder/Publisher

TRANSLATION

¿Cómo estás, mi amor?—How are you, my love?
Te arrepentirás mucho—You will be very sorry.
Hija—Daughter
Ven aquí—Come here.
¿Habla español?—Do you speak Spanish?
Un poquito—A little bit.

1

ANYSSA

ANYSSA'S THIRTY-BEFORE-THIRTY LIST

☑ Make love in a stairwell
☑ Hike the Rocky Mountains
☑ Ride an elephant
☐ Dance in the rain
☑ International road trip
☑ Learn an art
☑ Ride in a hot air balloon
☑ Go backpacking
☑ Make love to a stranger
☐ Perform on a stage
☐ Tattoo on my ass
☑ Scale a summit
☑ Learn a foreign language
☐ Swim at night, where you can see the stars
☐ Snorkel
☑ Parasail
☑ Make love on a train
☐ Take a cooking class in a foreign country
☑ Learn to ski
☐ Stand under a waterfall
☑ Swim with the dolphins

1

- ☑ Sing a karaoke duet with a stranger
- ☑ Ride a gondola in Venice
- ☑ Travel the world
- ☑ Send a message in a bottle
- ☐ View a sunrise from a place where you can see the horizon
- ☐ Do something along the lines of exhibitionism
- ☐ Find my father
- ☐ Try kinky sex
- ☐ Fall helplessly in love

"**E**levator's not working if you're heading to the seventh floor," the bored doorman says.

"Shit!" I mutter, turning in the opposite direction to head for the stairwell.

"We could take the elevator to five and the stairs from there," Connor says, tugging my hand.

"Can I just be Jeannie for one minute?" I groan, following him.

"Jeannie?" he asks, looking over his shoulder at me with that winsome smile as a blond lock of hair falls into his eyes.

"Yeah, like that old show, *I Dream of Jeannie*, with the chick with the genie outfit on. She'd fold her arms, close her eyes, and blink to make some shit happen. That's what I need right now."

Connor laughs, looking at my legs. "Calf muscles sore, huh?"

"Hell yeah, they are!" I mumble as the elevator doors open.

Connor's my tour guide here in Colorado. I've come to Estes Park for a hiking adventure in the Rocky Mountains. Since I've been here, I've ridden horses, gone kayaking, and seen a magic show in an underground speakeasy lounge underneath a carriage house. The last few days, I visited an aerial adventure park where I ziplined and navigated hanging chairs and even learned to throw axes.

Today, I rounded out my trip by hiking in the Rocky Mountains, and I thought I was fit . . . until I hiked that mountain. That venture alone kicked my ass. Every muscle in my body is sore. "You'll be good soon. We'll get you to the seventh floor, get you tucked away, and I'll read you a nighttime story."

"A nighttime story?" I laugh as the elevator doors open on the fifth floor.

"Yep. Make sure you have good dreams tonight," he says as his voice lowers slightly and his eyes flash with unbridled need.

"I'm already having one," I reply.

It's been this way with Connor and me all week, the back-and-forth easy banter of flirting. Surprisingly, I haven't scratched my itch yet. Flings while traveling aren't new to me. It's what I do. It's who I am.

Though I enjoy them, every now and then, I yearn for the comfort and security of a stable relationship.

"Stairwell's this way," he says, heading to the right.

Our tour group hung around for s'mores and beer over a campfire, but I was ready to return to the hotel. I'm the only one leaving tomorrow to prepare for my next destination.

"God!" I groan when we step into the stairwell, and I look up at my floor.

"Come on," he goads. "You can easily navigate this."

"Or . . . You could carry me," I challenge.

He winks and kneels with his back to me. "Hop on, ma'am. Your chariot awaits."

He ain't said nothing but a word. I quickly climb on his back, and he moves me up to his shoulders with a few quick shifts. My legs wrap around him, and he clutches my calves. As he takes the first few steps, his fingers gently massage the swollen, tired muscles, relieving my aches and pain but stirring up something far more potent.

There's a throbbing growing deep between my legs, and the swell of ecstasy that's taken over won't be contained. By the time we reach the fifth step on the first flight, I find myself shifting uncomfortably, trying to control the throbbing.

Yet, as I shift and my core rubs against his neck while the cloth of my cotton shorts rubs against me, I find I'm even more turned on. I'm so close to an orgasm that it's a damn shame. The man hasn't said boo, and I'm ready to drop my panties and bend over here in the stairwell.

"Anyssa?" Connor says.

"Hmm," I barely moan.

"Are you okay?"

"Mm-mm," I mutter.

He stops on the landing and slides me down from his shoulders and off his back.

"What's up?" he asks.

My eyelids are heavy like I've just smoked, and my breathing is erratic. A knowing smile crosses Connor's face, and he steps closer to me, backing me up against the wall.

Tilting my chin, he dips his head and kisses me. The sweet cherry and spicy aroma of the cigar he'd been chewing earlier comes to me, tempting me to want more. His slow kiss and the way he weaves his tongue into my mouth seduce me, making me feel light and at ease.

Connor's hands smooth down my shoulders, resting on my hips, but I grab one and shove it underneath my T-shirt. He pinches my nipple through my bra before pushing it aside as I jerk my T-shirt over my breasts.

"Fuck!" I cry when his lips take my budded nipple between them, and his tongue works it over.

My fingers tangle in his hair, pulling him closer, holding him in place all the while my hips jerk forward, pressing against him, begging for the hardness that I feel pushing through his cargo shorts.

Our heavy breathing echoes through the stairwell, and I hope no one else needs to take the stairs to the seventh floor. It's the last goddamned floor in this hotel, but hopefully, everyone who needs to get there is either safe and secure in their rooms or settled somewhere else for the evening. At least temporarily.

Connor lifts his head, kissing me once again as his fingers torture my nipples, tugging, pinching, and massaging them.

Boldly, I grab one of his hands and shove it into my cotton shorts. Connor moves his hand around in my shorts before satisfying himself by slicking his hand across my wetness.

"No panties?" he breathes heavily against my lips.

"None."

"Shit!"

I reach for his zipper, knowing that if it's about to happen here, we need not waste any time. His hands move away from my pussy and nipple to unzip the fanny pack at my waist.

"Reach inside," I mumble.

"Huh?"

"Protection inside," I say just as he's preparing to throw the fanny pack to the floor.

Within a minute, Connor is wrapped up and pushing inside me.

Disappointment floods me at his size, but he makes up for it with his movements. My back is flattened against the wall, and my legs are hiked up and pressed between us as he shoves inside me.

In this position, I'm wide open for his taking, and he takes and takes and takes, leaving me breathless. His dick stirring up my juices as he pumps echoes louder than our moans in the stairwell.

No way in hell could anyone enter the stairwell and not know what was happening. I don't care if they're down on the first landing; they'll hear Connor and me fucking.

I shift my legs slightly downward to wrap around his waist, and he bounces me up and down on his dick while sucking my breast.

"Connor!" I cry out, loving how it feels: so free, wild, and primal.

I've had sex in some crazy places but never in the hotel's stairwell. And just to think, that wasn't even on my "Thirty-Before-Thirty" List. I'll explain that later.

Connor's panting harder than before, and I know he's on the verge of an orgasm, but that's okay because I'm about to come myself. Wrapping my legs tighter around him, I kiss his lips, sucking at his bottom and then the top before I open my mouth to let his tongue inside again.

I hear a door banging closed somewhere a few floors down. I don't care; I keep going, hoping they don't see us, but if they do, I hope they're inspired too. I hear their footsteps growing closer, but their voices are softer.

No kids are at this hotel, so I'm not worried about scarring some poor kid for life.

"Nys," Connor groans throatily. "Aww, fuck!"

I whimper a few "Ahhhs" and "Mmms" of my own, and the footsteps I'd heard before slow up before someone snickers.

Clenching tightly around Connor, I gyrate hard, working him over slowly as his thrusts grow harder, slower, more intentional, and controlled.

He releases my mouth, takes one of my breasts in his mouth, and bites it.

"Oh shit!" I cry out just as I release all around him.

He's not finished yet. Connor's pumps increase in intensity and speed as he rocks upward, giving me everything he's got to give, and he finally releases as a whimper escapes his throat. He buries his face in my neck, biting down and stifling his groan.

"That was good," he gushes between deep breaths.

"Mm-hmm," is all I mutter between my labored breaths.

Clapping fills the stairwell with a couple of hoots and cheers.

I clap my hand over my mouth with wide eyes, staring at Connor, who's growing red. We both sputter with laughter as we adjust our clothes. I grab my fanny pack off the floor, and we jet for the final set of stairs.

The earlier pain in my calves is long forgotten, along with the abandoned condom wrapper. I think the actual condom may still be on Connor.

✓✓✓

ANNY'S ANNALS

Aloha!

Hey, it's me again . . .

Today, I crossed off number two on my list. Hike the Rocky Mountains.

We took the shuttle to the eastern trailhead and started at Spring Lake. I swear that must be the most peaceful place on earth. For a while, I just wanted to sit there and soak up the beauty of nature. It was still serene despite seeing a few people fishing in the lake.

Connor and Emily, our tour guides, led Tyler, Lisa, Gage, some others, and me around Bear Lake. Towering aspen, lodgepole pine, and fluffy spruce trees created an enchanted shoreline. When I say it was the stuff that fairy tales are made of . . .! There's nothing as magnificent and beautiful as this little haven in our backyard.

We followed the trail up to the little gorge, and I took some great pictures of Nymph and Dream Lakes for my channel. It was a perfect reflection of the beauty all around the lake as it mirrored the images of the trees, mountains, and skies. After we passed Emerald Lake, we took a more challenging hike, and I took pictures by Alberta Falls with my group.

I probably should have opted out for the more strenuous hike because I promise I'm paying for it now. Yet, as the ache in my body eases, I won't regret doing it.

The higher we climbed, the more we caught sight of beautiful elk grazing. Our travels brought us to this imposing granite barrier, which

Connor said was Timberline Falls. I took pictures there, as well. It was a breathtaking scene.

We turned around at the base of the falls and headed back. Lisa and Gage wanted to go further, but it was a one-hundred-foot chute, and Connor said it was best that we not try to hike it. Although it wasn't raining or snowing, he said hiking the chute was too dangerous for people like Tyler and me, who aren't experienced hikers.

I must admit the hike put some things in perspective for me. Made me think about all that I've taken for granted. It was like getting a glimpse of God in action. This was His handiwork.

With all my travels worldwide, who knew one of the most beautiful and peaceful places was here? I almost don't want to leave.

On another note, I left the group when they decided to stay behind for s'mores and beer. I'm leaving tomorrow morning and heading home for a few days before my next stop in Curaçao. I can't wait for that trip.

Anyhoo, Connor followed me back to the hotel because he didn't want me traveling alone. All our flirting this week finally led to some hot and heavy sex in the hotel's stairwell between floors six and seven!

Although his size wasn't impressive, he had some moves that made it worth it. We almost got caught, or maybe you can say we did get caught. We heard some people in the stairwell, but we didn't stop. We kept going like we were behind closed doors. The people were laughing, and they even fucking cheered us when it was over!

Can you believe it?

Connor and I died laughing when we got to my room. He returned to his room, and we planned to hook up again tonight after dinner. I should be sleeping and getting ready to travel again, but hell, that was the first time I had sex on this entire trip. I have to make it worth it.

After all, how can I find true love unless I test out what each destination offers?

Until next time, Anny!

Nys 🌀

2

NAZÁR

"**Y**ou should visit home more often," my mother says, patting my cheek.

"He's a man who has to find his way in the world, Maria José," my father says. "He's almost forty. No reason you should still be treating him like a boy."

"He's found his way, Papá. He owns a resort, a vineyard, and properties around the world," my older brother, Gabriel, says, speaking up for me as he's done since our youth.

"The amount of money or properties he can amass does not speak to his success, Gabriel. You should know this. What matters is the size of his family and how well he can protect and provide for them."

"He's got the provision down, Papá," my younger brother, Matias, says.

"I'm talking family. The man needs children," my father argues.

"Yes. I need grandchildren, Nazár," my mother says.

"You have grandchildren, Mamá," I point out. "Matias has two kids, and Gabriel has five."

"That is not enough. I need more. I need *your* children, little Nazários, to run around here that I can spoil."

"Mamá, even if I were to have children, they wouldn't be here. I'd still have to bring them to visit just like I visit twice a year now."

"But if you were to find a good Colombian girl, that might change, no?" she argues.

I smile and scoop some more ajiaco onto my spoon and into my mouth. I close my eyes, savoring the flavors of creamy, delectable corn, potato, and chicken soup.

"It's good, no?" she asks.

"Yes, Mamá. Excellent as always."

"That is why you need a good Colombian girl. Someone I can pass my recipe down to."

I chuckle despite myself because I know this is an argument I won't win.

"Your mother's right. Stay away from those American girls. They're too worldly and mean you no good. You see what happened with the last one that you married. Disgraced our name."

"God rest her soul," Mamá says, making the sign of the cross, although I know she didn't like my late wife, Bella.

"Bella wasn't American, Papá. She was French!"

"Dios mío! That's even worse!" Mamá says, shaking her head and pushing her bowl away.

She does the same theatrics every time Bella's name and nationality arise, as though she's just learning that Bella was French.

"What's worse about French women versus American women?" Gabriel asks, starting an argument that I want no part of.

"Women from both are shameless, but at least the American women try to have some discretion."

"No, they don't! I remember—" Matais speaks, ready to tell an oft-repeated story about some woman he had an affair with during college.

"Can we just stop?" I bellow, looking around the table at my parents and brothers and my brothers' wives, Salome and Luciana. It must be embarrassing to them to listen to my brothers' tales of ex-lovers every time this argument arises. Not to mention, the conversation will become heated and grow louder before long. And though everyone will kiss and make up at the end, that doesn't change the fact that their children are in the other room eating and listening to every word.

"What is wrong, Nazár?" Mamá asks.

"Every time Bella's name comes up, there's always a heated discussion, disrespect associated with my wife's name—"

"Well, son, she disrespected you," Papá points out.

"And an omission that we don't speak ill of the dead. At least that's what we believe, but somehow, when that comes to my late wife, it doesn't matter," I grunt over Papá.

I'm standing now with my fingertips gripping the table's edge so tightly that if they grow any tighter, I might rip the tablecloth free, clattering all their dishes to the floor. I'm tired of the disrespect that is associated with Bella, tired of careless remarks, the innuendos, and the callous humor.

"Where are you going?" Mamá asks as I stalk toward the door.

"Away!" I thunder, slamming the door closed behind me.

I don't care that they view it as disrespectful and rude. I'm beyond caring about the ways of our traditions when those traditions only extend to them when it's convenient. The rules never seem to apply to me.

It's the reason why I moved away from home. When I first became a real estate developer, I remained in Colombia, wanting to improve my town. I ventured out as my wealth, reputation, and business connections grew.

I bought my first property in Mauritius because Bella and I had visited on several occasions and loved the island. We met in America, but after I'd proposed, she'd agreed to return home to Colombia with me, excited about the opportunity to live in another new country.

Problems arose from the onset, from my family refusing to speak English in her presence when they very well could to them asking ignorant questions about her country and nationality. We tried to overlook them. As much time as I spent reassuring her that my family liked her, I spent that much time begging them to respect her and give her a chance.

When she had her miscarriage, my family began to suggest that she was cursed and our marriage was doomed. It was more than Bella could take. I knew I had to leave my family if I wanted my marriage to survive.

And so, we did. We bought the property in Mauritius because we loved it, and it was in neutral territory for us both. Now, here I am all these years later, and I still have the property, but I no longer have my beautiful Bella.

What's worse is the guilt I hold for often reliving my parents' words suggesting she was cursed. Looking back in time, it seems as if maybe she was.

"Hey, are you okay?" Gabriel asks, catching up with me as I walk down the street of our little town of Villa de Leyva.

"I'm never okay when I come back to this place," I grumble, shoving my hands into my pockets.

The sun is high in the sky and a little hotter than usual for Villa de Leyva. Sweat trickles from my hairline down the back of my neck.

"You know they don't mean any harm, don't you? They just want you to find someone to love you, settle down, and marry like they did."

"Yeah? Well, that didn't work out for me too well, did it?" I ask, turning to glare at my older brother.

"Look, I know there are a lot of insinuations out there about what happened to Bella, but . . ."

"But what?" I seethe when he doesn't say anything after several seconds.

Gabriel stops walking and shoves his hands into his pockets, mimicking my stance.

"But . . . You haven't given anyone anything to go on. No one knows what happened to her or why. We know that she died in a fatal car accident, end of story. It makes no sense, Nazár. She was familiar with the terrain, the roads . . . None of it ever made sense."

"So the family does what they always do, turn to their hodgepodge of superstitious beliefs about what happened to my wife, rather than respecting my privacy and decision not to discuss it? You all would rather believe the worst?"

"That's not true, and you know it, Nazár. You're angry right now."

"As if I don't have the right to be!"

"You do, but . . . Those same beliefs once guided you before you moved away."

"They were never my guiding principles. I just didn't argue with them out of respect for my parents. Never once did I expect they would turn on me."

"No one has turned on you," he says, reaching for my arm.

I jerk away from him, seeing the wounded expression in his eyes, but I'm beyond caring.

"It's been five years, Nazár. Don't you think that it's time you moved on?"

"Moved on to *what*, Gabriel?"

"Found a good woman who loves, respects, and cares for you."

"As opposed to what?"

"What you're doing now. Becoming a recluse on that island."

Shaking my head, I mutter, "It's a damn shame. My own family doesn't even know me."

"We could if you'd let us in again."

I start walking toward the bar once more, and Gabriel picks up the pace, catching up with me.

"I don't live like a recluse on the island. I travel to other places, meet people, and have friends worldwide."

"Not when you're at the resort."

"You don't know what you're talking about."

"For God's sake, Nazár, no one is allowed to visit the fucking resort without a personal invitation from you! You won't even allow your family to visit. Matias and I showed up unannounced and weren't permitted entry beyond the gates. You actually met us down there and escorted us to another hotel. What the hell?"

"It was in your best interest, as well as my own. I have precautions in place for a reason, Gabriel. If you can't respect that, then I'm sorry."

"We wouldn't have had to show up unannounced if you'd invited or allowed us to visit once. You don't even share pictures of that place. If it weren't for the beauty I could see from the road, I'd question if you'd let it go to the dumps."

"Never that."

"Then you're just in a prison of your own making behind guarded walls?"

"No. That's you thinking that."

My brother is trying to pilfer information about my private resort. I won't disclose anything because my family isn't good at keeping secrets and are judgmental assholes.

I open the door to La Cava de Juan Carlos and bask in the cool air flowing through the bar. Dim lighting, walnut overhead beams, orange walls, and liquor bottles hanging from strings overhead set the tone of the bar.

On the wall leading up the stairway to the second level are album covers from old bands of the seventies and eighties. Salsa music and the low hum of lively and hushed conversations create a laid-back atmosphere.

Gabriel and I sit at the rear, giving us a full view of the door.

"So, tell me this, at least. Is there anyone meaningful in your life?"

"That depends on what you mean by meaningful."

"A potential love interest who has the possibility of turning into a wife, turning into a mother," he says as he waves a finger at a server.

The woman smiles flirtatiously at us and winks at me as she takes our orders.

"Daniela, this is my younger brother, Nazár."

"Hello, Nazár. Are you visiting or coming to stay?"

"Visiting."

"Maybe I can show you around in your downtime."

"This is home for him, Daniela. He moved away, but he's very familiar with our town."

"There are a few changes that I'm sure you're not acclimated to. Maybe I can help out in those areas," she flirts, leaning a little too close for my comfort and overwhelming me with the scent of cheap perfume.

She leans so close I can see the tip of her nipples pointed upward in her blouse.

"Don't think you're into what I'm into, my love."

"Oh . . ." she says, looking between my brother and me.

I know that she's assuming that I'm commenting on my sexuality. Many people make that mistake when I say that, but it's fine by me. They can think whatever the hell they'd like. I'm secure in my masculinity and owe no one explanations. Besides, their assumptions keep them from the truth. Only those who delve into the world that I prefer catch my meaning.

"Um, what will you have?" she asks.

We order and return to our conversation.

"So, wife, mother?"

"Neither. I'm not looking for a family, Gabriel. I'm perfectly happy with how my life is set up."

"Then why are you always scowling? You're never happy anymore."

"I have a lot going on in my life. It has nothing to do with my lack of happiness."

"So, what . . . Have you become an international lover or something?"

Smirking, I spin the red frayed coaster around under my fingertip. "Or something."

"You're being extremely evasive, Nazár."

"You don't leave me any choice. I know the moment I spill a single detail about my life, you'll say something to Luciana. She will tell Salome, who will tell Matias, and he'll run to either Mamá or Papá."

My sisters-in-law are sisters and share everything with each other.

"That's not true."

"It is, and the fact that you deny it lets me know that I can't trust you. Don't blame me if I don't want to be the fucking content of gossip over the next family dinner."

Daniela returns with our beers and a bowl of nachos, cheese, peppers, and jalapeños. We nibble at it while Gabriel talks about his wife and kids and catches me up on what's been happening in his life.

When he finishes, he says, "You want it too, Nazár. You're just too stubborn as fuck to admit it."

"Want what?"

"What Matias and I have. Marriage, kids, family, home."

I shake my head and say, "There will never be another Bella. She's the only woman that I was capable of loving. Losing her . . . Let's say it fucked with my psyche, Gabriel. I'm no good for any woman, and no woman is good for me. That's why I get what I need before moving on to the next woman."

Gabriel pulls his beer bottle from his lips and eyes me closely. "What?"

"You poor bastard. You believe that shit, don't you?"

"It doesn't matter whether I believe it. It's the way that it has to be. I'm happy with it, and that's all that matters."

Daniela walks by again, and I imagine her on her knees with a leash and collar, a ball gag in her troublesome mouth, preparing to be spanked. In my fantasy, those dusky-colored nipples are clamped, turning redder by the moment as her screams of pain are muffled. My dick hardens, and a smile takes over my face.

3

ANYSSA

ANYSSA'S THIRTY-BEFORE-THIRTY LIST

- ☑ Make love in a stairwell
- ☑ Hike the Rocky Mountains
- ☑ Ride an elephant
- ☑ Dance in the rain
- ☑ International road trip
- ☑ Learn an art
- ☑ Ride in a hot air balloon
- ☑ Go backpacking
- ☑ Make love to a stranger
- ☐ Perform on a stage
- ☐ Tattoo on my ass
- ☑ Scale a summit
- ☑ Learn a foreign language
- ☐ Swim at night, where you can see the stars
- ☐ Snorkel
- ☑ Parasail
- ☑ Make love on a train
- ☐ Take a cooking class in a foreign country
- ☑ Learn to ski
- ☐ Stand under a waterfall
- ☑ Swim with the dolphins

☑ Sing a karaoke duet with a stranger
☑ Ride a gondola in Venice
☑ Travel the world
☑ Send a message in a bottle
☐ View a sunrise from a place where you can see the horizon
☐ Do something along the lines of exhibitionism
☐ Find my father
☐ Try kinky sex
☐ Fall helplessly in love

"**H**i, guys! It's Nys again. This time, I'm checking in from Curaçao. For those of you who aren't familiar with Curaçao, it's a beautiful Dutch Caribbean island known for its coral reefs teeming with marine life and, as you can see behind me, gorgeous beaches tucked into coves," I say, panning the camera so that my viewers can see the beautiful green waters rolling behind me.

The wind picks up, forcing me to speak a little louder.

"Curaçao is part of what's known as the ABC islands, which are Aruba, Bonaire, and Curaçao. I just arrived yesterday, and I'll be leaving Sunday evening and heading home to Atlanta, so that's six days and five nights in this tropical paradise. I'm here as part of a press trip, but I've extended my stay by two days just to have fun.

"As you can hear, it's quite windy now, and they're expecting storms, but it's still beautiful, and I've been getting as much beach time in as possible. I'm staying at the Blue Bay Curaçao Golf and Beach Resort. They have luxurious accommodations and excellent, attentive, and friendly staff," I say, flipping my camera around so the viewers can see the resort where I'm staying.

"Now, for those curious about where I am on my 'Thirty-Before-Thirty' List, I've ticked off all but a few items. To check out my list, *find my website in the comments below. I'm still searching for my next destination to find true love. Drop your comments below for suggestions on where I should travel next. Bye-bye for now."*

I click the camera off and wink at my partner, who's beckoning me back to the chaise lounge with him. He smiles and waves a delicious orange-yellowish drink with cherries and pineapples bobbing on the surface of the fruity concoction.

Laughing and shaking my head, I return to the dark-skinned, gorgeous man with deep dimples, light brown eyes, and thick, curly hair.

"How do you know that you have not found true love with me," he asks in his thick island accent.

He reaches for my hand and pulls me gracefully onto his lap as thunder rumbles in the sky, causing people to look up.

"Mm, Aarlin, you're spoiling me," I moan as he presses his cool lips against my neck while holding the straw of my drink to my lips for me to take a sip.

"That, my love, is my intention: to make you fall helplessly in love with me."

Giggling, I shake my head. "No, you've been watching my channel too much. You know about my quest."

Shrugging, he replies, "I am guilty of watching your channel, which is why I sought you out when you first arrived. Can you blame a man for wanting to be part of your quest for love and happiness? I hope that your journey ends here, in my arms."

He wraps them tightly around me as I set my drink on the little table beside us and lean further into him. A soft rain falls around us, and people start packing up.

It's no secret that I've had many lovers. I've enjoyed almost as many lovers as countries I've visited, and that's quite a lot.

After each trip, I debrief with my followers on my channel. I share my highlights, whether food, culture, or shopping. Yet, it's still my flings that they look forward to hearing the most about.

And when I leave Curaçao, Aarlin will be no exception. I'll talk about the wonderful time that I had with him, as well, and I'll highlight his good points and share his flaws.

"I don't think my journey has concluded, Aarlin."

"How can one know?"

The rumble of thunder grows louder, and more people rush to leave the beach, but we remain.

"Oh, trust me. My heart will know when it's found true love, but I'm happy to have fun on the voyage in the meantime," I say as he tweaks one of my nipples through my bikini top.

We kiss for a while as the rain continues. Despite all the movement, we continue kissing and hugging each other. I know it won't be long before we head inside like everyone else.

"Shall we return to my suite, my love?" he asks after a few minutes, nibbling my ear as my nipple hardens at his torturous touch.

My pussy throbs, and I can't resist the irresistible tug that his mouth has on every part of my body as his kisses move from my ear to my shoulder and his hands grip my hips.

Hopping up from the chaise lounge, I grab my drink and camera and smile playfully at him before I sprint toward the resort hotel. Aarlin is right behind me, and though I know I'm in great shape at twenty-nine, he's quite athletic, in bed and out for a thirty-six-year-old.

"We're going to get soaked if you don't hurry!" he shouts, passing me up as my sprint turns into a light jog and then a stroll.

"Don't you hear that?" I ask as we approach the hotel doors.

"What?"

"The music."

"That's coming from the hotel lobby. It always plays music into the parking lot."

"Wait."

"For what?"

"I want to dance in the rain."

Aarlin stops and stares at me as if I've lost my mind.

"Please!" I shout, stretching my hand toward him as he stands in the doorway.

He looks back into the confines of the dry hotel and then back to me. Reluctantly, he steps into the rain with a hesitant smile.

"How can I deny a beautiful girl her wish?"

Aarlin takes my hand into his left and wraps his right arm around me. Pulling me closer, he moves slowly to the beat of the music.

He hums softly while the rain falls around us, bouncing off his curls, curling mine into springy coils, and kissing our eyelashes. The soft vibration of Aarlin's baritone wraps me in a cocoon of peace.

Rain pelts the sidewalk, and thunder rolls through the air even though the sun still shines.

"It is kind of peaceful and romantic, isn't it?" he says.

"Yes. It's one of the things on my 'Thirty-Before-Thirty' List."

"How did you come up with that?"

"My list? I watched my mother sacrifice so much for me. I want to have a family someday, but there is so much that I want to experience before starting a family. So, I created a list of things I want to happen before I'm thirty when I plan to focus on a family. I've been working on them for the last few years but slowed up."

"This was an easy one to make come true. I'm glad you chose me to be your partner," he says, his eyes sparkling with humor.

We continue swaying in the rain as cars pull in and out for valet parking, and people rush into the hotel. People coming and going glance at us. Some stop and watch under the safety of the hotel's awning, and others shake their heads at our foolishness.

When the song ends, we head into the hotel with water dripping from our bodies, heads, and faces. Some people mill around the elevators, waiting for a car to free up. When one arrives going up, Aarlin tugs my hand, pulling me back.

"What?"

"Not yet."

We let two more cars go before no one is left at the bank of elevators except for those departing.

He presses the button for our floor, and as soon as the doors close, Aarlin pulls me close to him.

"Have you ever fucked on an elevator before?" he asks.

"Quite a few," I moan as he presses the stop button on ours.

I met Aarlin the first night of my arrival, and we instantly clicked, sharing drinks, talking about our travels, and finding places we've both traveled to muse about, and we've flirted a lot. On the second day, we flirted more and became extremely physical but not quite having sex. The third day was a no-brainer for me. I found myself in the pool late at night with him thrusting inside me.

To my amusement, the resort manager came out, clicking on the lights just as we finished. I retied my bikini, and we slipped out of the water, claiming we were training for the Olympics for the next year and that he was my coach.

I don't think she bought that lie, but it was enough for her to smirk and get that twinkle in her eyes. She left us alone, and we rushed to Aarlin's room from the pool area.

"You don't have any protection on you," I mumble as his hand slips into my bikini.

"I don't need it for what I'm about to do," he says, kneeling before me as he slides my bikini aside.

Greedily, Aarlin sucks at me, wasting no time teasing me. He's hungry, and he wants what he wants. I'm horny and need what I need, so I readily give it to him. Splaying my legs wide and slumping against the elevator wall as he grabs a leg and props it over his shoulder, I shove my hips forward.

His tongue is hot, and his mouth covers me entirely as he drinks and drinks from my well. My nipples ache, and my back thrusts forward with my hips arching out, giving him more and more until I beg him to release me.

"Mm-mm," he mutters with his mouth full of my pussy.

Aarlin slips a finger inside of me along with his tongue and rotates it inside of me as his tongue pulses against my clit. My body shudders, and a thought occurs to me. Is this all that it will ever be for me? One lover after another who makes my body feel good but doesn't touch my soul or my heart? A lover who knows how to finesse my body and take me to deeper heights but cannot move my spirit?

I want more than this, and I *need* more than this. I am a strong, independent woman who needs my king. A man who sees my value and strength as an asset to him and not a hindrance, not a barrier to his success or a threat to his manhood.

I'm looking for someone who knows himself, yet I don't mind humbling myself to him to be my leader, protector, and strength.

Aarlin lifts my other leg over his shoulder, and I'm now sitting on his face as he buries himself inside me, rapidly rolling his head back and forth. His hands squeeze my ass, and I feel one finger slipping inside of my ass, and it's the most incredible feeling in the world, being penetrated back there.

I don't hold back the scream that's building within. Although I'm uncertain what floors we're trapped between, it doesn't matter. The scream that unleashes from within me is nothing less than earth-shattering, mind-blowing, and mountain-moving.

Anyone who hears the scream knows that I'm caught in the throes of a very enthralling orgasm. They know that someone is bringing me great pleasure and that I'm in no danger other than death by orgasm.

My legs tighten around Aarlin as my hand braces the wall to the side of me and the one behind me as we are wedged in the corner. Slowly, Aarlin lets me down, and a smirk dances on his lips as he winks at me.

"Still don't think that I'm the love of your life?"

"Maybe the love for this week. Can we be satisfied with that for now?" I ask as he presses the button to start the elevator again.

He winks, takes my hand, and doesn't reply but tugs me off the elevator and down the hall to his room once the doors open.

☑ ☑ ☑

". . . I'm starting to think that you purposely look for a man's imperfections to have an excuse as to why you can't settle down."

"Don't start that shit with me, Kayla Michelle."

"I'm just saying. There's always a reason why 'he' can't be the one, yet you claim you're looking for love. If you want to be an international ho, then just say it. No one's judging you."

"*That* sounded very judgmental, and I have no problem being an international *lover*. I mean, men do it. Why can't we?"

"You do realize that your reasoning is implausible."

"How?"

"You're the one who always says that men have their place and women have theirs and that we shouldn't try to compete. You always say that we should excel in our different spaces and that it's okay not to want to be the same as men because we weren't created like them. We're a different species; therefore, we should operate differently, accepting and embracing our differences. Now, you're comparing yourself to a man. That's counterproductive to the stance that you're always making, that's all."

I sigh and fall back on my bed, closing my eyes.

"Kayla," I whine, dragging her name out. "I did not ask for you to be logical tonight, did I?"

"I'm just saying. Why can't this guy Aarlin be the love of your life?"

"For one, he's stalkerish. Two, his cunnilingus game is on point, but his dick action could use some work."

"Thought you said he was good in bed."

"Good ain't great. Three . . . My heart isn't jumping out of my chest whenever I see him or hear him calling my name, that's why."

"And you believe that when you fall in love, you should experience rapid heartbeats, sweaty palms, loss of breath, and fainting."

"No. You sound like you're describing atrial fibrillation or panic or anxiety attacks. I'm not saying that at all, but I should feel something other than the pulsating in my va-jay-jay, shouldn't I? Hell, *maybe* I'd even settle for a man who entertained me continuously with good conversation, an excellent sense of humor, and made my pussy feel like she had a heart attack."

"That's crass."

"It's true."

"When did you decide you want the love that romance novels and movies are made of? You once told me that was enough and that you didn't need more. You said if the man could have your toes curling and have you screaming to the top of your lungs, that was good enough."

Sitting up on the bed and pulling my knees to my chest, I rest my head on my knees. "Mm, that was when I was dating Tony and needed a real man to give me what I needed."

Kayla laughs in my ear. "You've got plenty of them, don't you?"

"Men?"

"No. Excuses."

Laughing, I flop backward on the bed again and say, "You're right."

"I'm not judging you, Nys. I just want you to be open to love, truly open without all the expectations you place as a barrier to keeping a man from your heart and not true signs used to vet a good man."

"Because you're looking out for my best interest."

Laughing, she says, "Someone's got to. After all, you don't care about that poor heart of yours at all. The only thing you're looking out for is your va-jay-jay."

"Nothing wrong with that," I say, thinking about Aarlin.

I promised to meet him and a few of his friends tonight for dinner on the beach and then spend the night with him.

"All I'm asking is that on your next venture, you're open to more than just sex with a man. Look at him as a potential partner, especially a lifetime one, and not just a bedtime partner for the next week or so. Think you can do that?"

"You make it sound like I'm shallow."

"Not shallow, just thinking with your hole and not your brain, girl."

"Goodbye, Ms. Wyndham. I have a dinner I'm supposed to be at in half an hour, and I haven't showered or dressed yet."

"Okay, just promise me that you'll be open."

"Oh, I'm always open," I quip, scissoring my legs back and forth through the air, giggling.

"Not talking about that hole of yours either," she says knowingly.

"Okay, I promise that the next man that I meet on my next venture, I'll be open to the possibility of more than just a casual fuck."

"So tactless," she groans, ending the call.

I met Kayla at a vlogger's conference eight years ago, and the two of us clicked and became fast friends.

I glance at the clock again, groan because I have no idea who these friends of Aarlin's are and if I want to be bothered with them, then hop off the bed to shower and dress.

If nothing else, I should get a good screw out of tonight, literally or metaphorically, depending on how dinner goes.

4

ANYSSA

"I don't see it."

"It's usually that way when a person has a doppelgänger," Paisley, one of Aarlin's friends, says.

"Yep, happened to me," Aarlin agrees. "There was this one time when I was working for a communications company, and I saw this man every day. I never thought twice about him, but people kept telling me that I had someone who looked like he could be my brother. I had no idea who they were talking about, even with the flowery descriptions they gave. One day, one of my colleagues pointed him out, and it was the guy I'd seen all along. Nothing. I could find absolutely nothing about him that looked like me. We took pictures together because he'd been getting the same responses as me. I showed my mom and pop, and they agreed. Said he could be my twin."

I stare at the cinnamon-colored woman across the table with the chin-length bob, nut-brown eyes, and a slight overbite. She's beautiful, but I still don't see it.

"Nope," I say, shaking my head.

Camila Martinez smiles goofily at me and says in a slightly accented voice, "Don't think that just because I'm Dominican, we

28

can't look alike. I see the similarities in your rounded face, pouty lips, and wide-set, down-turned eyes. Even our coloring is similar."

"Don't see it," I mumble, returning to the seafood pasta.

"Pass the wine, Lena," the elderly gentleman across from Aarlin says to the middle-aged woman to his right.

"You're going to drink the entire bottle," Lena complains, moving the bottle out of his reach.

"It's okay. There's more where that one came from. This," Camila says with a flourish, brandishing another bottle of wine, "is a bottle of our vintage two-thousand-two Vino de Lujo. It's rare, the only one produced of its kind. Anyssa, you're the wine connoisseur. Tell me what you think."

I wait until she's opened the bottle of wine before passing my glass. She carefully pours my glass half-full before she pulls the bottle away and sits back in anticipation of my reaction. I swish the wine in my mouth, savoring the coffee, tobacco, blackberry, toasted oak, and plum flavors.

"It has a polished style, very lush. It has harmony and is firm, but it's also fluid. There's a long finish, but the fine-grained tannins give grace to that. This is nice," I say, holding my glass up for a refill, though I have yet to finish the first pour.

She smiles happily at me, eager to give me more as everyone else holds up their glasses, and the older gentleman, Jacob, I think is his name, greedily eyes the entire bottle.

"I think you and I could become great friends and business partners, Ms. Kelley. I need someone with a delicate palate on our marketing team."

I smirk, knowing I may never see her again. Or I just might. Not for business, though. I have enough on my plate as it stands. But I could end up visiting her vineyard and taking on a lover. I bite back the giggle that wants to usurp the seriousness of the conversation.

"What's so funny?" Aarlin asks, leaning into me and nuzzling my neck before nipping my earlobe.

"Nothing. Just thinking about how delicious this wine tastes."

We tune the others out as they continue chatting. "I know something that tastes better than this wine. Something very lush and fine, whose fluids are the perfect harmony my mouth is searching for," he says.

I'm squirming in my seat, trying my damndest to behave, but barely. Turning to him and kissing his lips sweetly, I reply, "After dessert."

"You're the only dessert that I need."

I bite my bottom lip and look up to meet Camila's gaze. She's observing me, and I can't help but wonder what she's thinking.

"You need to behave. You're being rude to your guests," I tell Aarlin, who sits up, clearing his throat.

"That's a shame," I hear Lena say, clucking her tongue.

Turning away from Aarlin, I look up to see Camila's gaze on her phone. Her lovely features are marred by a scowl and a pinched look around her eyes.

"What's a shame?" I ask, reaching for the rare bottle of wine again.

"Camila has to turn down a once-in-a-lifetime opportunity," Lena explains.

As if pulled back into the conversation at the mention of her name, she jerks her attention away from the phone and says, "I have to cancel my next trip."

"Which is where?" Aarlin asks in a bored tone.

"Mauritius. A beautiful island nation in East Africa. I was supposed to tour the Belle Baie resort and their rum distillery."

"Isn't that an exclusive resort?" Aarlin asks, seemingly more interested.

"Yes. One can visit by invitation only, and the resort owner has to invite you," Lena explains.

"Rich people," I say drily.

"Not exclusively, but yes, the guests are predominantly wealthy. The owner is after anonymity more than anything and wants his guests to uphold discretion, honoring his privacy but enjoying the land and the fruits of his hard work," Camila says.

"This would have been the perfect opportunity to expand my vineyard. I've been traveling to various resorts that offer similar experiences to those I'd like to offer, such as wine tastings, horseback riding, and touring and learning about the land, the culture, and the history of our area and my family."

"Though this was just one of her destinations on that journey, it was the best opportunity for her to expand her knowledge," Courtland, another of Aarlin's friends and the man who's been paying close attention to Camila all night, says.

Until now, he's been quiet for most of the evening, carefully studying her instead.

"What's worse is that if I don't make it, he won't honor it later."

"Why can't you make it?" I ask, pouring myself yet another glass of wine.

Camila holds up her phone and explains. "My father is having surgery in a couple of months. I can't miss it. I'm his only child, and there's no one closer to him than I am. I'd hate to disappoint him or for him to go through this alone. My mom will be there, but she's a worrier, and they'll both drive each other crazy."

"Maybe you could tell the resort owner that, and he'll honor it," I suggest.

Camila shakes her head. "He won't. I've already mentioned it to my friend, who referred me. Usually, if people visit the resort and have a wonderful experience with him and a great time, they're invited back for future visits. Any cancellations, rule-breaking, photography, or video leakage will get you banned and potentially sued. You have to sign an NDA before entering the property," she laments.

"From everything that I've heard, the resort is beautiful," Jacob slurs, reaching for the second bottle of wine. At this point, Lena smacks his hand and pulls the bottle to the other side of her.

She earns a scowl for her efforts. "Mauritius is beautiful. A resort created to take advantage of the simplistic beauty and natural landscaping would be stunning," Lena says.

"What's the name of the resort again?" I ask, pulling out my phone with one hand and holding up my glass for another refill with the other.

This delicious and powerful wine gives me more courage than usual. There's a plan brewing in my mind, and I know it's foolish, but I can't stop its tendrils of power and persuasion from putting its hooks in me.

Camila waves her hand as Aarlin chuckles. "Chica, you may as well put that away. There are no pictures of the resort online. Haven't you just heard a word of what we've said? The owner doesn't allow photography or videos."

"Damn. Sounds a little cultish to me," I say.

"Not really. It's beautiful and romantic, and how the owner preserves its integrity and does not allow anyone to capture it on film lends a certain mystique to the place," Camila says.

"People have offered to pay millions for a chance to visit," Lena adds with a bemused expression.

"How can you know it's all that engaging if you've never visited or seen pictures?" I ask.

"Easy. I've had wealthy friends who have visited and gone on and on about their wonderful time and how romantic it was. I know of at least three couples who visited for their honeymoon.

One of those couples was the one who got me an invitation," Camila explained.

"They always say it's not what you know but who you know," Lena expresses.

Courtland nods his agreement but remains silent on the subject.

"How much does a trip cost?" my intrigue now piqued at an all-time high.

"For three weeks, it's roughly twenty-five thousand."

"Damn!" I yelp as the others chuckle and giggle.

"Many a lover has found their soul mate on that island. Or so I've heard," Lena says.

"You didn't find me there," Jacob states, gazing at Lena. I hadn't realized they were together until now. She rolls her eyes and waves off his comment.

"I don't have twenty-five K in my account, but I'd empty what I do have to make that happen if it's everything that people say it is."

The conversation eventually moves to talk about other travels the group has ventured on, and that's when I learn that they usually vacation together, which is how they know one another. Only Aarlin is from Curaçao. He met the others when they'd vacationed here about five years ago, and they've been traveling together ever since.

"So, where's your next stop?" Courtland asks, eyeing me over a beer mug.

"Honestly, I don't know. I usually allow my viewers to suggest where I should travel next, but so far, no one has come up with anything interesting," I inform them, holding my phone aloft as evidence before letting it plop back onto my lap.

"Your website says you're looking for love," Lena says, holding up her phone.

"Among many other things," I confirm, polishing off the bottle of wine.

"The woman is talking foolishly. I've told her she needs to look no further than me," Aarlin says.

"Same game that you've been spitting at other women for far too long, my guy. It's about time *you* settled down," Courtland states.

He and Camilla are the only ones in the group with an American accent.

"I'm trying to, but she's not working with me," Aarlin says, nuzzling my neck again.

I shake my head and say, "It'll come one day, and I'll know when it's right."

"Sounds like you should get yourself an invitation to that mysterious resort. You might find just what you're looking for," Lena tells her.

"Problem is . . . I don't have twenty-five K, and I don't know anyone with those types of connections," I explain.

I grab my wineglass and excuse myself from the table where Aarlin is engaged in playful banter with Jacob and Lena's entertaining Courtland. I push my chair under the table and glance up when I feel someone staring at me, only to find that Camila's gaze is on me.

"Hey," I greet when Camila comes to stand beside me by the water's edge.

"It's beautiful, isn't it?" she says, waving her glass toward the water.

"It is. I always find myself returning to Curaçao, hoping one day to have someone to enjoy it with."

"Maybe you will."

I sigh and sip my wine.

"In the meantime, I might have a way for you to take advantage of the opportunity of a lifetime."

"What do you mean?"

"How much would you be willing to pay to go on that trip to Belle Baie?"

"To Belle Baie? What's going on?"

"You said you'd be willing to empty your bank account to make that happen. How much can you come up with?"

"Uhhh . . . I do *not* have twenty-five grand."

"How much *do* you have?"

"I mean, I can check to see what I can come up with, but why are you asking me this?" I ask, pulling my phone from my pocket.

"The reality is that I've already been referred, and been accepted and paid for the trip. There's no way that I can make it, and I won't get a refund. As I said, my father's surgery is coming up, and I have to be there for him. It's a risky surgery, and while we're praying that all goes well, I honestly don't know what will happen. I will never forgive myself if he doesn't make it through and I wasn't there."

"I'm sorry, Camila."

"Thank you. But listen, I have an idea that will help us both out."

"What's that?"

"You go to Belle Baie in my place as me."

"How would I make that happen, Camila?"

"As much as you want to deny the resemblance between us, it's more than just a passing resemblance. We could pass for twins to anyone who doesn't know us."

I roll my eyes. "Okay, we look a *little* alike—"

"Anyssa," she says patiently.

"Okay, okay. We look alike."

"Thank you. We could make this a win-win situation for both of us. Although I won't recoup the full amount of my twenty-five thousand dollars, I will salvage some of it. And I won't ruin my friends' reputation by prohibiting them from being allowed to refer any future guests because I didn't show up. I'll still have the option to return someday, and I can gain some valuable knowledge for my business expansion if you'd be willing to help. Not to mention, you'll have the perfect destination for your next vacation, *and* you just might find the love of a lifetime," she says, ticking off each point on her finger.

"Well, damn. When you put it like that, it sounds like an offer I can't refuse. I can come up with ten grand if that works for you."

"That's better than a total loss. But there's one thing that I ask."

"What's that?"

"I need information on the distillery and vineyard to help expand. That's why I was going there more than just vacationing. So, I'll need you to complete the research I was going to do."

"Tell me what you need, and I'm your girl!"

"I'll put a packet together with my questions, concerns, ideas, and suggestions. We can set up a few Zoom calls to discuss the packet and teach you about my business and personal things about me, but don't go too deep, and we'll go over any questions you might have."

"Sounds great. Hey, is there anyone that might be able to identify you when I arrive?"

"No, I've never been there before. My friends who have been there are vacationing in Greece for that month, and I don't know anyone else there. Besides, I'm not on social media or famous, and it's not like my photo is splashed all around the internet."

"What about your vineyard?"

"No photos of the family. Just visitors to the vineyard and the actual property. Eventually, that may change as my business operations expand."

"Are we seriously about to make this happen?" I ask excitedly. A wide smile blossoms on her face as well. "I think so! It would be a beautiful partnership, and as I stated before, maybe this will lead to getting you on my marketing team."

Laughing, I say, "I don't know. I love to travel too much."

"We can incorporate that as well."

"Maybe," I say.

"I've got some bright ideas, Anyssa, if you're open."

"Let's see how this trip pans out, and we'll go from there."

She extends her hand. "Deal."

"Deal!" I say, shaking her hand.

"Now we have to figure out the IDs."

"Don't worry about it. I've got a guy who can take care of that," I say, thinking about my friend Logan.

"Three things. No pictures or videos can be taken there, or I will be banned forever."

"Agreed."

"I'll have you sign an NDA because this has to be kept between you and me, no one else. No best friends, parents—nobody."

"Agreed."

"And finally, no questions about the owner's wife."

I hear the group's laughter behind us and turn slightly to look over my shoulder. Everyone's still engaged in deep conversations, but Aarlin's eyes are on me. I know I don't have much longer before he joins us; his attention is already drawing further away from the group's conversation.

"Who is his wife?"

"Actress Bella Fouché. Everyone is constantly speculating about how she really died."

"I've heard of her. Haven't really seen her movies, but I know who she is."

"Stay clear of that topic, no videos, no photos, stick to the terms of the NDA, and you should be okay."

"This will be easy peasy," I assure her.

"I knew we'd be great friends," she says, smiling as Aarlin approaches my side.

Later, I will lie in bed, long after the fun with companions, long after sex with Aarlin, and my heart will yearn for something more. Someone to hold me through the night, kissing my temples, telling me he loves me. My heart will yearn for someone who makes me his sole focus.

And I will wonder if I'll find everything my heart dreams of at Belle Baie.

5

ANYSSA

Two Months Later . . .

"**Y**ou can't manipulate love."

"Who says that I'm trying to?"

"This entire quest that you're on says it all. Who knows, maybe you're not destined for marriage."

"Whoa! Cool your heels, Prophetess Wyndham. No one said anything about marriage, and how do you know what I am or aren't destined for? I just said that I want to fall in love and be loved. Everyone deserves one shot at happiness. Belle Baie could be mine."

"You're starting your journey on a lie, Nys. It would be different if you were going as yourself, but whatever Romeo you happen to meet over there will think you're someone you're not. How can they possibly love you for you if they don't know you?" Kayla groans.

I'd thought about that exact scenario a million times over, but I also believed that if I was destined for love and if it was meant to be between me and some great guy, then nothing could stop us.

"Look, I will eventually disclose my identity. If I'm falling for someone, there must be a trust factor there, don't you think?"

"Preferably."

"Right. And whoever he is, I should be able to trust him with my secret, allowing me to remain at the resort without him outing me."

"Mm-hmm."

"Whaaat?" I whine.

"It's just that I don't think you're starting off on the right foot. There's the NDA you've had to sign and what if someone there recognizes you?"

"Girl, it's not like I'm some celebrity or something. My YouTube channel has a decent following, but we're talking about wealthy and über-rich people here. They don't get that way by watching some travel girl's YouTube channel. They're off doing the things that I'm doing or better."

"I guess you're going to simply overlook that you're also the Travel Channel's Romance Abroad host? Or that you've written articles for *Ebony, Coastal Living, Travel & Leisure, Condé Nast Traveler*, and *Marriott Bonvoy Traveler*?"

I sigh dramatically into the phone and roll my eyes, dropping back on my bed as I fling my arm over my eyes.

"Why do you have to be such a spoilsport, Kayla?"

"I'm not, sugar pop. I'm just a realist. I don't want you to get hurt or hurt someone else."

"And you think that I'm capable of that?"

"We all are. And it's not just by cheating on someone like Rick did you."

Groaning, I reply, "And you just *had* to mention his name?"

"Well, he's why you started journeying around the world having sex with random strangers in different countries."

"I have romantic *flings*," I object.

Laughing, Kayla replies, "Call it what you want. You're having random sex with random guys in random countries."

"You do realize you're sounding chauvinistic now, right?"

"Whatever, Anyssa. Do what you feel you must, but just be careful. Please."

"Don't I always?"

"This is different, though. You're getting fake IDs to pretend you're someone you're not. God forbid that the authorities find out and you get arrested for impersonation in some foreign country where you'll be tossed in jail and denied food and have to eat crumbs off the cold, concrete prison floor, bathe once every thirty days, drink dirty water, and sentenced to bad hair days for the rest of your life."

Laughing, I ask, "A flair for the dramatic much?"

"Okay, Ms. I've-Got-the-World-in-My-Hands-and-Who's-Gonna-Stop-Me-Now. Don't say I didn't warn you if shit goes awry."

"Not gonna happen."

"Well, if it does, I promise to start a 'Free Anyssa Kelley' campaign, and my family's paper will do a national write-up about it and the denial of American rights in foreign prison systems. Who knows, we may even be able to get American ambassadors and dignitaries involved on your behalf."

Rolling my eyes, I pull the phone closer and say, "Kayla?"

"Hmm?"

"Come closer to the phone."

"Why?"

"Do it."

She approaches the phone, and I say, "Kiss. My. Ass."

Laughing, I hang up the phone and hop off the bed, ignoring the phone when she calls back. I slide into my denim cutoff shorts, pull on an orange tank top with matching orange sandals, and look around for my keys and handbag.

Armed with those items, my phone, and my glasses, I head out of my apartment into the bright afternoon sunshine. It's hell-hot in Hotlanta today at a sultry ninety-five degrees, and the heat index is off the chart. I instantly toss on my sunglasses when the blinding sun compromises my vision as I trek to my car.

The twenty-minute drive to downtown Atlanta doesn't take long at all on a Thursday afternoon. Most people are at work, and though the connector is always crazy, it's not as bad as rush hour.

My bags are packed, my airplane ticket has been purchased, and Uber is scheduled for a late evening pickup.

I'll be on the island for three beautiful weeks. I won't be able to use anything I capture for the magazines I write for, but I plan to use it as inspiration for my channel.

I've talked to Camila nonstop the last couple of months about her business and little things about her personally. Neither of us think personal details will come up, but her business might since that's why she was traveling there.

I remember Camila's warnings and the fact that I have more than just myself to protect.

Camila grew up on the vineyard and took over when her father got sick. She said that as her parents aged, it was a no-brainer that she would be responsible for running it as she knew the ins and outs of the operation like the back of her hand.

Now that she oversaw the vineyard, she wanted to expand, something her parents had been reticent about.

"Hey, beautiful," Logan greets me as I walk into his shop.

"Hi, Lo," I say, wrapping my arms around him and basking in his full-bodied embrace.

Logan knows how to hug a girl and make her feel secure, comfortable, and sexy. He's not my type, and I'm not his, but we're cool enough. We have been for a long time.

He pulls back and holds my hand, lifting it into the air and twirling me around.

"Girl, I swear you get finer and finer every time I see you!" he says, whistling.

"Keep making comments like that, and I'll pluck your eyes out when you fall asleep tonight," Karin, his girlfriend, says, walking from the back of the shop.

"Karin!" I greet excitedly.

She smiles, pulling me into her embrace, and kisses me on the cheek. "Seriously, beautiful, you need to stop by and visit us more often."

"I know . . . but work and all that . . ."

"Honey, I wish my work were as glamorous as yours," she says.

"This bigheaded boy been taking care of you?" I ask, nodding at Logan as I rub Karin's growing belly.

"Keep my woman well-fed and that bigheaded boy of mine inside of her," he quips, winking at me.

I consider them the perfect couple and the epitome of Black love. As much as Logan can talk shit, Karin can not only take it, but she can talk him *under* the table. Despite his flirtatious ways, he loves Karin with all his heart and wouldn't do anything to hurt her and vice versa.

"Hear you're going undercover on your next venture," Karin says.

I'd lied and told Logan that I needed a fake identity for research purposes that I was doing at a facility overseas. I hadn't told him the identity wasn't so much fake as I was impersonating a real person.

"Yeah, doing some deep research for a magazine article that I'm writing," I lie, now feeling the weight of that lie on my shoulders.

Karin and Logan are my friends, and I always keep it real with them. I trust them, but this is something different. It's bigger than me, and I must keep this secret safe to protect my reputation and Camila's.

"Mm, must be supersecret if you're going all discreet sleuth on us," she laughs.

"Something like that. I had to sign an NDA before I accepted the job, so I can't talk about it," I say, thinking back to the NDA Camila had me sign.

It terminated any rights that I had to revisit the resort under the identity of Camila Martinez and negated all liabilities if any legal issues should arise.

"Okay. So, will we get to see some pictures of this place?"

Shaking my head, I say, "No. That was part of the NDA."

"Then what will you have to share in the article?"

"Trust me . . . It will be creative and different than anything I've ever done."

"Okay," she says, looking doubtful as Logan returns from the back of the shop with a manila envelope.

"Here you are, Ms. Martinez," he says, chuckling.

"Martinez?" Karin asks dubiously as I slide out the passport, driver's license, and birth certificate. They look legitimate.

"Girl, yeah. You didn't know? I'm part Dominican, so I can get that off," I tease.

Karin places a finger to her chin and slightly tilts her head assessingly.

"Girl, don't even think about it. I was just playing with you."

"You might be playing, but I've told you so many times you don't look completely Black," Logan says.

"How much do I owe you?" I ask, pulling my credit card out of my wallet.

"For you, lovebug? Give me a Benjamin," he says, ringing up my purchase.

I swipe my card, and he hands me the receipt.

"Why don't you come upstairs with us for a bit?" Karin invites.

"Nah, I need to get ready for my flight."

"Tiana, Kyrie, and Alycia are upstairs," Karin says.

"What? You didn't tell me the boogie bunch was here!" I say ecstatically.

Kyrie and Alycia are Karin's siblings, and Tiana went to high school with Karin, Logan, and me.

"My baby made smothered pork chops, sauteed green beans with garlic and lemon butter sauce, potatoes au gratin, her homemade yeast rolls, and her caramel cake," Logan says, walking ahead of us up the stairs that lead to their loft apartment over his shop.

"Damn! Why didn't you tell a sister you were about to feed her?" I ask, rubbing my belly.

Karin is between Logan and me on the stairs, looking over her shoulder and grinning. "Girl, you know I'd have fixed you a plate if you couldn't stay."

"Yeah, well, good food, good company, and good wine go hand-in-hand," I reply as Logan opens the door to their apartment.

No sooner than the door opens, music pours out, accompanied by a peal of boisterous laughter and soft, feminine voices.

When I step inside, I see Kyrie's long legs stretched out on the floor, and he's sitting between Tiana's legs where she's retwisting his locs. Her smooth brown face lights up when she spots me, and a wide, toothy smile takes over. The gap between her front teeth is endearing, as is the smattering of freckles over her nose.

"Nys!" she hollers, causing Kyrie to pop open his eyes.

"Baby girl!" he calls out, pulling away from Tiana.

He stands and lifts me from the floor, swinging me around.

"My first love! Where have you been, baby girl?" he asks, kissing my neck as he settles me back on the floor.

"Traveling the world," I say.

"Yeah, I've been reading your articles and watching your channel, and you've got me wanting to cross the oceans finally," Tiana says, pulling her bare feet up on the couch underneath her.

Kyrie's arm wraps affectionately around my waist, and I see Tiana's gaze go to it before her eyes and posture droop slightly.

Kyrie and I had a thing back in the day during our senior year of college and the first year after, but it fizzled out over time. I wonder if something's happening between them or if the feelings are unreciprocated.

I pull from his arm and head to Tiana as she unfolds from the couch and wraps me in her embrace. Tiana is tall, just a couple of inches shy of six feet. She's thick and curvy, but it looks good on her.

"Good seeing you, girl. You gotta stop being a stranger," she says.

"Not trying to be. I'm just hardly ever home anymore."

"It's been . . . six, seven months since we last saw you?"

"Eight!" Kyrie says.

"Yeah, she only comes around when she needs a favor," Logan adds, playfully punching me in the shoulder.

"I don't!" I argue.

"Okay, you don't," he replies.

"Nys, do you want everything on your plate?" Karin calls from the kitchen.

"Yes, please," I call back.

"Hey, baby girl!" I hear from behind me.

I spin around and see Alycia coming from the bathroom with a large grin. She was the first to start calling me "baby girl."

As the youngest of the Walter siblings, it made her feel good to have someone else smaller than her hanging around, so she dubbed me that nickname, and it stuck with all the others. Not because I was younger, but just smaller in stature than her.

"Look at you all loc'd up. When did you get them?" I ask, tugging on one of her locs.

"Tiana did them for me about . . . six months ago."

"They're growing really fast," Tiana says.

"Yeah, they are."

"Red locs look good on you," I reply.

"Here you go, baby girl. Sit down and eat," Karin says.

"Thanks, Rin. You didn't have to bring it to me. I could have done this," I say, accepting the fork and plate.

Logan follows with a glass and napkin.

"I'm pregnant, not immobile," Karin replies as I sit on the couch. Kyrie returns to his place between Tiana's thighs, and Alycia flops beside him, burying herself in her phone.

They all take turns catching me up on what's going on in their lives and then ask some questions about my travels. I fill them in and update them where I am on my "Thirty-Before-Thirty" List.

We play a few rounds of Dominoes after I finish eating. My friends are settled in with a beer, water for Karin, and wine for me. Ro James pours from the speakers, and before I know it, we're all getting high on some weed that Kyrie pulled from somewhere.

Karin has stepped into the bedroom. After we pass it around a few times, Tiana steps away to take a call.

"So, what's up with you?" Kyrie asks, nudging my knee.

"Nothing much. Just trying to live my best life."

"You still haven't figured it out, huh?"

"What?"

"That you belong with me. Maybe we can reconnect tonight and figure some things out," he says in a low, raw tone that sends a thrill of excitement through me as he rubs my thigh.

I remove his hand, staring into his eyes, and see that he's serious.

Ignoring the physical feeling and memories he invokes in me, I reply, "It wasn't meant to be, Kyrie."

"Why?"

"Because it just wasn't. No particular rhyme or reason. It didn't work, and I think we're better friends. We had this discussion before. Why are we returning here now?"

"I miss you, girl," he says, nuzzling my neck. "You walk up in here looking fine as hell. I'm thinking we should hook up for the night and see where it leads."

Pushing him away, I reply, "Or you could follow that trail with Tiana and see where *it* leads."

"Huh?"

"She's feeling you, Kyrie," I say.

"Nah, we're not like that."

"Sure?" I ask.

"Dead ass."

"I don't think she got the memo," I say, turning to face him.

"What memo?" Karin asks, stepping out of the bedroom with Logan, who'd just gone in to get her.

"The one that Tiana is clearly feeling the man."

"Told you," Karin says, giggling at her brother.

Alycia waves her hand and says, "He's ignorant. I've told him that a million times. The stuff she does for you, man? Women don't just do that for a man unless they want that man. Stop acting dumb."

"Watch your mouth," he says, pointing his finger at his sister.

"Seriously, Lycia has a point. You need to be up front if you're not about her like that. Don't play with her feelings or accept shit if you're not feeling her that way. It only leads women on," I explain.

Tiana walks back into the room, and I decide it's time for a conversation change.

"So, when will I be a godmother?" I ask.

Logan laughs. "You think I want *you* for a godmother?"

"What's that supposed to mean?" I ask, offended by his tone and its implications.

Shrugging, he replies, "You know . . . I love you, Nys. But you're not exactly the role model I'd want for my kid growing up."

"Why not?"

"Logan!" Karin says at the same time.

"Come on, girl. You and all your 'lovers'? Just saying it's not exactly a good look for a kid. If something were to happen to Karin and me, you could not be traipsing with my kid all over the world for your love affairs."

"Logan! That's *not* cool."

Shrugging, he says, "Nys knows she's cool, babe. Just saying."

Kyrie is eyeing me closely but not saying a word.

"You do seem to have a long list of lovers, Nys," Tiana says.

I'm unsure if she's just giving an opinion or throwing shade.

"And you would know this how, Tiana?"

"Girl, because of your channel. I follow you. You're always talking about the lovers you take in these different locations. I can tell by the things you say they're not the same man," she explains.

"You always did know how to pull a man without even trying," Alycia says enviously. "Maybe I should start traveling *with* you."

"No, baby girl. You're not about that life," Kyrie says.

"It really isn't that hard. Lycia can travel at a minimal cost, and if she follows any of the tips I've shared on my channel, articles, or TV show, she'll be good. Speaking of which, we have a new season of *Romance Abroad* this fall."

"Nah, I'm not talking about *that* life. I mean, she's not . . . That's just not her flow," Kyrie says.

"What's not her flow?" I ask.

"Yeah. What's her *flow*, Kyrie?" Alycia adds.

"Lycia's not an easy girl. She's more reserved," Tiana says.

I look at her, and for the first time, I see the anguish and the spite in my friend's eyes.

"You guys don't think I want to be in a committed relationship?"

"I see you talk about it on your channel, but it's not that difficult," Tiana says.

"For some people, it is. Everyone doesn't want to settle for the guy they think should be 'it.' Some people want the passion, the heat, the yin to their yang. They need more than great sex, someone who speaks to their soul," Alycia says.

"Beautifully put," I say, smiling at her.

"Something like what we have, Lo," Karin says softly.

He rubs her belly and kisses her forehead.

"So, is that why we didn't work, Nys? I didn't speak to your soul? Because you damn sure spoke to mine," Kyrie states.

I roll my eyes. "You're too much."

He stretches out on the floor. "Nah, I'm trying to be serious here."

"Dude, you just called her 'easy' a little bit ago," Alycia expresses.

"No. That was T who called her easy," he counters, lifting up onto his elbows to shoot a smirk at Tiana, who rolls her eyes.

"Can we just chill with all this?" Logan asks.

"You think that I'm easy, T?"

"No, but clearly Kyrie and Logan do," she answers.

"Look, I'm not trying to bash you, baby girl. I just have to be cautious about my decisions for this kid's future," Logan says.

"You don't get to choose. You're choosing the godfather, and *I'm* choosing the godmother!" Karin snaps, getting up and coming to stand by my side.

I rest my hand on her shoulder and say, "It's all good. Really, it is. Anyhoo, I need to get going. I have a few more stops and errands to run before my flight leaves."

Karin hugs me tight and whispers, "I'm sorry they're being an ass."

I kiss her cheek and emphasize, "It's good, girl. Thanks for the food and the fun."

Turning to look at Logan, I narrow my eyes. "You hold it down, Lo."

"You're leaving, Nys?" Alycia asks sadly.

"Yeah. It's time for me to head home."

We hug, and I see Tiana over Alycia's shoulder. Her lips are twisted, and she's staring at her phone.

Kyrie steps up with his arms wide after Alycia releases me. Squeezing me tight, he says, "You're still my girl. I'll be waiting whenever you're ready to come home and settle down."

"Don't," I mumble, pulling from his embrace.

"T, you take care, girl," I say.

She nods and mutters, "Yeah. You too, Nys. Be safe out there." Not once did she look up at me. I pull the door open.

Holding his arms out at his side, Logan asks, "What? No love for me? A brother can't speak his truth?"

"Not yours, Lo. Mine. Not yours," I say, shaking my head and closing the door behind me as I jog down the steps to his shop and out the door.

I won't lie; my spirits are dampened as I drive away and head out of the city and back to the suburbs. I'm feeling a way about my friend's words, though there is some hint of truth to them.

While I've been gallivanting around the country and loving my life, I haven't created any roots. Yes, I have an apartment, and yes, I have friends who happen to live all over the world. But my life isn't exactly stable, and I haven't been in a relationship in more than five years.

All because a guy I'd been dating for over a year broke my heart. I can't even really say that I loved the guy. It seemed as if the moment I opened up and allowed him to get close, he showed me his true colors. I vowed not to be that accessible to anyone again.

Looking back, maybe that was where I went wrong. Instead of dusting myself off and trying again, as Aaliyah advised, I shut out the possibility of finding love and settled for what I considered the next best thing . . . scratching an itch.

6

ANYSSA/CAMILA

"**W**hat the entire fuck!"

Creamy, puffy white clouds float overhead in the cerulean sky. Gentle waves hit the shore with a soft whooshing sound, foaming and rolling away until they repeat the cycle.

I arrived late last night in the cloak of darkness. I allowed my imagination to concoct vivid imagery of how beautiful this tropical paradise could be with its lush landscaping, frothy blue waters, white beaches, and majestic green trees. This place is stunning, a haven, a lover's paradise. It's everything that I imagined it would be and so much more.

Oh, *so* much more.

The people on the beach are nude! Like literally walking around with asses, tits, swinging man poles, furry jungles, and bare ones all on display!

Don't get me wrong, I'm no prude at all, but this shit is some other-level shit! I glance left and right and notice everyone casually sunbathing, playing volleyball, or strolling by like everything is good . . . except for me.

I'm stuck staring and sticking out like a sore thumb. Not because I'm the only one dressed because I'm not. There are some with thongs or a G-string and no tops, and a few in complete bikinis and bathing suits, but I'm the only one staring like I've lost my mind.

"Contrary to how brochures and commercials look, there are insects in exotic destinations like this. I'd advise you to close your mouth. Wouldn't want a bug to get trapped inside."

I turn to my right, gaping at the smiling brunette beside me.

"Hi, I'm Felice," she says, extending a hand.

I take it and shake it slowly, closing my mouth.

"Hi, Felice . . . I'm An . . . Camila," I hurriedly correct.

"Nice to meet you. It is something to get accustomed to, and I was as shocked as you were my first time visiting."

"I wasn't warned."

"No one ever is. That's part of the discretion of this place. People can enjoy the exclusivity and anonymity of enjoyment without fear of recrimination or having their fetishes being disclosed."

We take a few steps further onto the beach, where she lays down her towel, bag, and umbrella.

"Fetishes?"

She smirks knowingly, setting up her umbrella, and says, "The nudist beach isn't the only proclivity that Belle Baie caters to. It's a resort with all the amenities of a regular resort, plus a few more."

"Such as?"

"I wouldn't want to spoil the fun for you. Later, you'll get the grand tour . . . after you've signed the second half of the NDA."

"Second half?"

She nods, removes her T-shirt, and unbuttons her shorts. I'm not into girls, but I can't help but look at how comfortable she is. Her slender body doesn't have an ounce of fat. From her tiny handful of perky breasts with the strawberry-tipped nipples down to her slim ankles, she's toned, athletic, and healthy-looking.

"Care to join me?" she asks, glancing at me over her sunshades as she slides out of her flip-flops.

Blue eyes mock me, almost challenging me to do the same as she's done.

"Um ... I'm good."

"The best way to become acclimated and to experience everything that Belle Baie has to offer is to experience *everything* Belle Baie has to offer."

"I don't know. I didn't exactly sign up for this."

"Oh, but you did. Remember the statement in the original NDA that said something to the effect of 'exploring your complete self with an open mind'... and the other little ditty about not objecting to exploring different facets of life and embracing new adventures?"

"I recall something like that."

"That's what this is. Step out of your comfort zone, Camila, and relax and enjoy the experience. How long are you here for?" she asks, pulling out suntan lotion.

"Three weeks."

"And you're going to stay closed up the entire time?"

"Maybe not closed up, but definitely clothed up."

She chuckles. "I like you. Suit yourself," she says, lying on her belly. "Do you mind rubbing some of this on my back?"

I glance at her holding the bottle aloft, and as much as I want to run and say hell no, I don't. I accept the bottle, squeeze a little into my palm, and then rub it on her back.

"Lay out your towel and get comfortable. Just soak in the ambiance first. No need to rush. It'll come in time. Before you know it, you'll be walking around here with no inhibitions about anything like the rest of us."

And though this experience is uncomfortable for me, I will ease myself into it a little at a time.

I flip out my towel and lay it in the sand, kicking off my flip-flops and settling down on it. I'm not removing a stitch of clothing, though.

Plopping in my earbuds, I relax and read for a bit before I put away my phone and lie back, closing my eyes.

☑ ☑ ☑

After my time at the beach, I returned to my suite, showered, dressed, and checked my schedule. I was due for the grand tour. Yet, I was a bit nervous about it after what I'd discovered thus far, paired with Felice's mocking words.

The nudist beach isn't the only proclivity that Belle Baie caters to. It's a resort with all the amenities of a regular resort, plus a few more.

I walk into the reception area, basking in the cool breeze caressing my sun-kissed skin.

"Hello, Ms. Martinez. I hope your stay last night with us was comfortable and relaxing," a woman named Leona, according to her name tag, greets.

"It was very relaxing," I reply.

"Great. Well, it's time for your tour, but before we start, I need you to sign this second half of the NDA," she says, offering me a clipboard and pen.

I accept it and take a seat in a large, oversized armchair. My stomach rumbles with nerves as I worry about what the paper will state and whether I will agree.

I glance over it and see nothing that would cause me to go on red alert. It discusses sensual pleasures, embracing erotic experiences, and the concept of open-mindedness as it relates to absorbing the complete encounter of what Belle Baie offers. Then I'm reminded that I am entering into a binding legal agreement not to disclose anything I have seen, heard, or experienced at the resort.

Damn!

I sign away, swallowing my fears and trying to appease my conscience that whatever happens here, surely, I can run to the altar and pray for forgiveness when all is said and done.

"Okay, are you ready?" Leona asks when I hand her the signed NDA.

"As ready as I'll ever be, I guess."

She leads me down a long corridor to a glass door that looks out on a lush tropical garden. Beautiful pinks, magentas, bright oranges, and yellows dance with green, blue, and purple.

She shows me the gym, nightclub, restaurants, juice bars, winery, and indoor and outdoor pools before we move to the next amenity, the spa.

I follow her along the cobblestone path to another set of double glass doors with BBS scripted in a fancy font on both.

"Hello, Delilah. This is Camila Martinez, a new guest. Camila, this is Delilah, our resident spa manager."

"Leona," Delilah says with a nod before turning to me. "Welcome, Camila. I hope you enjoy your stay at Belle Baie and take advantage of the spa's amenities. We offer several deluxe packages, both conventional and unconventional," she says, pulling out a leatherbound menu and spreading it open on the marble countertop for me to examine.

My cursory glance at the menu with the fancy gold script embossed on black linen paper shows the usual massage offerings: aromatherapy, hot stone, Swedish, full-body, and so forth. I'm just about to close the menu when something catches my eye.

Clitoral stimulation massage. Anal stimulation massage. Sexual reflexology. Erotic massage.

Those are just a few!

Reading the descriptions under each heading has turned me on, except for anal stimulation. This girl is in no way letting anyone touch my ass other than to grip and squeeze.

I close the menu and turn to Delilah, who points at the board behind her. "These are our masseuses, along with a listing of their credentials and backgrounds. The price of a massage is covered in the cost of your stay here; however, we encourage guests to tip the staff. If you prefer a particular staff member, request that person's service again, and we will schedule you with them. Do you have any questions?"

"Yes, with your erotic massages, do they bring you to the point of . . . orgasm?" I ask somewhat shyly.

I can't believe that I'm asking this question.

"Yes, if that is your preference. Believe it or not, we have several guests who just want to be teased, and then they return to their partner later to complete the process. Then, some are into orgasm denial. Whatever your preference is, our staff is happy to help."

Okay. Why the hell didn't Camila tell me this was a sexual resort? Did she know?

"Is there a particular staff member you suggest?" I ask, looking at the ten members' pictures on the wall.

There are five men and five women who are equally attractive and sexy.

"All of our staff members are well-trained and skilled in the art of erotic and traditional massages. It all comes down to your preference and whom you wish to connect with. We have a weekly meet-and-greet for staff to interact with new guests. That will be tomorrow night at seven if you'd like to return then."

"Sounds great," I say. "What if I'm interested in a massage before then?"

"We'll simply get you scheduled at a convenient time for you. Is there a particular service you would like?"

Shrugging, I say, "No. Just curious. Maybe I'll come back later after the tour."

"Why don't I show you around the facility?" Delilah suggests.

Leona nods in encouragement, and I follow Delilah, who's already taking off as if it's assumed I will be following. Leona's right behind me as we tour the unoccupied rooms.

Each room is painted a different color. There's a pink one with cherry blossoms, another with grass-green wallpaper, dove grey, a deep red, a vibrant red, and teak. Several others have closed doors with Do-Not-Disturb signs, and Delilah explains they're in use.

Each room has a tall floor-to-ceiling mahogany cabinet with frosted glass doors to house supplies; some have one massage bed, and others have two. A couple of rooms have a whirlpool, others have a jacuzzi, and they all have sinks. Beautiful green trees stand in the corners, and varied-colored orchids are on the counters.

When we finish, we end up at the front desk again, and I realize the spa is one large circle.

"So, will we see you here this evening?"

"Maybe," I say, not promising anything.

I can't imagine relaxing under a full-body massage, knowing where the hands of my masseuse have been and what they could be doing. Would I be turned on? Would they accidentally forget I'm not here for a clitoral stimulation massage but the hot stone massage instead?

"Thanks, Delilah," Leona says before leading me from the massage parlor. "So, what do you think?" she asks, gazing at me as we walk along the stone path to another building.

"It's beautiful, serene, and smells great."

"And the offerings?" Leona asks with a knowing smirk.

"They're a bit more than I expected. I think it's sexy and unique, but . . . I won't lie; it caught me off guard. I guess everyone has a thing."

"What's *your* thing, Camila?"

Smiling, I say, "I don't know, really. I love traveling, and while I don't consider myself a prude, some of this is beyond what I could have imagined. I want to be open to exploring new things while I'm here, and hopefully, I'll figure out what my thing is by then."

"Maybe we can help you figure out your thing while you're here. Help you explore and develop your sensual awareness."

She opens another glass door to a large, open space. A reception desk is centered there, with a man and woman talking. They stop when we enter and smile in greeting.

"Hi, Jules, Nelson. This is Camila. She'll be staying with us for the next three weeks," Leona introduces me to the redheaded man and blond woman.

"Welcome to Belle Baie," the woman, Jules, says warmly.

"Would you like for us to give her a tour?" Nelson asks.

"No, thank you. I'll handle this," Leona says, turning to me. "Follow me, Camila."

We walk down a long hallway with luminescent mosaic wall tiles. On the wall hangs several brightly colored erotic paintings of couples in various sexual positions and poses.

"What's this place?"

"This is Studio BoDSMe. Guests come here to experience various levels of eroticism, whether pleasure, pain, or both."

"Pain?" I ask as Leona pushes open a door, showcasing a large bed in the center of the room with straps and various devices hanging overhead from the ceiling and some leather attachments on the bed.

The room has two windows, one behind the bed and one on the left wall, but both are covered by heavy black drapery. Against my better judgment, I follow Leona inside, and the heavy door closes behind us without any prompting from me.

My heart jumps as I wonder what this room is and if I'm locked inside. Before I can ask the question, Leona pulls a key card from inside her blouse and slides it against a card reader on the side of the cabinet.

When she unlocks it and gestures to it with a flourish, I take a step closer and look inside. My hand touches the candles, oils, towels, and a broad display of rather harmful-looking instruments.

"BDSM?" I ask, facing her as my fingers stroke the flogger's leather falls.

"Yes, and the studio's name is a play on that word. BoDSMe is an acronym for Boudoir of Desirable, Stimulatingly Mind-bending Experiences. Have you ever indulged?"

"No, I haven't," I said, shaking my head. "Not that I'm averse to it, but . . . I guess I haven't found the right partner to try it with or someone knowledgeable and willing to teach me."

"Have you gone online into any chats to find meetups?"

Laughing, I reply, "No. I've never been comfortable with that. So, I've stuck with finding out what my lovers liked. Unfortunately, most of my lovers are only interested in one thing . . . getting a nut. No matter how it comes."

"Selfish lovers."

"Not all of them. Some have been more skilled than others, and plenty are interested in bringing me pleasure. But they're not very creative, or . . . Let me correct that. They're not into anything beyond a 'traditional' affair."

"So, you're a virgin to this world, but I detect you *might* be interested."

I chew on my bottom lip as I mull that over.

"I mean, I don't know anything about it, but I'm not ruling it out."

"Are you sure?"

I hesitate for a moment before a small smile takes over my lips. "Yeah, I am. I'm very sure."

She taps her bottom lip and says, "I may have just the perfect partner for you."

7

NAZÁR

"You should at least consider it, Nazár."

Shaking my head, I fork the Parmesan-garlic-encrusted asparagus tip and place it in my mouth. Chewing slowly, I watch Leona across the table as she traces the rim of her wineglass with her fingertip. She looks up at me and tilts her head.

"It's been a long time since you've had a suitable companion. Someone who complements you well. I gave her the tour, and she seemed a bit standoffish until I took her to Studio BoDSMe. Her interest was piqued by what we offered there. She said she hasn't indulged in it, but she might be interested with the right partner."

I can feel her gaze on me as I cut my steak and take another bite.

"Well?"

Staring at her, I stop chewing. She knows better than to push me or pressure me. She lowers her gaze briefly, and I finish chewing.

"You're a bit talkative tonight."

"I'm sorry, it's just that . . . She's perfect for you, Nazár. She's a beautiful, intelligent woman who, while she may be comfortable in her sexuality, seems to be looking for something more. Something I'm well aware that you can provide for her."

Leona and I had a brief fling three years back, and while it worked for me, it didn't work for her. She eventually wanted more, and I had nothing more to offer. She's engaged to a man who is more her speed now, and I'm happy to have her as my assistant and nothing more.

"You have no right to speak out of turn, Leona. Not about something like that."

She lowers her gaze to her plate and begins eating her food before looking at me again.

"I think I'm well within my right. I know your appetite better than anyone else, Nazár."

I push away my plate.

"I have a meeting in Switzerland next month. Have you made the travel arrangements for that?" I ask, changing the subject.

"I have. Everything is in place, including your special requests. Shantel Graf has cleared her schedule to entertain you for your visit."

Shantel is a casual acquaintance with whom I indulge in a few nights of pleasure whenever I'm in that area of the world.

"That will work," I say with a nod as I remove my linen napkin from my lap and wipe my mouth before placing it on the table.

Niles, my house attendant, comes to the table, instantly removes my dinnerware, and looks at Leona.

"I'm finished, Niles. Thanks."

"What's my schedule for the day after tomorrow?"

"You have an early-morning flight at six thirty to attend the nine o'clock meeting in Madagascar. So, when you arrive, it will be—"

"Seven thirty their time. I know they're an hour behind us."

"Right. So, you're scheduled to be served breakfast in-flight. When you land, a car will take you to the conference center, but you will have time to review your notes and the agenda before the meeting."

"My return?"

"Is scheduled for three our time. After your meeting, they set you up to tour the property. On your return home, you have a vineyard tour scheduled for five in the evening."

"Move that to tomorrow morning."

"But, sir, you have a—"

"Move it to tomorrow, Leona! Cancel the meeting with Palmer and Trope. I won't be buying their property after all. Schedule my vineyard tour for the time of my meeting with them. I'll take a lunch break and then do the distillery tour later that afternoon around three."

I look at Leona as she quickly jots down my notes and then excuses herself to place the phone calls she needs to make.

I push back from my chair, step out onto the lanai, and sit on the chaise. Every evening at ten minutes to five, I come out on my lanai to watch the sun set over the ocean.

Lush palm trees, giant fig trees, and ochrosia borbonica, an endangered plant on the island, all grow in abundant supply on my property.

"Your drink, sir," Amara says, setting my glass of spiced rum on the little table beside me.

"Thank you, Amara."

"You're welcome, sir. Will there be anything else?" she asks politely.

"No, Amara."

She walks away with her hips swishing provocatively. I wonder again, not for the first time, about my sanity. Women, guests, and staff alike have often propositioned me for a night of pleasure, but I don't indulge. It's not that I don't want to because there are more than a few women whose sexuality and attraction are beyond tempting.

I choose not to indulge because I don't need the complications that broken hearts and messy affairs lead to. My reputation, net worth, and financial holdings don't allow for those impediments on my resort. I have brief affairs with women who have never visited my resort.

It's been awhile since I've had sex, though I don't know why I bother to hold off. This place is a sexual den with all we offer. Waiting another month for sex won't kill me, but I swear it's making me grouchy and on the verge of losing control.

Turning my attention beyond the lush setting of my backyard, I watch as the sun slowly sinks over the horizon, sending a brilliant display of orange, red, yellow, pinks, and purples radiating across the sky.

My thoughts return to dinner and Leona's suggestion that I meet one of our guests, a vineyard owner from California. She says the woman is signed up for our rum distillery and vineyard tours. I do recall receiving an email from Camila Martinez stating that she was interested in expanding her operations and was touring various resorts around the globe.

Camila Martinez's interest in my operations would have been largely ignored had it not been for a mutual friend, Dale Weatherall. He and his wife, Yvonne, said Camila Martinez would benefit from visiting the resort.

They expressed that she had a beautiful and successful vineyard. Although it was thriving, it could be more profitable with expansion, and she could learn a lot from me. They'd also said that while she was a hard worker, she needed an extraordinary vacation to remove her stress.

My guests are hand selected and receive invitations at the behest of past guests who suggest them to me. Guests who are inclined to be discreet and who have a palate for the offerings we extend receive invitations to visit the resort after a thorough background check. I had accepted Camila as one of the few guests I allowed to visit the resort.

After the sun sets, I decide to stroll around the property. It's not often that I engage with my guests, but I will walk around once a week to greet a few familiar acquaintances and to see if there's anything that I want to indulge my appetite in.

Belle Baie was created to share the beauty of this stretch of the island in Mauritius with those who want to escape the real world for a while and indulge in sexual activities that cater to their needs without the fear of recrimination.

We offer twenty suites and twenty-five guestrooms, with world-class romantic dining. Guests can choose from various activities such as sailing, horseback riding, scuba diving, hiking, biking, private sailing, kite surfing, paddle boarding, snorkeling, and windsurfing.

Unlike many resorts, we also have a vineyard and rum distillery, offering tours and wine tastings. My rum distillery is my pride and joy, and I offer personal tours of that, along with the vineyard sometimes.

Although construction began on the resort six years ago, a tragedy set me back by a year. When loneliness and depression set in, I refocused my attention on my original mission and proceeded to open the resort four years ago. It was a success right away but for the wrong reasons. It took me less than six months to restrict the guests to those I chose.

Four months later, I expanded the resort's services after a rousing conversation with a few like-minded guests who wanted to experience a genuinely adult-only resort. Our beach is a private one, which allowed me to change it to a nudist beach. Not that people must go nude, but guests prefer that option.

Along with the nude beach, we opened an entire facility dedicated to BDSM or kink. While I've found that many couples enjoy engaging in it, many single women don't seem interested because they have an incorrect concept. The few single women who have visited and are interested are Dommes.

I have not found the perfect submissive, not only on the island but also even in my travels. Not that they're not submissive, but there's no genuine connection with me. No one wants the pain I have to offer, nor can they endure the deep-seated emotions that I sometimes experience, which causes me to be reserved.

"Nazár, come and have a drink," I hear a familiar voice say.

Turning around, I see Jason Cunningham, senator of the great state of Georgia. He holds his glass aloft, and I see the Mexican woman sitting beside him, curling under his arm. It's not his wife, that's for sure, but that's none of my business.

She often accompanies him here, but I've never formally met her.

I head over to the outdoor tiki bar and sit beside him.

"Liliana, this is Nazár, the owner of the resort. Nazár, this is my longtime friend, Liliana," Jason says, turning back to the woman and smiling at her.

"It's a pleasure to meet you, Liliana."

"Please, call me Lily. What a wonderful resort you have here, and I *love* the offerings," she says.

"Thank you. I hope you enjoy the duration of your stay," I say, turning to the bartender, who offers me a fresh glass of rum.

"What's next on your ventures?" Jason asks.

"I have to tour a property in the morning in Madagascar, but there's not a lot planned right now."

"I have a piece of property in Georgia that I've been eyeing for some time. I'd like you to come and look at it. Let me run some ideas by you about what I'd like to do, and then give me your thoughts, okay?"

"How about this? You send me the specs for the land, an aerial video, and your ideas for developing the property, and then I'll decide if I should come and check it out."

Jason smirks, tosses down his drink, and slowly shakes his head.

"It's hard getting this one onboard with any project," Jason says.

"Not true. I just want to ensure it will make money before investing."

"You think coming to the States to look at the property is a waste?"

"Could be. Jason, you're greedy for gain. You remember that property the last time you showed me in Alabama surrounded by obscure swampland?"

Jason chuckles, and I finish my drink, setting it on the bar top.

Squeezing his shoulder, I say, "Send me everything I need, and we'll go from there."

He holds up his glass and says, "You got it, man."

I head further down the beach and loop around through the gardens and the cottages on that side of the resort. By the time I've come to the end of the walking path that courses through the cottages, I'm facing the hotel of my resort, and I stop for a moment to gaze up at the beautiful stucco building.

A woman steps out onto a balcony on the fifth floor, leaving the door open. She grips the railing and holds her head back, the wind tossing her curls around her. She pushes her hair away from her face but doesn't open her eyes.

The breeze picks up more, plastering the sheer blue nightgown against her body. I see nude bodies around my resort daily, but she's the first one in a long time that's intrigued me completely.

The light in the room behind her casts an angelic glow about her face and body. She has a handful of small breasts that are erect and tipping upward as if sending a kiss to the moon and stars, broad hips, a slim waistline, and curvy but toned thighs. I can see a darker outline at the apex of her thighs, making me wonder what she tastes like.

I can't help but stare at her even when she lowers her head and opens her eyes. They scan the grounds briefly before they land on me.

I'm leaning against a palm tree with my hands stuffed in my pockets, watching her like some damn stalker. She doesn't allow that to deter her, though. If anything, she steps closer to the railing, pressing her body against it, and stares back at me, almost challenging me. To what? I don't know.

A small smile tilts her lips. She waves, and just like that, she's returned to her room with swishing hips and jiggling ass. The door shuts, the curtains close, and the lights go off. Fuck!

I walk off into the night, heading home again to be alone with my thoughts. It's not easy being wealthy, private, and cautious. It leads to a very lonely existence.

I can only hope that I'll sleep a dreamless sleep tonight. If not, I'll be teased by thoughts of the temptress and stroking my cock alone.

I have to find out who the woman in room five-thirty-one is.

8

ANYSSA/CAMILA

I tossed and turned all night, thinking about the man I flirted with. I couldn't see his face in great detail, but I could see enough to know that his features were sharp, striking, and handsome. Today, I'm ready to go in search of this man.

I have three weeks at this resort, but I have no idea how long he will be here. For all I know, he could have left this morning already. A quick glance at the bedside table's clock has hope soaring through me.

I know the shuttle from the resort hasn't come yet because there are two in the morning. One leaves at nine and the other at eleven thirty. It's just a little after seven, so I may still have time to run into him if I hurry.

Leaving my hotel room, I search each floor as I take the glass elevator, praying that he's not in his room. There are four suites on each floor, and each floor is a perfect square. My room takes up one length. There is a room opposite mine, one to the right and another to the left.

I make my rounds on the first floor, looking for him among the guests who are eating, by the bar, and at reception. When I come up empty, my feet take me down the path to the nude beach, and I pray that no one is sunbathing in the nude this early.

Unfortunately, God has a sense of humor because there are sunbathers out this early, and there's an old man with a wrinkled ass and a crooked, long, skinny dick. I thank the stars that I haven't eaten breakfast yet. Otherwise, I would have puked it up on this beach.

Why, oh, why couldn't the man from last night have been here?

Yet, something tells me that this isn't his thing.

I wander around the resort before I end up at Studio BoDSMe.

"Hello, welcome back," Jules, the woman from last night, greets.

"Thank you. I uh . . . I was just wondering if I might check out some of the rooms. Are they in use right now?"

"No. Feel free to look into them," she says cheerily. "Usually, they're locked, but not this early."

There's no point in moving on if no one is here because that means he isn't here either. Yet, I smile and head to the rear, peeking into each room to keep up the façade of my visit just to check out the rooms.

When my tour of each room confirms what Jules told me, I stop in the largest room in the back. Black walls have a luminescence to them as though sprinkled with diamonds. Heavy black drapes block the floor-to-ceiling picturesque windows. A black chandelier with diamonds and pearls draping it hangs from the ceiling.

A tall, ebony wardrobe sits at the rear of the room. There's a lock on the wardrobe, so I step away and walk to a black table opposite the bed.

I tug on a drawer handle, surprised to find that it opens. It holds an assortment of knives, and I can't help but pick one up and run my finger along the blade.

I cannot imagine what they use this for. I replace the knife and close the drawer before turning to admire the large California King dungeon bed. My hands stroke the steel bedpost.

Kneeling, I check out the underbed that holds a cage with padded floors. Excitement at being locked inside hums through me. "Who the hell knew?" I ask myself as I marvel at my reaction to this room. I sit on the mattress, surprised at its comfort, before I reach up and grab one of the restraints looped through the restraint hoop.

Thinking of being restrained to a bed like this one as the man from last night has his way with my body turns me on. My nipples harden, and I squeeze my thighs tight, trying to stem the desire building inside me.

I climb onto the bed and grab one of the restraints, locking it around one ankle and then the other. I've closed the door, so I'm not worried about anyone coming in and catching me in a compromising position.

I grab one of the restraints and secure my left hand. Leaving my right hand unrestrained because I can't restrain it, nor can I release it. I smooth my hand across my belly.

Closing my eyes, I imagine the man from last night being here with me. I know that he could see through my gown. I wonder if he's here with anyone.

My nipples bud at the thought of what I'd want him to do to me with me lying on this bed. The soft click of a door closing causes my eyes to flutter open in alarm. I hadn't heard anyone outside the hall, nor had I heard the door open.

"They say that black is a mystery. It's inviting yet foreboding. It calls out to the deep within us, inviting you to take the risk. Most women are attracted to the purple, orange, red, and violet rooms here. Seldom do they come to the black. Are you a risk taker, my love?"

"Uh . . . I, um . . ."

"Black is my favorite color," he says, pulling his fingers through the black leather tails of a flogger.

I don't say anything. I just stare in shock with my mouth wide open.

"Next time, you may want to lock the door. It clicks a 'Do Not Disturb' sign in place," his deep, raspy, heavily accented voice says as he slaps the flogger against his palm.

Fuck! It's *him*—the man from last night. I know I didn't see his features. Yet, those broad shoulders, masculine chest, the slight curve in his legs, and the cocky way he stands let me know that it's him. He's just as beautiful as I thought he was last night.

Dark green eyes glitter like broken emeralds scattered amongst a sea of glass. Full lips are slightly parted as his gaze pierces me. Long, thick, dark brown hair covers his head and face. He looks moody and angry yet curious all at once.

"I'm . . . I'm sorry. I didn't think anyone would be here," I say, rushing to unchain my wrist.

He moves to the foot of the bed just as I sit up to unwrap my ankles. His hand holds my left one firmly as his thumb rubs tiny circles on my instep. Who knew something so gentle could be such a turn-on?

"They're usually not this early in the morning. Which is what provoked my curiosity about the closed door."

"Oh," I say, too afraid to jerk my foot from his grasp or reach down to free my ankle from the cuff myself.

"Do you like it?"

"Um . . . Like what?"

"The room."

"Uh . . . Yes, it's different. Interesting."

"What's your guilty pleasure? Pain or tenderness?"

Shit! How could I answer that?

I'm never speechless. Hell, I'm a prolific writer for some of the most world-renowned magazines. How are words failing me now like some schoolgirl with a casual crush on the star basketball player?

"I'll take it that you're a virgin. Am I right?" he asks, his fingers still rubbing small circles on my ankle.

"No," I say softly.

Laughing, he says, "You are. I can smell it on you. This is all new to you."

I watch as his hands spread to encompass the room.

"Oh, you mean . . . BDSM?"

He licks those thick lips of his.

"I mean sexual exploration. Removing the barriers and testing the limits of pain and suppression. Unearthing your body's deepest secrets and the ability to submit to another, yielding control to someone else, and trusting them with your life."

"I, um . . . Well, I haven't considered that before, but it sounds sexy."

"So, you're in this room for what? Trying it on for size?" he asks, finally unlocking both my ankles.

"Something like that."

He nods, walks to the locked cabinet, and pulls out a key card, unlocking the cabinet as I swing my legs over the side of the bed and stand.

"Tell me, Princesa, how much do you know about this world beyond what you may have read or watched on TV?"

I closely watch as he displays an assortment of toys I know nothing about. Some look fun, others interesting, and some downright scary.

Floggers, paddles, restraints, hoods, blindfolds I'm familiar with, but there are metal instruments in there, some with chains and others with hooks and spikes that I've never seen.

I want to lie, but at the same time, I don't. I'm not trying to run him away, but I don't want to come off too knowledgeable and find myself in deep shit.

I search for an answer that's somewhere between the two extremes.

"Not that familiar with it, but that's because I haven't had a partner knowledgeable about it or interested enough to try it."

"Everyone always has their firsts."

I bite my bottom lip, holding my breath, hoping he'll suggest what I think. He doesn't. Instead, he closes the cabinet and relocks it, pocketing the key.

It's going to be up to me to make it happen.

"I want . . ."

I swallow, trying to find the right words.

"The woman I want knows what she wants and is unafraid to express it."

"I want what you want," I boldly say.

He turns around and stares at me; the wicked gleam in those eyes is frightening. It's as if I'm looking into the eyes of the devil himself.

What the hell have I just done?

☑ ☑ ☑

ANNY'S ANNALS

Aloha!

Hey, it's me again . . .

I met the man that I saw outside of my balcony last night. It was embarrassing as hell how I finally ran into him. I'd set off this morning determined to find him before he left the resort, but he found me . . . bound to a kink bed of all things!

Yes! Me.

As if that wasn't bad enough, he asked if I was interested in this world. I didn't tell him that I knew nothing about his world. I pretended I was into it but hadn't found the right partner.

He tells me he's looking for a woman who knows what she wants and isn't afraid to say it, and I tell him I want what he wants.

After that, he just walked out of the room. No plans for later, no questions, no goodbye or nothing. He simply walked away as if we'd never engaged in a conversation in the first place.

Now, I hope I don't see him again, and even more so that he doesn't tell anyone about our encounter. I'll bet he has a girlfriend at the resort and is just toying with me.

It'll be my luck that he's setting me up for some freaky threesome, which I'm Not down with.

Maybe he wasn't Mr. Right, but he looked like he'd feel so good being Mr. Wrong.

After my vineyard tour, I think I will head down to the beach later this evening. I'm excited about that, as it will be the first time I'm doing anything related to my promise to Camila. After all, if it weren't for her, I wouldn't be here.

I haven't reached out to her since my arrival. Maybe I'll do that after the vineyard tour. I hope Mr. Dark and Kinky isn't on this tour.

Until next time, Anny!

Nys 🖊

I close my diary, lock it, and secure it in my bag again. I'm itching to film some video or go live, but I know I can't.

I've thought about going live on my channel and reading from my journal, but even that would be a breach of contract, going against everything in the NDA. After all, anyone could glimpse my background, and I haven't found anything here that isn't unique to the resort.

Sighing, I grab my phone and decide to call Camila now.

"Hello?"

"Hey, Camila. It's me, Anyssa."

"Anyssa! How are you, honey?"

"I'm doing pretty good. What about you? Has your dad had his surgery yet?"

"Yes, he did. Thanks for asking."

"How did it go?"

"It was touch and go for a while, and he had some complications that the doctors will have to go back in and resolve, but they're giving it a couple of days. Right now, he's in a medically induced coma to help relieve the pressure on his brain and reduce the pain. I'm here at the hospital with him now. Mom needed some sleep, so I'm giving her a break."

"I'm so sorry to hear that, Camila. You and your parents are in my thoughts."

"Thank you. But that's enough about me and my sorrows. Tell me all about Belle Baie. Is it as beautiful as I've heard? Exciting? Exotic?"

Laughing, I tell her, "Girl, it's everything you told me it would be and much more!"

"Wow! As much as I want to ask you for details, I won't. I know that you had to sign an NDA."

"I did, but since it's you that's actually here and not me . . . for all intents and purposes, I will say that there are many things that I didn't expect, and I'll tell you that one of those things is a nude beach."

"A what?" she screams in my ear.

Laughing, I say, "You heard me."

"I can't freaking believe that! Have you gone nude?"

"Not yet."

"Yet? Hmmm . . . Sounds like there may be plans to."

"I was thinking about it. I'm going on the vineyard tour now, though," I say, changing the subject.

"Perfect. Did you get the questions that I emailed you?"

"I did, and I've downloaded them to my notes app on my phone to ask them while on tour. I don't know if they would allow it, but I considered asking if I could record the audio of the tour. It'll be easier for me to share that with you later as you can relate to their discussion."

"Sounds like a great idea," she agrees, "but I doubt they'll let you do that."

"Yeah. Well, I'll just take some great notes, Camila. I promise to represent you well and get everything you want."

"Thanks, Anny."

Laughing, I say, "Wow. That's what my mom calls me."

"Really? My dad calls me Cami."

"Pretty. Anny sounds homely, but I love it because it's her nickname for me. Something only she and I share," I say softly.

"Aww . . . That's sweet."

"Well, I won't hold you up any longer, Camila. I know you need to be with your dad, but if you have anything you can think of before or during my tour, just text me, okay?"

"Sounds great, Anyssa."

I end the call and glance at the clock. After changing into a yellow floral maxi dress, ballet slippers, and a denim jacket, I grab my crossbody purse and pull it over me before snatching up a big, floppy hat and sunglasses.

I head out of my room, wave at a couple going into their room to my right, and board the elevator with another couple.

"Are you going on the vineyard tour?" I ask.

"Yes, we are. Have you been to one before?" the man asks in a British accent.

"Actually, I've been to plenty."

"Please tell my wife that the heels and perfume are a no-go. She wants to be cute."

"You're beautiful," I say.

"Thank you," she replies, preening before sticking her tongue out at her husband.

"I hate to admit it, but your husband is right. We'll be doing lots of walking, and if this trip is anything like others I've been on, we'll be touring not only the vineyard but also the fields and caves. After walking all day and drinking, your feet and back will kill you. Not to mention, stumbling from too much wine might have you falling down or tripping up a hill."

"Crap!" she groans. "What about my perfume?"

"I say don't wear any at all, but I have a couple of friends who opt for a lightly fragrant lotion. I wear deodorant and skip everything else because the fragrance impacts your ability to taste the flavors of the wine and sniff the glass. If you truly want to experience it, you should listen to your husband."

"Thank you, ma'am," he says, graciously taking a bow as the elevator doors open on the first floor.

She shoves him playfully on the shoulder. "Well, at least ride back up to the room with me to change shoes."

"We're going to miss the tour."

"We won't!" she exclaims as the door closes on their argument.

I giggle and make my way to the front of the hotel, where the bus pulls up to take us down to the vineyard.

We're boarding five minutes later when the couple comes racing through the door and running up to the bus.

"Just in time," the driver announces. "We were just getting ready to pull out."

The drive to the vineyard is only five minutes, and I enjoy the serenity of the ride, taking in the beautiful foliage around us as I listen to the couple from earlier engage in lively banter. Others talk softly or sit back, relax, and enjoy the ride.

We climb off the shuttle bus and gather in a large circle as the driver tells us what to expect. Just as he finishes his speech, someone steps out from one of the rows of vineyards, and I swear I want to disappear.

"Ladies and Gentlemen, I'm leaving you in the expert hands of your tour guide, Mr. Nazário Rivas, the owner and operator of Belle Baie and Sérénité Vignoble," the driver says, pointing at the signage for the vineyard.

I can't do anything more than stare at my feet as my senses block out everything except an awareness of him. Although I'm not looking at him, I can smell him, hear his voice, and feel his energy rolling off him in waves.

"You probably are wondering why I would give this tour when I have so many capable staff who do everything else and even run this place in my absence. Well, it's because the vineyard is my heritage. It's in my blood, and it lives and breathes in me. Were it not for a vineyard back home in my hometown of Villa de Leyva in Colombia, I would not have had the opportunities I've had in life to be successful or even run my own vineyard."

His accent is thick and bold. His tan seems to be deep and rich in the late-morning sun. I didn't notice these things as much this morning because I was mortified at being caught in a compromising position. But he looks like he has spent the morning in the sun.

He's wearing tan khaki pants, a crisp, long-sleeved white shirt rolled up to his elbows, showing off a smattering of dark hair on his arms, and a casual pair of loafers on his feet.

"Care to join the rest of us, Ms. Martinez?" he calls out.

My head jerks up, and I realize that everyone is moving forward. I've been lost in my thoughts. My eyes widen in wonder as I keep up with the others, taking notes as we go.

When we stop again, I close my eyes and inhale the crisp, sweet air tinged with the ripeness of the grapes, which glisten with moisture from the morning dew. I can almost taste their bitter sweetness on my tongue.

Nazário's long, tapered fingers pluck a grape, and he holds it up for us to see.

"As you can see, the harvesters are out here, harvesting the grapes we will use in our sparkling wines. Then the grapes for the still white wines will be harvested next."

"When does harvesting end?" the woman who had to change her shoes asks.

"We'll finish either late October or early November. Those are for the red varieties," Nazário explains.

"Oh, my favorite!" someone else gushes, causing the rest of us to laugh.

"This is a perfect grape. It has no sunburns or blotches. It's perfectly round, big, and full. It's not misshapen at all. This is what we're looking for."

He pops the grape in his mouth and chews slowly, a twinkle in his eyes as he stares at me.

"Delicious. Juicy. And ripe," he pronounces, making my panties wet.

Shit! It takes a while before I can get my mind back on track while he's moving along, as though that didn't just happen.

My notepad is full when the vineyard tour ends, but I have many other questions.

And they all revolve around one man.

9

NAZÁR

I wasn't surprised to see her at the vineyard. I'd gone over the roster the night before. I was surprised to see her this morning in the Noir Room. Although Leona had insinuated the woman had an interest in what fascinated me, I didn't expect her to dive right in. When I first arrived at Studio BoDSMe, Jules had told me the center was empty the way it typically is in the morning, except for one guest who just wanted to look at the rooms. I always go to the Noir Room in the mornings to center myself. It helps me feel close to my true self and create new scenes in my head for the next time I'm with a woman who shares my desires and interests.

I hadn't expected to find anyone in that room, and when I approached the closed door, I knew it had to be the guest she had mentioned. The door was not only unlocked, but it wasn't closed completely, and I took the liberty to see who'd encroached on my sanctuary.

All the guests know that the room belongs to me. While I lock it occasionally, I haven't lately because I've known all the guests visiting. Camila Martinez is new to me, and while she was referred to me by a mutual friend, she still has to learn the unwritten rules. The unspoken rules that staff and guests alike know to respect.

I could feel the sexual energy humming off her when I stepped inside that room. It took everything in me not to leave her bound the way she was, binding her free hand and having my way with her.

I desperately wanted to extract pain, pleasure, and moans. The greatest arousal would have been to dip her gorgeous body into the depths of pleasure that only my hands can bring.

Instead, I chose to keep my hands to myself. Well, mostly. I couldn't help but touch her. It was amusing watching her writhing there, trying to maintain her control, speechless and so damn aroused. Her nipples poked through her shirt, and her scent reached out and tickled my nose.

Despite her need and mine, I chose to mindfuck her instead with just a few well-placed suggestions.

Yes, I can't wait to feast on her.

I want what you want. That's what she said. She has no idea what I want, but I will get it. And she'll be the one to give it to me.

The woman never should have offered herself to me on a platter like she had. I could feel her eyes on me throughout the vineyard tour and the wine tasting. I never had to look directly at her to determine if she was looking at me. I could see her out of my peripheral vision, staring at me. I could feel her watchful gaze on me.

I'm an enigma to her, one that she wants to figure out, but at the same time, she's scared.

I maneuver through the tasting room, stopping at tables to chat with my patrons as they indulge in charcuterie plates or chocolates with their wine pairings.

"This wine is delicious, Nazár. This Albarino has notes of peach, citrus, and stone fruit," Sheila, one of my guests, says.

"It's very dry and crisp on the palate with some lemon. I love this white wine," her sister, Gayle, chimes in.

"Perfect! I'm glad I could make you ladies happy," I say, squeezing each of their shoulders.

I move on, leaving them in giggles.

Ms. Martinez, or "Princesa" as I call her, is chatting with Felice. I see the occasional glances Princesa tosses my way, but I prefer to engage with everyone else first, saving her for last.

I stop by three more tables to chat with other patrons about our selection. When I'm finished, I exchange my empty glass of white for a full glass of red, and I slowly make my way in Princesa's direction.

"Nazár! This red is simply amazing," Felice gushes, holding up her fifth glass of red wine since the tasting began.

She prefers the reds to everything else, and while she may sample some of the others, she'll always return to the red.

"Thank you, my love. As are you. Are you enjoying this trip?"

"I am, thanks," she says as I lean in, and we exchange air kisses.

My gaze lifts slightly to meet Princesa's gaze, and she's blushing. I wink and blow a kiss at her just before I pull back from Felice.

"You have to join me for dinner tonight," Felice invites, resting her hand intimately on my wrist.

"You know that I don't stop at dinner, Felice. You know that my hunger is never satiated," I say as my eyes remain on Princesa.

She chokes on her wine, and Felice turns to pat her softly on the back.

"You are such a flirt," Felice says, turning back to me.

"And yet, no words have ever rung truer."

"I'm afraid I can't keep up with your appetite, Nazár."

"There's only one type of woman who can do that."

"Oh? I'm surprised that you found someone who could," Felice says genuinely, lifting a cracker loaded with cheese and tomatoes to her mouth.

"Oh, she's not fully developed yet. She's ready . . . waiting for me to shape and train her into the perfect rendition of what I need and want."

"Good luck to the poor woman," Felice says, looking at Princesa, who's been watching me with wide-eyed wonder the entire time.

"Nazár is an excellent lover. Very dominating and controlling, but it makes it all worth it—*if* a woman can keep up," she says.

"You're speaking from personal experience, I suppose," Princesa says before sipping her wine, eyeing me, and then Felice over her rim.

"Loose lips, Felice. Loose lips. Don't be a woman of indiscretion even after drinking. Alcohol is no excuse and can ruin even the greatest women."

"I know how to be discreet," she says proudly.

"You'd damn well better hope so, lest you find that you won't get reinvited to the resort."

The threat and warning in my voice are apparent, and Felice's face reddens as she nods and places her glass of wine on the table.

"If you two will excuse me, I need to use the ladies' room," she says, scooting her chair back as I hold it for her.

She tosses her napkin onto her plate and walks through the maze of tables.

I take her chair and push her plate and napkin back. Crossing my ankle over my knee, I run my finger around the rim of my glass.

"You understand the need for discretion, don't you, Ms. Martinez?"

"I, um, of course, I do."

"I would think so. A businesswoman such as yourself, with a successful vineyard of your own, knows that certain secrets that every business holds close to their chest make the operations so successful."

"Well, of course, but I can understand how that relates to the business aspect of this place. What I'm not so sure of was your barely concealed threat to Felice as it related to personal matters."

Chuckling, I lift my glass to my lips, taking another sip.

"Make no mistake about it. That wasn't an attempt to conceal my threat. I wanted to be very clear. And let me make this clear. I'm as private about my personal life as I am about this resort and all my businesses. A woman who wants what I want would understand that, no?"

She pushes her plate back and says, "You have made yourself very clear. What you didn't have to be was rude to Felice."

"I am blunt if nothing else, and I make no apologies about it. Felice knows me very well. She knows what I expect, what I like, and what I do not like. As I respect her wishes and feelings, I expect the same to be reciprocated. Is that a problem for you, Princesa?"

"Why do you call me that?"

"You give off an air of royalty, entitlement."

"I don't," she hisses.

I chuckle and lift my glass to my lips. After another sip, I look into her eyes and say, "Oh, what fun I will have in showing you that you're wrong and I'm always right."

I see the fire flash in her eyes, along with curiosity.

"Is that what you think?"

"It's what I know."

"Mm . . . Challenge accepted."

"I hope you're a woman of your word," I say, setting my now-empty glass on the table as I stand and leave her there sitting alone as Felice makes her way back toward the table.

☑ ☑ ☑

"Well, well, well. I see I was right," Leona says over dinner.

"About?" I ask, wiping my lips with my linen napkin.

"She's the right one for you. Camila Martinez," Leona says cheekily.

"What makes you think that?"

"Oh, little birdies talk."

"Maybe those little birds need to be knocked off the telephone wires," I say glumly.

"Hmm . . . Well, I heard you ran into her in your room this morning. How did that go over?"

"Jules was the only one who could have told you that Ms. Martinez and I had any kind of encounter in the Noir Room."

"Don't harass her, Nazár."

"I won't. She's lucky she's your baby sister, or she might be fired."

"She only gossips with me," Leona says, shaking her head.

"I don't trust gossiping women, Leona. You know this."

"Yet, you trust me with your life," she says, smiling cheekily at me.

"Humph," I grumble, lifting a glass of bourbon to my lips.

"Enough of that. I'm sure you've had enough to drink tonight. You have an early-morning flight."

"I do, but if you know me as well as you claim to, you also know that I only have two glasses of wine at the wine tasting."

"What will you do about *her*?" she asks, changing the subject as Niles brings in two dessert plates with key lime pie and forks for each.

"What's there to do?"

"Are you going to engage her in play?"

"I think you're too invested in my sex life, Leona."

"And I say that you're not invested enough."

"How does Gary feel about you being so invested in my sex life, Leona?"

She waves her hand and shakes her head. "He's more invested than I am. He hopes you'll find someone soon to keep you occupied."

"Why? Is he worried I'm about to snatch you up again for my lair?"

Laughing, she says, "Please. He knows that there's no chance of that. No, Gary wants you happy because he cares about you, Nazár. Just as the rest of us do."

Gary, Leona, and Jules are the closest people to family to me here at Belle Baie. Gary, Leona's fiancé, runs the rum distillery. Leona met him through me. And while my family balks at not being invited to the resort, I don't have to worry about Gary, Leona, and Jules. They're a part of my world.

Gary and Leona also engage in kink, though not here at the resort. They save that for the privacy of their home. Jules, Leona's baby sister, engages with some guests visiting our resort and is not ashamed of it.

My family would have much to say about my lifestyle and the resort I run. They would shame me and pressure me into leaving and returning home. I couldn't do that because Belle Baie is who I am. It saved me through some years that could have crushed me. How can I turn my back on the one thing that breathes life into me?

"I care about you and Gary's happiness too, Leona. Which is why you should stay out of my personal life," I say.

She smirks. "You know that I can't do that. Now, tell me. What did you two discuss at the wine tasting while Ms. Felice ran to the restroom? I have it on good authority that she had flaming hot cheeks when she left the table and was subdued when she returned."

"There were only three staff at the tasting room this afternoon. When I find out who's blabbing, they're fired."

"No, they won't be," Leona argues. "But you should ban Felice. She does gossip too much."

"Felice is harmless. She's a good woman, Leona."

"No, she's a woman scorned. She only returns, hoping to claim a place in your life. The fact that you ridiculed her this afternoon—"

"I didn't ridicule her."

"Well, the fact that you said something to embarrass her tells me she'll be looking to do something vengeful."

Shaking my head, I say, "No. This isn't the first time something like this has happened to us."

"Just make sure that she doesn't ruin what could be a beautiful friendship between you and Ms. Martinez."

"I would never do anything to sacrifice what the Princesa and I could have."

"She even has a name," Leona says knowingly, smirking at me above her wineglass.

"This is amusing to you, huh?"

"No, I just like to see you happy, and I believe she can bring you happiness."

I stare at Leona for a while before slowly nodding. "I believe she could be trained to be the perfect partner with time. Unfortunately, I don't know that I have much of that before she returns to her life."

"Well, you could allow me to speed up the process."

"Meaning?"

"Siphon out what her intentions are through meaningless conversations between two women. Decipher if she really is a perfect fit for you. Prepare her."

"You're a nosy busybody, Leona. Stay in your place."

"If you insist."

"I do."

Somehow, I doubt that she'll listen.

10

ANYSSA/CAMILA

ANYSSA'S THIRTY–BEFORE–THIRTY LIST

- ☑ Make love in a stairwell
- ☑ Hike the Rocky Mountains
- ☑ Ride an elephant
- ☑ Dance in the rain
- ☑ International road trip
- ☑ Learn an art
- ☑ Ride in a hot air balloon
- ☑ Go backpacking
- ☑ Make love to a stranger
- ☐ Perform on a stage
- ☑ Tattoo on my ass
- ☑ Scale a summit
- ☑ Learn a foreign language
- ☐ Swim at night, where you can see the stars
- ☐ Snorkel
- ☑ Parasail
- ☑ Make love on a train
- ☐ Take a cooking class in a foreign country
- ☑ Learn to ski
- ☐ Stand under a waterfall
- ☑ Swim with the dolphins

☑ Sing a karaoke duet with a stranger
☑ Ride a gondola in Venice
☑ Travel the world
☑ Send a message in a bottle
☐ View a sunrise from a place where you can see the horizon
☐ Do something along the lines of exhibitionism
☐ Find my father
☐ Try kinky sex
☐ Fall helplessly in love

"**H**i, beautiful people! I wanted to drop in and check on you. I know you're used to seeing videos from me everywhere I go, but I'm taking a bit of a hiatus. So, I'm checking in with you from a personal and undisclosed location. However, I dropped in for a couple of reasons. I wanted to see where you guys think I should go next. Two, I wanted to show you something cool I did today, which allowed me to check off item eleven on my list."

I'm in the glassed-in shower in the bathroom of my suite. Sitting on the shower bench with my back against the tiles, I know my viewers can't possibly discover my location. The black and clear glass shower tiles against my back don't give too much away.

I've been going crazy all morning not connecting with my viewers. I'd gone down for breakfast earlier and chatted with some of the guests, then made my way to the Black Room in Studio BoDSMe. As expected, no one was there this early in the morning, and it wasn't Jules who was on staff this time, but Nelson.

I waited around for half an hour, and he never showed up. After his cryptic message yesterday evening, I was sure that I would be seeing him again soon.

Honestly, his arrogance and treatment of Felice had pissed me off, *and* the fact that they'd been lovers at some point. Yet, after tossing and turning and seeing him in my dreams overnight, I couldn't help but look for him this morning.

Unfortunately, I never found him. So, I caught a ride off the resort to a little tattoo shop about fifteen minutes away. I ended up with my ass exposed and getting inked up. Afterward, I shopped and grabbed some lunch before returning to the resort.

I came to my hotel room looking for something else to do. Hence, me on my YouTube channel.

"Hi @kitten357. Yes, I danced in the rain, and it was so much fun! So simple, and this sweet and beautiful man I met in Curaçao graced me with that wish."

I smile as the comments flow and scroll through a few until I get to the next one.

"Yes, that's what I wanted to share with you tonight, @jorje_7821. I went to this awesome little tattoo shop today and got my ass tatted up," I say, laughing. "It didn't hurt, not like my other tattoos, and I guess that's because of the fatty meat back there, but there are also muscles in your glutes. Anyway, it took him a while to complete it, but I love the results," I say, shifting on the shower bench.

I angle my phone in such a way as to show my viewers my left cheek, where a lioness paw is tatted. The lioness's face can be seen through the individual features depicted in each claw.

When I pull the phone back up, I laugh at the comments.

@philbryan701: "Great ass."

@cruztrader: "Nice tone."

@tripled3889: "Can I kiss it?"

@dedrickbabymama517: "Where did you get your work done?"

@adamridge_00: "Great body. You stay in shape."

@damarisxxx: "Who's your trainer?"

Several more comments like those come through.

"Okay, peeps, I upheld my part. I showed my ass, literally and figuratively. Now, I need to hear your suggestions about my next destination."

Again, the comments roll through, and people suggest places like the Philippines, Madagascar, Sweden, Finland, Turkey, and Chile. There are several others, but I notice that I have several suggestions for Colombia so that I can see the Rainbow River.

@egyptdiamond: "No, I haven't found my true love yet. However, I met a very interesting man on this trip. He's different from any of the others that I've met. At first glance, he seems detached and unapproachable, but I sense some layers need to be peeled back."

@derbywright: "No, he's not one I want to leave behind like the others. Yet, I don't know him well enough to call it love, but I do know that I would like to know him better. It's not a sexual thing with him, but . . . Honestly, I don't know how to explain it."

I laugh at the responses and answer a few more questions unrelated to love and Nazário Rivas to keep my ass out of hot water.

"In my next video, I hope to have more to tell you about my next destination. Again, I'm taking some time away to rejuvenate and refresh. So, don't freak out if you don't see me on here for a week or so. Everything's fine. Don't send out any BOLAs or Ashanti Alerts because I'm tucked away in a quiet little corner of the world, getting my spirit together. Until the next time . . ."

I blow a kiss and end the video. My thoughts wander back to my last conversation with my friends before leaving the States. While I haven't said as much to anyone and have barely acknowledged it myself, I can't help but feel heavy about their comments about my life.

I stare at my phone for several minutes before giving in and calling Karin.

"Hey, beautiful."

"Hi, Mamas. How are you and the baby?"

"Oh, ready to pop, but doing great. My feet are swelling, but other than that, all is well. How about you?"

"I'm good."

She's quiet for several seconds before saying, "How are you *really*, Nys?"

Sighing, I say, "I've been thinking a lot, especially after the conversation at your place."

"I'm sorry that Logan was such an ass. We had a long talk about that."

"No apologies needed. It forced me to do some thinking too. Don't get me wrong, I was thirty-eight hot leaving out of there, but I'm really considering the meaning behind his words."

"Such as?"

"Logan's words could have reflected many people's thoughts. People who are too kind to voice their comments or too distant even to care."

"People like who?"

"Like my viewers. I wonder what my viewers really think about my numerous affairs. I don't have sex with men everywhere I visit, but I have a lot of sex with many different people. I'm always cautious, and I use protection. Usually, the men are guests at the hotels I'm staying at. Occasionally, the men are random strangers in the city," I admit, realizing that I feel the confines of depression creeping in on me.

"Are you happy with your choices, Anyssa? Because at the end of the day, you're the one who has to live with those choices. Not Logan, not me, not your viewers, or anyone else."

"For the most part, I am. I'm just ready to settle down."

"Have you ever considered just being alone and not having a man in your life?" Karin challenges.

"This shouldn't be a thing, but just hearing you ask me made me afraid."

"Why?"

Blowing out a breath, I say, "I think about my mother and know that I don't want to live life as she did. Mommy took me away from my father before I was born. He was abusive, and it was the only way she could ensure she didn't lose her life and, potentially, mine. She ran away and never looked back.

"Unfortunately, that's all that I know about my father. I don't know his first or last name or even what he looks like. I only know that Mommy took her maiden name again, which became my last name. I saw her lonely throughout the years as she worked to provide for me and make a decent home for us. Although she never begrudged me anything that she could afford nor friendships, she did place limitations around allowing people into our home. We have no family other than the two of us."

"Damn, Nys. I never knew all of that about you and your mom. That's hard."

"Throughout the years, I resented that, especially during the holidays when other kids were surrounded by family. It was always just Mommy and me. In my teen years, she would allow me to spend some holidays with friends after spending the first half of the day with her."

"She must have been lonely, but how much does that speak of her love for you to make that sacrifice to ensure your happiness?"

Tears prick my eyes, and I say, "Does it make me selfish that, while my heart was breaking for me, I was angry with Mommy?"

"Not at all. You were just a kid, honey, and as kids, most of us have selfish thoughts. It takes training, bumping our heads, getting up again, and then maturing and growing to get through those years. I will say that you're the least selfish person that I know now. You give endlessly to everyone you love. And your mom? She's your world. You take such good care of her, Nys," Karin reassures me.

"I have been so heartbroken for her because her life centered on me. I know that she's lonely even after all these years. My travels don't help matters because all she has is her church family. But at night and throughout the week, except for Wednesdays, her Bible study days, she's alone after work."

"You know my mom and dad have been together for a couple of lifetimes. I admire what they have. It's strong genuine, and they've weathered many storms together. Just like your mom chose not to take a risk on love again, they chose to take that risk. That's who I modeled my relationship with Logan after. I saw what my parents had and how happy it made them, and that's what I knew I had to have in my life. Maybe that's what happened to your views on relationships and men. You chose to run so hard and so far in the opposite direction that you created something that maybe you didn't recognize or possibly even want. Have you ever considered that?"

"That's true. I vowed that I didn't want that for my life. I know that a therapist would look at me and say I have abandonment and commitment issues all rolled into one. I fear being alone like Mommy, so I always seek male companionship. I worry that one day, I'll look up and have no one, not even a child, to share my life with, create new memories, and share my deepest secrets, greatest fears, and biggest dreams.

"My fear of being abused or left behind prevents me from being able to commit to any man, which is why I can't hold a relationship. The same thing that happened to Kyric and me, the fizzle going out, was the same excuse I've used with others before and after him."

"Honcy, you have to make a choice. You can either keep going the way you are to avoid being hurt, or you can do what my parents and Logan and I chose to do: Take the risk, fall, and fall hard. If you get hurt again, get up and dust yourself off again. Wash. Rinse. And repeat. Trust me, baby girl, it's worth the risk to find the right one."

"We'll see," I say.

"I love you."

"Love you too, Rin. And thanks for listening."

"Any time," she says before I end the call.

I push off the shower bench and step outside the bathroom. Grabbing my beach bag and sunhat, I tuck my phone into the bag and head out of my hotel room.

Within ten minutes, I'm on the beach. It's a little after two in the afternoon, and I decided that I'm going to conquer one of my fears today . . . the nude beach.

"Hi!" I hear a voice call.

Turning around, I see Felice waving from her spot on a sunflower yellow and navy blue towel. I walk to where she's set up and roll out my towel.

"You're back. I was sure the wrinkled asses, shriveled dicks, and hairy cooches had run you off."

Laughing, I reply, "I wish I could say you were wrong. I'm not as brave as I might pretend to be. Initially, they did run me off."

"And?"

Sighing, I say, "I'm tired of living in fear. I want not only to live life but also embrace it. So, I decided today to conquer one of those fears. I'm going to get off this stunning white sand and walk my sexy ass down to those gorgeous, turquoise waters in all my naked glory."

I punctuate that statement by removing my top and, slowly and cautiously, look around. No one's watching me except Felice, whose eyebrows lift slightly above her sunglasses. Beyond that, I can't see anything.

I untie my string bikini and let it fall onto my towel before I sit down.

Clapping, Felice says, "I'm proud of you. Don't worry; they may check out your body from afar, but no one will approach, assault, compliment, or condemn you."

"I didn't think that," I say shyly, pulling my knees up to my chest to cover it.

"Word of advice?"

"What's that?"

"With a body like yours, you don't need to hide anything. Besides, in that position, you may be covering your tits, but you're exposing your ass and twat from the other angle."

Mortified, I stretch my legs, crossing my arms over my breasts.

Felice laughs at my reaction and lies back, shaking her head. It's not long before she's returned her attention to some book with a beach cottage on the front.

"Hello, friend!" I hear another voice call.

Looking up, I see the couple from yesterday. Unfortunately, they set up on the other side of me as if we didn't have this large expanse of beach to choose from. I turn to Felice, who's still reading but smirking her ass off.

The husband is the first to remove his clothing, but I don't look. Hell, I'm afraid to turn one way or the other. A nude man standing beside me is hard to ignore, especially when I want to look. Damn, I want to look so bad, but I don't. I continue staring forward even after knowing he and his wife are undressed.

"Claudia, rub some lotion on my legs, baby."

"Greg, you can't do anything for yourself, can you?" she asks.

"You love me like this."

"I do," she says.

After a few seconds, I risk a glance at them. She's got her back and ass turned to me, and she's rubbing lotion on his shoulders. His dick is hanging free, resting on his upper thigh. Not that I'm trying to check for either of them, but they're both in great shape.

I turn my eyes away again and wonder what I was doing coming down here like this. I thought I was ready, but obviously, I'm not.

"Breathe," Felice says, resting a hand on my shoulder.

"Huh?"

She leans closer and whispers, "You look ready to bolt."

"That's because I am."

"Conquer your fears. You're greater than they are. Besides, this is easy work compared to what will be asked of you in the coming days."

"What are you talking about?"

"Nazár."

"What about him?" I ask, going on alert.

I wonder what she's heard or what he may have said to her. After all, I haven't seen him all day.

"He's set his sights on you. When Nazár wants something, he gets it."

"I'm not a toy or some property."

"No, you're not. Trust me, he recognizes that. But you're a beautiful girl. Young, fresh, and naïve. You're a dream for a man like him. Nazário is very persistent and persuasive. He'll take good care of you, but be careful with your heart. If you give it to him, he'll never give it back. And he won't give you his in return."

"I'm not . . . I'm not interested in him like that."

"Liar," she scoffs.

"Well, I'm not," I say calmly.

"Honey, your nipples are hard, you're clenching your legs together, your fists are balled up, and your tone and posture are all defensive. Trust me, when you were looking at Buddy Balls next to you, your nipples did *not* get hard."

I instantly cross my arms over my chest again.

"He's an attractive man, but I'm involved with someone. I don't want Nazário."

"Do yourself a favor, hon."

"What's that?"

"Give in to the attraction. I promise that you won't be disappointed."

"Why? Because he's good in bed?"

"He's a master in the bed, but he's the lord of mind games. Whew! That might be almost as good as him fucking you."

The last thing I want is to have this conversation with a former lover of Nazário's about Nazário. Besides, my curiosity is begging me to ask her if she's seen him, and I don't want to give her ammunition against me. That would be as good as admitting that I do want him.

Instead, I stand and say, "I'm going for a walk on the beach. Trying to get comfortable with this new me."

Shrugging, she says, "Okay. I'm taking a nap, but holler if you need me."

I glance at the couple on my side, and they both look up, smile, and wave. I give a tiny wave and head away from our little group.

I swear it feels as if one or both are watching my ass. Or maybe that's just my imagination.

☑ ☑ ☑

ANNY'S ANNALS

Aloha!

Hey, it's me again . . .

I had a very disappointing day. I'd gone out this morning to meet the sexy man again. By the way, his name is Nazário Rivas. How sexy is that?

After meeting him yesterday in the BDSM room, I found he was the tour guide for the vineyard and the wine tasting. It was so damn embarrassing. I hoped I wouldn't see him again after the kink bedroom incident.

Worst-case scenario . . . I was hoping it might be a day or two. But no, to my dismay, it was only hours later. He was watching me when I didn't think he was, and whenever I'd look up, he would look elsewhere.

He's Felice's former lover. The only person here that I kinda know. After dropping that tidbit on me, he chastised her about it. She left us and went to the restroom for a moment. He made a cryptic comment to me yesterday before he left me. He said, "Oh, what fun I will have in showing you that you're wrong and I'm always right."

I hoped to see him today, but I've been everywhere, and there are no signs of him.

On another note, I returned to the beach today and got up the nerve to remove my clothes. A couple that I met on the vineyard tour yesterday was there, as well as Felice. They acted as if it were the most natural thing in the world.

It was before Eve bit that damn apple and enticed Adam to do the same. Damn, we women have been hell since the beginning of time.

Anyhoo, I shed my clothes and strolled down that damn beach like I was born to do it. No one bothered me or made me feel uncomfortable. Just some waves, hellos, or head nods.

A group of people playing volleyball invited me to come and play. It was funny watching all of them playing in the nude. Guess the same could be said of me because I damn sure played . . titties and ass bouncing all over the place.

Well, maybe tomorrow I'll go on the hunt again in search of Mr. Dark and Kinky. I hope I find him.

Until next time, Anny!

Nys 💋

11

NAZÁR

"Deeper, Nazár?"

"Yes."

"Harder?"

"I can barely feel it."

"What about now?"

"Yes, love. That's the perfect spot. Stay right there for a moment and work it out."

My eyes shut momentarily at the sheer perfection of how good my body feels. Suddenly, a sharp pain forces my eyes to open, and I tense.

"Relax."

"I can't. It hurts."

"Nazár, you're a big baby. I've told you about allowing yourself to get this worked up. It's been two months since your last massage. You're tense all over, and the stress of your work, your workout regimen, and failure to get routine massages have every muscle in your shoulders, neck, and back knotted like a pretzel."

"Not being a baby," I mutter.

"You even sound like one," Yoni chides.

"Whatever. Just . . . Can you work the shit out, please?"

"Well, since you asked nicely," she teases, rolling her fingers over my left deltoid muscle while her thumbs rotate in tight circles.

I relax under her careful manipulation of my muscles, thinking about what I want to accomplish the next day.

"How did your business trip go?"

"It went well. The property was just what I'd hoped it would be. Now, my lawyers will have to play hardball with their lawyers, and we'll see who wins in the end."

"Your lawyer knows your final number, I'm assuming."

"He always knows."

"If they don't meet you where you want them to, what happens next?"

"They'll find another buyer, and I'll search for another property."

"So, is there ever a time you would go beyond your final number to secure a property?"

"At the end of the day, it's about business and about making money. I set the final number for a reason, and I'm not in the business of incurring losses, Yoni. It would take a special property and circumstances to change my mind."

"Do you apply that same tactic to your relationships?"

"Where is all this coming from?" I ask, turning over to look her in the eyes.

Her face flushes a deep shade of red, and her brown eyes flitter away momentarily before landing back on me.

"It's just that there's this guy I've been seeing. He's a businessman who is a shark when it comes to business. He reminds me a lot of you with those same hard limits as you, but he seems softer and more caring in our private lives. He's attentive to my needs, making me feel like I'm the most important thing to him."

"What's your problem then?"

"Whenever I want to discuss where the relationship is going, he clams up and becomes business-minded."

"Why do women always want to discuss where the relationship is going? Why can't you be satisfied with where we're at now? Enjoy every day and moment and take advantage of the opportunities to appreciate each other now. Relationships don't have to have limitations, restrictions, and rules. That's what messes them up in the first place."

"You believe that?"

"I do."

"So, we're what? Just a piece of meat to you guys? Convenient for sex?"

Shrugging, I say, "You said that. Not me. I love good conversation with a woman and comparable companionship. I like to bond with them. I just don't happen to think that one woman can satisfy all my needs."

"Why not?"

"Women fight for their identity, and a man wants a wife to come home to. A woman who takes care of the house, the kids, and business concerning the family so that he can handle his business in the world. A yin and yang that works out. If her fight for her identity clashes with his goals and objectives, she wants him to compromise or sacrifice his hopes and dreams. Women walk through the door saying what they will do and then change somewhere along the road. They don't always know what they want sometimes but want you to believe what they say.

"Women play mind games to control a man and want to be judged equal to men where there is no equality. Men are men, and women are women. Women no longer want to be narrowed down to wife and nurturer; they want to be out there chopping trees with the men. But who cares for the house and the kids if she's out chopping trees?"

"That's why you hire a housekeeper and a nanny if necessary," Yoni says.

Shaking my head, I reply, "And why would I do that when I don't want another woman caring for my kids and home? In that case, I should marry the nanny and housekeeper, don't you think?"

"The two are not the same."

"But they can be. Sometimes, for a man trying to be the best he can be, committing to a woman can be his worst mistake. Rather than stressing out the woman, I'd rather allow her to serve her purpose in my life for the space she thinks she should fill and vice versa. Wherever the gaps lie, I can find someone else to fill those areas. Why should I impose my desires on a woman who isn't interested in being that woman?"

"And yet, I never see you with any woman," Yoni says smartly.

"Point made. No one can claim me as theirs, and I'm okay with that, Yoni. Right now, I have no time to cater to any woman's emotions or needs."

"And what about your needs?"

"Conversation? That's fulfilled with family, friends, and constituents. I can have engaging conversations with a stranger. Companionship? I have that with travel partners."

"And sex?"

"I have no problems in that area."

"So, you agree that's all that men want or need from a woman?"

"Why does a woman work so hard to be enticing, and when the man falls for it, she turns around and says he only wants sex? Many times, the woman is only offering up the possibility."

"That's not what I'm asking of this guy, though."

"Only time will tell."

Yoni grows silent and returns to massaging my muscles. Though I know I've given her a lot to think about, and she doesn't understand why my beliefs are what they are, she doesn't take it out on me. She remains the consummate professional caring for my body as she always has.

After all, she's the only one to whom I trust my body, other than the casual relationships I engage in.

"Sir," Nigel calls near the end of my massage.

"Yes, Nigel," I reply with my face still buried in the hole of my massage table.

"Your mother is on the line."

"I'll take it," I grouse.

Yoni steps away and begins packing up her items as I climb off the table.

"Hola, Mamá," I greet after stepping off the lanai and into the garden that overlooks the ocean.

"Nazário! ¿*Cómo estás*, mi amor?"

"I'm fine, Mamá."

"Gabriel just found out he and Luciana are expecting another little one."

"That's great, Mamá."

"And Matias said he and Salome are trying for a third."

"Wonderful, Mamá."

"Your cousin Selene and Antonia just had their sixth child."

"Amazing, Mamá. You want me to send them a gift?"

"Nazário Sebastian Rivas! Behave yourself!"

"Mamá, I was busy with a business call. If you only called to talk about kids—"

"There is no call that is ever more important than your family. I don't care what type of business you are taking care of. I called to talk about kids because children are a reason to celebrate. If you were to have your own, you would understand. But you have lost your sense of family in the world!"

I don't mean to disrespect my mother, but this is my second conversation about what women want in less than half an hour. What the fuck ever happened to what a man goddamned wanted?

"Mamá, I have to go."

"No! You waltzed out of here angry when you visited last. Then when you returned, it was so late that your father and I had gone to bed. The next morning, when I woke up, you were gone. Is that any way to treat your family, Nazário?"

Pinching the bridge of my nose, I close my eyes and breathe deeply several times.

"Nazário! Answer me!"

"It is the way to treat my family when they cannot respect my wishes," I say slowly.

"What do you know about wishes?"

"Mamá, I am not a little boy anymore."

"So your father keeps telling me. As a man, you should understand the importance of appreciating and respecting family."

"As I said, I am a man with his own thoughts, ideas, and opinions. I have given you everything I have to offer, but you won't continue taking my dignity. I tolerated your and Papá's opinions about my marriage for so long that I allowed them to weave into every aspect of Bella's and my lives. She's no longer here to defend herself. But I won't tolerate the two of you continuing to disrespect her or impose your opinions on my life."

"What has gotten into you, Nazário?"

I don't think she will ever see what she does to me in a million years. This argument is in vain.

"I have to go, Mamá. Te amo. Tell Papá that I love him too."

I click the call off without waiting for any further responses. It's too much, and I just can't take it. I need to unleash all this pent-up anger inside of me.

"Why don't you go to Noir tonight?"

Turning around, I spot Leona leaning against the door frame with her arms crossed. She knows that whenever I speak with my family, I'm not often in a good place afterward.

"Thank you, Leona, but I don't have a suitable companion. And I'm not in the mood for meditating and creating a scene tonight."

"Maybe you should invite the 'Princesa' and see if she's up to the challenge."

My eyes darken and flash, and Leona shakes her head. "At least it will allow you to put that thing to good use," she says, waving a hand at my dick before she walks away.

The next time I get a massage, I'll be sure to wear a towel. Running into the house after her, I call, "Leona."

"Yes, Your Majesty," she teases.

"You're testing my patience. You must be up for a spanking tonight."

"We stopped playing those games with each other years ago."

"And yet, you continue to provoke me."

"I doubt Gary will be happy about that."

"Then stop testing my limits, woman."

"If you were to stop playing games and tell the Princesa what you really want from her, then you wouldn't have to worry about me or any other woman testing your limits."

"I think it's time for you to head home for the evening. I'm sure Gary would love nothing more than to spank that tight little ass of yours for that snarky mouth."

She blows a kiss at me, grabs her bag and keys, waves goodbye, and disappears. My chest rises and falls in frustration. I have nothing or no one to take out my frustrations on.

God, how I would love to spank Camila tonight. To see how she creams at the feeling of my hand on her ass, caressing and spanking her. I head to my room to shower and dress. Sometimes, a walk on the beach settles my spirit when I'm agitated.

12

ANYSSA/CAMILA

It's an old warehouse with brick walls, oak floors, heavy pine beams, and exposed ductwork overhead. Windows positioned three feet under the ceiling give the illusion that it goes on forever, but I would guess the room's height is around twenty-five feet.

Rows of circular stands and T-Stands display T-shirts with the Belle Baie Rum Distillery logo on the front. Wooden shelves hold trinkets, from personalized shot glasses to name bracelets, copper mugs, and hats. There are even delicacies like chocolate-dipped, rum-coated lollipops, fresh-baked rum cake, and rum cookies.

It's not what I expected at all. I'm taking notes to share with Camila when I return. I wish I could take pictures, but that's out of the question.

A set of stairs to the left and right lead to a bar and grille area upstairs. The staff is welcoming and friendly, which may be due to the owner's presence. After all, if Nazár Rivas were my boss, I wouldn't want to disappoint him either. And not just for the sake of my job.

The man is beautiful, simply put. With his dark, brooding looks, long, dark hair, and deep moss-green eyes, Nazár is breathtaking. Pair that with his broad shoulders, defined biceps and ass, and that thick Colombian accent, and he's the stuff that dreams are made of.

Nazár leads us past the rows of merchandise and beyond a bar at the back to a large, open lobby area. Where the store had a more rustic appeal, the lobby area is slightly more polished and gleaming with a sunny yellow coat of paint, a glass chandelier hanging from overhead, and sleek polished oak floors.

"What's the TV for?" an Indian man asks.

"For those who choose to get the quick history recap of our facilities and how we started making our rum, as well as the history of the rum-making process on the island," Nazár explains.

I glance at the row of three pews in front of a large-screen TV mounted on a wall. Along the walls are framed posters of old pictures and articles about the factory.

Nazár explains how Americans purchased slaves from Africa and then traded them to the West Indies for molasses. After the rum was made in New England, they would trade the rum for more slaves in Africa.

After donning aprons, face masks, and gloves, we step into another large room with five stills and other equipment and I have to ask for the correct spelling for my notes. I try not to focus on the man standing so close to me that I might get singed at a simple brush of his skin against mine.

"This control box allows our operators to control the heat supplied to these machines," Nazár explains.

"How hot does it have to get?" I ask.

"One-hundred-ninety degrees," he says, turning that heated gaze on me.

He steps away as though becoming aware of how close we are to each other.

"As it travels up the tower into each plate, the alcohol content increases and the boiling point decreases."

"How long does this process take?" I ask.

"Eighteen hours."

He continues with his spiel, and the others look as if they're partially interested but more focused on when they can return upstairs for the tasting. I'm the only one asking questions, and although I don't want to act like a teacher's pet, I have to get these notes for Camila.

Besides, Nazár looks impressed that I'm interested in this process enough to ask the questions.

"The boiling point increases as we remove the alcohol from this equipment," he says, pointing at a giant vat that looks like a commercial-sized hot water tank. "When the machine reaches the boiling point of 212 degrees Fahrenheit, we're done."

Nazár's explanations are more detailed throughout the tour, eliminating my need for further questions. I'm satisfied with what I've gathered, and I plan to return to my room this evening to transcribe my notes into a detailed document that I can send to Camila.

For the most part, my obligation to her is complete, and I can now relax and explore this resort and island the way I want to.

We return to the front of the store, but I make my way to the lobby with the history articles to read each of them. I've finished reading the framed articles about rum making and its impact on slavery, and I've moved on to the articles about the history of this location when he returns.

"Did you get everything that you needed?"

I spin around and see Nazár leaning against a wall with his hands shoved into his front pockets. His gaze travels from my eyes down to my legs and then slowly back up again before it lingers on my mouth.

The heat from his predatory gaze consumes me, and I desperately want to have just one night with him.

Shaking my head, I recall the purpose of my visit. "I did. Thank you for being so forthcoming with all the information."

"You're welcome. I hope it's useful in the changes you want to make to your vineyard."

"I think it will be. I'm looking for new ideas to continue growing the operations, and I want us to have viable options for other income. Investing in other business ventures aside from the vineyard alone is smart and will set my future family up for generational wealth."

"Your future family?"

"Yes."

"Mmm," he murmurs but doesn't elaborate.

"So, I read the history of this place, but why was that your attraction?"

I have to switch subjects to uphold my promise to Camila. I can't delve into a personal conversation with this man because I'll feel too close to him, and that's the last thing I need. His proximity to me is turning me on. I need some sort of distraction.

"My family owns a vineyard and have for centuries. My grandfather had a whiskey distillery when I was a boy, and the process was more interesting to me than the vineyard my brothers and I worked."

"How many brothers?"

"Two. One older and the other younger."

"Did you enjoy working in the vineyards?"

"Initially, until I got older and started having my own dreams. My grandfather's distillery interested me the most, though. It allowed me to spend time with my grandfather one-on-one. He would take me to work with him early in the morning, and we'd have breakfast and coffee together at his desk before we'd do the rounds, talk to the workers, and then return to his office for him to do paperwork.

"My assignment was to read up on the distilling process. By lunchtime, we'd go to the local pub that his best friend owned, and we'd head to the back table and have lunch together. He would take me home after lunch, and I wouldn't have to do anything the rest of the day."

"This happened on the weekends?"

"Summer. Every summer since I was nine until I went off to college."

"That's sweet. Do you still visit with him?"

"He passed away my freshman year of college."

"I'm sorry, Nazár."

He shakes his head and then asks, "What about you? Is this something you want to carry on because you inherited it from your parents, or are you passionate about it?"

"A little of both. I want to honor my parents, but I love fine wines and the process of creating them. It is my lure to the vineyard as it relates to a possible resort that feeds my passion for traveling and providing others with wonderful experiences like the ones I seek. Right now, I'm not married to the idea of creating a distillery or resort, but I'm looking around and keeping my options open. I want to do this, but I must complete my research, run the numbers, and weigh the pros and cons before committing myself completely to the idea."

"Well, if there's anything that I can do to help you make up your mind, just let me know."

"Thanks. Do you do these tours on your own that often?"

"Sometimes. All the staff is well versed in giving tours, but I like to stay close to the operations. It allows my guests to see my face and involvement occasionally."

"Is that so?"

"Yes."

"How often?"

He smirks, looks at the floor, and then back at me.

"Maybe once every six months."

"Ahh, I just happened to have fallen in that six-month window."

"No. It's only been two months since I last did this," he says, standing and winking at me.

Without another word, Nazár places his hands in his pockets and heads back to the store with the other guests, who are either shopping or drinking.

✓ ✓ ✓

ANNY'S ANNALS

Aloha!

Hey, it's me again . . .

Sooo, today was pretty interesting. I spent all day yesterday looking for Mr. Rivas and couldn't find him. He shows up today at the rum distillery tour looking hot and gorgeous.

Yet, he remained professional the entire time. The only time that I felt he noticed me was when we were in the distillery and he explained the process.

The man was so close to me that I could have bent over, pulled down my shorts, and he could have slipped inside. When he realized how close he was, he instantly moved away.

Gah!!!

He remained in professional mode and kept his distance until the tour ended. We talked while everyone else was drinking or shopping, and I learned a little about him. Not much, but just enough to feel like I know him better.

I'm uncertain what my attraction to him is. I mean beyond the tight ass, the broad shoulders and chest, the gorgeous face, alluring eyes, and the sex appeal. Hell, I'm not sure what it is because, if anything, he gives off vibes that scream, "Run!" I can tell he's hung, and he'll fuck up my whole uterus—or maybe even my life!!!

Because you don't get "love" with a man like Nazár Rivas. He doesn't utter sweet whispers and make promises he can't keep. Hell, the man doesn't look as if he's capable of loving anyone other than himself.

Nazár is the type that will have you eating out of the palm of his hands. You'll be down on your knees begging to please him, and he'll snatch your soul out of your body while you love every minute of it.

Yeah, he's a heartbreaker, that one. The knowledge of his existence alone is intoxicating, suffocating me until I have to see him again just to breathe. And then when I'm around him, I'm drowning in sensual awareness and sexual desire like I've never known for any man. And drinking? I have to stop the damn drinking around him because he has me wanting to rip my panties off, spread my legs, and tell him to take me. Just have your damn way with me already!

Will I be ashamed in the morning?

Probably. But dammit, it will be worth it.

Maybe next time, I'll offer myself to him on a platter.

Maybe not.

Or . . . Yeah, just maybe.

I'm hopping off to write up a paper for Camila. Then I'll head to dinner to see what I can get into.

Until next time, Anny!

Nys 💋

13

NAZÁR

It's been some time since I've been this restless. Every time I find myself near her, I want to see her kneeling in front of me. I want to see her bound and breathless with a complete loss of control.

My desire, tension, frustration, stress, and confusion . . . I find that I want to take it all out on her body. Yet, I know that she's not ready. I don't want to ruin her with my loss of control. And I fear that because I want her so bad, I just might lose control.

The best thing for me to do is find a suitable partner to have a scene with. Someone other than her so I can release my pent-up frustration and unrestrained desire.

When I left her at the distillery today, that was the hardest thing I've ever done. I wanted to leave the rest of the customers in the hands of my staff, throw Princesa over my shoulder, take her to my office at the distillery, and fuck her until she forgot her name.

Those are the thoughts of a foolish man—one who loses control.

Why am I that way with her when I'm ordinarily disciplined and restrained?

She's fresh, innocent, and pure. No one has marked her body; no one has tainted her soul. She's pliable, a malleable instrument in my hands. I want to teach her how to yield to my needs and control her desires. I want her to learn what it means to sacrifice for the greater good of another and know what it feels like to have someone sacrifice everything for her.

I pull a hand down my face and get up from my bed. It's late, and the day is almost done, but I know that I won't get any sleep. My mind is too muddled with confusion over this woman.

I'm in a vulnerable place right now. It's been almost five years since my life turned upside down. Almost five years since I realized that maybe there was no woman out there for me. No one that I could ever destroy again.

It's been awhile since I've had sex or acted out a scene. I need some sort of release. Walking down the pathway from my house into the resort, I veer to the left, heading for the beach.

It's empty at night on this stretch of beach. It's the closest to my private property, and seldom does anyone wander this way, especially with the "No Trespassing" sign.

A gentle breeze blows, and there's nothing but the instrumental sound of the ocean's waves to accompany this starry night. Stepping out of my slides, I remove my shirt and shorts and wade into the water.

Lately, Bella has been on my mind more than she has in a long time. She intrudes upon my thoughts at the most inconvenient times, and I find it throws me unexpectedly into depression.

The warm water is refreshing against my hot skin. The muscle soreness from my earlier workout dissipates with every stroke I take in the water. Images of Bella on that final day rush through my mind.

Her tear-streaked face was red and puffy, and anger pinched her features. I still loved her even as she stood in my face, lying to me. I only wanted things to be better for her. I prayed that she could live up to her promises, not just for my sake but for both of ours and any future family we might have.

Not in a million years had I expected the doorbell to ring that late at night with a visitor. We didn't have unannounced visitors. Only dinner guests and the foreman from the construction crew working on building our resort came to our home.

Yet, none of them would show up at my front door at ten at night. It wasn't unusual for Bella to be gone for hours at a time, especially when she was upset. Sometimes, I knew where she was going; other times, I didn't.

I knew something was wrong when I heard the doorbell ring. Dread made my footsteps heavy as each step took me closer to the door . . . closer to the turning point in my life.

I hadn't heard the words spoken to me. I hadn't even read their lips. I'd known in my soul that my wife was no longer in this world.

Although my mind is active and alert with memories from that day, my body is extremely exhausted. I hope to return home and fall asleep after a glass or two of bourbon.

Surprisingly, a shadowy figure walks on the beach in my direction, roughly seventy-five yards down the shore.

No one should be down here this time of night. Surely, they've seen the "No Trespassing" sign by now.

The closer I swim to the shore, the closer the figure draws to me. Rather than turning back, the person continues walking in my direction, but their head is down, and they're not looking at me.

"Hey! Did you see the 'No Trespassing' sign down there?" I call out.

"I'm sorry. No, I didn't."

I would recognize that sultry southern voice anywhere. It's impossible for me to turn her back, although I know she's not expecting what she's about to see.

"It's okay, Princesa. I didn't realize it was you," I say, stepping from the water.

The moon shines brightly on her face as her steps falter and her eyes rest on my cock. When I approach her, gathering my clothes as I go along, she stares at me with her wide-eyed gaze.

"I'm sorry. I didn't mean to intrude on a private moment."

"And private property," I say, pointing toward the "No Trespassing" sign.

She turns to look in the direction I point and then back at me. She's so damned cute biting that bottom lip the way she is. I wish I were immune to this woman the way I am with most women, but I'm not. And only God knows why.

That reason alone has me wanting to know more. I find that I'm intrigued by her, and that's the exact thing that will get me into trouble that I just don't need.

She turns to go, mumbling that she's sorry.

Rather than push her away, I want to keep her with me. I don't want her to leave, and I tell her as much.

"You don't have to leave."

She stops and turns around, staring at me and uncertain if she should stay.

"I really didn't mean to invade your privacy," she says again, her eyes purposely avoiding looking at my cock.

"Does it bother you that I don't have clothes on?" I ask.

Shrugging, she replies, "Your beach. Your property. After all, it is a nude beach, so . . ."

Chuckling, I ask, "That bothers you?"

"It did when I first arrived, but not anymore. You should really warn guests before they come."

I step into my shorts, zipping and buttoning them up with my eyes trained on her. There's a visible exhalation of relief as her shoulders sag and her face, previously tight, relaxes. I toss my shirt over my shoulder and slide into my shoes.

"Why were you out here this time of night?"

"I couldn't sleep, so I decided to take a walk. I've found that there's usually no one out here at this time of night."

"You've been down this stretch of beach before?" I ask as we walk back down the beach toward the public area.

"No. I was caught up in my thoughts and just kept walking. I knew a sign was there, but I didn't pay it any attention."

I nod, making a mental note to light the path around the sign in case any other new visitors inadvertently miss it.

"What had your mind so preoccupied that you didn't see the sign . . . or me until the last minute?"

She gazes up at me and then turns her head toward the ocean.

Smirking, I ask, "Me?"

She turns her head back toward me with a slight lift in her eyebrows, a mocking smile, and a gleam in her eyes. "You're a bit arrogant, aren't you?"

Shrugging, I reply, "Not really. Just how you looked at me and couldn't meet my gaze told me everything I needed to know."

"Are you a mind reader or a people reader?"

"No. Just observant."

"I was thinking about what changes I need to make to my property to get a resort started and possibly a distillery and if it might be worth it."

"What type of resort would you have? Are you near water?"

"We are near water, but not like this. There are a lot of rivers and lakes around us, so there wouldn't be any scuba diving or snorkeling. However, I could offer horseback riding, vineyard tours, wine tasting, kayaking, canoeing, and other activities on the grounds."

"That's a good start. Have you started running the numbers to see what the expenses might look like?"

"I have a rough estimate, but I haven't dug too far into it because I haven't decided which route to go. That's the purpose of this visit. Research. I have a question."

"What's that?"

She clears her throat. "Why are you out on the beach at this time of night swimming?"

"Like you, I couldn't sleep. Swimming at night is a good way to become exhausted. You should try it."

"I'd be scared to try it by myself. Anything could go wrong."

"So, if you had a partner, you'd try?"

She looks up at me, and I know she hears the challenge in my voice. A smile slowly tilts her full, pouty lips, and she nods, "Yeah. I just might."

Tossing my shirt on the sand, I slide out of my shoes and unbutton my shorts.

"I'll race you," I say.

She shrieks at the challenge and begins ripping off her romper. I run ahead just as she unbuttons her bra and removes her panties.

"No fair! You're cheating!" she screams out behind me.

I rush into the water, swimming a short distance before waiting for her to join me.

When she runs in, I swim out further.

"You're going out too far!"

I laugh, shaking my head at her.

"Where are you going? Don't leave," I call out encouragingly.

She hesitates briefly, looking back to the shore and then back at me before she decides to remain in the water and swims closer to me. We swim several yards before returning and then do it three more times. I'm thoroughly exhausted now, and I think she is too.

We grab our clothes and dress, silently sitting in the sand and staring at the sky for a few minutes.

"I've never done that before."

"What, swim at night?"

"No. I swam at night in a pool. I've just never swam on a starry night like this before. I have always wanted to, though. There are so many beautiful stars in the sky," she says.

I stare at her face as she keeps her gaze turned upward. Wide, luminescent eyes glow with wonder, and the moon lights her cinnamon face. Full lips carve up into a beautiful smile.

"What are you thinking about?"

"This place is romantic. I'd heard that it was, but since my arrival, I've been shocked by the unexpected."

"Then I did my job."

"You're into shock and awe?"

I want to say, *No, I'm into you*, but I don't.

"I'm into providing an experience for my guests like no other. An experience they can't get at another resort."

"Well, I've traveled many places and . . ." She bites her lip and turns away.

"And what?"

"Um . . . I haven't been to any place that compares to this. Belle Baie does provide a unique experience," she says as a cool, crisp breeze whips off the water and lifts her hair from her shoulders.

Her eyes sparkle with happiness, and I would like to see that look on her face more often.

"And the romance?"

"It's not just in the oceanside dinners, the candlelit paths along the beach and around the hotel, or the music always playing. Not even the allure of having your fetishes catered to or the relaxing and erotic spa offerings. It's in the beauty of this place. The beaches, the water, colorful flowers, and the coconut, palm, and flamboyant trees give it an exotic appeal. It's what dreams are made of."

"That's the same thing I thought when I first visited here."

"How long ago was that?"

"Ten years."

"You stayed and never left?"

"Not quite. I did return home to Colombia for a while, but then . . . I knew I wanted to return."

"I could see wanting to come here and escape. Hide away from the world and all of my problems and cares."

"Do you have a lot of those?"

"What?"

"Cares. Problems."

She turns, gives me an assessing look, then smiles and says, "About the same as everyone else."

"How do you manage stress, Princesa?" I can't help the way that my voice darkens. My thoughts go elsewhere, and I can't control my wants and urges. At the same time, I don't want to run her away.

"I travel, or I write."

"What do you write?"

She looks away again, and I feel that whatever she says won't be true.

"Umm . . . about my travels. I write about them in my journal."

"Is that all?"

"Yes. What about you? How do you manage your stress?"

"I'm not sure you really want to know, Princesa."

She turns to look at me again and stares at my lips before her eyes drop to my hands and then down my legs. "What if I said that I do want to know?"

"I'd be worried about what I'd do to you if you learned the truth."

A soft gasp escapes her, and then she giggles. "You're funny. I didn't expect that."

"I wasn't trying to be."

A stark look returns to her face. "Are you threatening me?"

"Never that. If I tell you what I do to relieve my stress, I might just have to teach you a lesson or two."

"I've always been an A student. Willing and ready to learn."

Leaning forward, I rub my thumb over her bottom lip and say, "Don't play with magic you don't understand, Princesa."

She sucks my thumb into her mouth and bites down on it.

"You've been warned," I growl.

14

ANYSSA/CAMILA

It's a stroke of luck, really. A fifteen-minute walk down to the vineyard turns into an evening of bliss. I wanted to get some pictures to share with Camila, and I had no plans other than to return to the resort hotel for dinner at the bar and grille and perhaps spend some time on the beach this evening.

I've lost track of time taking pictures and selfies, but I know that no more than fifteen minutes have passed when I hear a grumble behind me.

"What do you think you're doing?"

Spinning around, I see a scowling Nazár stalking toward me.

"Taking pictures of the vineyard . . . for research," I say when I realize my grievous mistake.

"What part of 'no film or pictures allowed' do you not understand? Don't you respect any rules?" he thunders, drawing the attention of some of his workers.

"Nazá—"

"Dammit, I said no pictures! No film!"

His rage is astounding and even a bit frightening. Okay, maybe I'd been careless and hadn't been thinking, but I meant no harm. I can't tell the man I'm taking these pictures for the real

Camila, who will only use them to enhance her business, not when I'm supposed to be Camila.

"I just want to study the varieties of grapes that you have. I'm not trying to encroach on your business but rather figure out how to improve mine. These pictures are harmless, and I haven't taken any others. Not of the property, the buildings, or the people. I swear. Look, I'll even erase them," I say, flipping to my camera and making a big deal of deleting the pictures and emptying the trash folder.

Holding my camera out to him, I say, "See, all gone." The following pictures are just random ones of me on the plane. I stop flipping before he realizes this phone doesn't have many pictures. It's not my real phone, so I don't need him figuring that out, either.

"I promise I won't take anymore."

His energy is dissipating, though his scowl is still intact.

"Nazár, I promise I didn't mean to break your rules. It was an honest mistake, and it's easy for people to forget a rule like that when it's not the norm. Usually, when people are on vacation, they take plenty of pictures to commemorate their time. I'm not trying to do that. This was nothing more than trying to improve my processes for my business."

He shoves his hands into his pockets, and I'm growing nervous the more he stands staring at me and not speaking. After all, Camila did say that he would kick people off the resort if they broke the rules. I don't want that any more than she does, but for different reasons.

"I'm sorry. I'll leave now," I say, turning around and walking away.

"Camila!"

His commanding tone sends thrills of pleasure through me. I shouldn't get excited at how he's barking my name, but I can't help that his aggression and commandeering attitude turn me on.

I wonder if this attracted my mother to my father for the first time. Was he domineering? Commanding? Was that what drew her in, making her blind to his personality flaws? I wouldn't know, as she doesn't talk about him. I only know a little about my father, and that's not enough to amount to a hill of beans.

Slowly, I turn around and find that he's standing in the same spot that he was.

"Yes, Nazár?"

"Have dinner with me."

Of all the things that I expected him to say, it wasn't that.

"Dinner? When? Where?"

"Yes. Now. Here."

I look around and spread my arms. "I don't see anywhere to eat."

"That's because you lack vision."

I don't know whether to be insulted or intrigued, but before I can respond, he's pulled out his phone, and he's speaking rapidly in Spanish to someone in that same commanding tone.

"Are you always this rude? Barking orders at people?" I ask when he ends the call.

"You call it rude. I'm simply protecting my investments and running my corporation."

"Do you have to be so mean while you do it?"

"Do you think I'm mean?" he asks as he walks and leaves me behind.

I have to double my strides to catch up to one of his.

"If I didn't, I wouldn't have said it. It's like you've got this Dr. Jekyll and Mr. Hyde personality going on, but contrary to popular opinion, it isn't attractive."

"Who's opinion? You think that I give a damn about opinions?"

"If you didn't, why would you close off this resort to the world? Why keep people out and make all these peculiar rules?"

"To keep nosy people out of my life and to stop the speculations that—"

He cuts himself off amid an angry tirade but keeps walking ahead.

"Stop speculations that what?"

"Nothing," he mumbles, shaking his head.

Reaching out to touch his elbow, I say, "I promise, Nazár, I won't judge you."

We stop, and he stares down at me, searching my eyes as though he's trying to figure out if I'm sincere. I take a gamble that may cost me in the end.

"The speculations about what happened to your wife? The world will always look for gruesome or scandalous topics to gossip about. It's the way the human psyche is made up, unfortunately. Not everyone, but most people are like that, especially when talking about a famous celebrity like Bella. People want to know. They want to feel sorry for her and think you're a monster. The reality is your aloofness is probably out of self-preservation and hurt.

"Nazár, you can't live your life behind iron bars trying to keep people out. Instead, you should learn how to say, 'Fuck them.' In time, it will pass, and no matter whether you keep them out or in, people will believe, say, and think what they want, and nothing you can do will ever stop that. If anything, let this beautiful property be a legacy of your love for her."

He's back to staring at me again, and no words are coming out. I don't know what to think. Did I cross the line and say too much? Did I offend him?

"You're a bold woman, Camila," he says as we begin walking again.

Shame runs through me when he calls me *her* name.

"Not really. I'm just as cowardly as anyone else. Maybe more so."

"No, you're not. You said to me the things that people want to, but they're scared to. Instead, they generate conversations with my staff, hoping to glean a nugget or two from them."

I shake my head and say, "I don't care about that. I'm here to learn how to expand my business while enjoying a vacation. It's just a perk that the property owner happens to be handsome."

The dark cloud hovering above him lifts for the first time, and he smirks at me. The wink he sends me shoots heat straight to my core, and I want him so badly.

Stopping at a row of vines, he stretches his hand out and says, "Flattery will get you a delicious meal, Ms. Martinez."

I step around him and look down the row and see a white tablecloth-covered table with two wrought iron chairs set up in the middle of the vineyard. There's a bottle of wine, two covered platters, and two wineglasses turned upside down on linen napkins.

"How . . . where did . . . Were you expecting me?" I ask, turning accusing eyes his way.

There's no way he could have expected me when I hadn't even expected to be down here today. This was a random, last-minute decision to visit the vineyard.

Chuckling, he says, "No. You're the most unexpected person I've ever met, Princesa."

A fire lights in my belly when he calls me that term of endearment in his gravelly tone.

"Then how did this come to be?"

"It came as the result of running a well-oiled ship and my staff knowing that I expect nothing but the best from them."

"Do you, in turn, give them the best?" I ask as we make our way toward the table.

"They wouldn't be here if I didn't. They also wouldn't be as faithful as they are," he says.

When we reach the table, he pulls out a chair for me before seating himself. This man is doing everything to my heart.

We have grilled tomato, chèvre, thyme baguette sandwiches, creamy squash soup, and a side salad. The food and wine are delicious, but the company is even better.

"You have the best selection of wines. I swear, each time I taste one, they only get better," I say after dinner.

"I have one that I'd love for you to taste. It's in my private selection."

"Oh? Well, bring it on."

"It's at my house."

His eyes glow, and against my better judgment, I accept the invitation.

"I'm ready whenever you are."

☑ ☑ ☑

We rode a golf cart back to his place from the vineyard. He'd gone into his cellar and returned with a premium bottle of Pinot Noir, and I couldn't help but notice the year nineteen-ninety-nine marked on the label.

"You had to have been a kid when this wine was produced," I say as he pulls two glasses from a cabinet in his kitchen.

Smiling, he says, "I was. It was a stock from the wine served at my parents' New Year's Eve party. They preserved it all these years and gave it to me when I bought this property. I've kept it in the cellar all this time."

"This has to be what . . . a ten- or eleven-thousand-dollar bottle of wine?" I balk.

"Eleven-thousand-three-hundred-seventy-four, to be exact. That's the price I could command for this."

"Why are you opening it now?" I ask as he takes the wine bottle from me and pours some into the glasses.

His gaze deepens as he says, "A special wine for a special occasion. Good company deserves good wine."

He holds a glass out to me.

"What's the special occasion?"

"Cultivating a beautiful friendship," he remarks, lifting his wineglass.

Hesitantly, I clink mine to his and inhale the fragrance.

"Musk and leather," I murmur appreciatively before I take a sip. Closing my eyes, I allow the dry wine to coat my palate before I open my eyes and find his resting on me.

"Well?"

"It has a soft entry . . . The concentration just hit my palate. It has harmonious notes of leather and plum with a sweet finish. I like it. It's complex and multifaceted with a long finish. Excellent."

"Thank you."

Turning around, I set my glass on the counter before murmuring, "Still don't know why you wasted this expensive bottle of wine on me."

I feel his heat encompassing me as he steps closer, and I'm afraid to turn around. The touch of his fingers on my arm incinerates me.

Nazár traps me between the counter and his hard body when he places a hand on either side of me, gripping the edge so I can't move.

"It's never a waste. Not when the company I'm keeping is worth the wait," he whispers.

My head tilts forward, and my eyes close at the touch of his lips against the nape of my neck. He trails a finger down my arm to my left ring finger.

"Are you married, Camila?"

"I think that you already know the answer."

"You're right. I do. I'd just like to hear it from your lips," he says, his finger grazing my lips.

I find myself licking my lips and clenching my thighs as fire shoots to my pussy, causing it to throb. "No, I'm not."

He bites my neck, and I purr, "No. No. And no."

"What were the other three 'nos' for?"

Nazár kisses my jaw and then licks along my earlobe.

"No, I'm not engaged. No, I don't have a man. And no, I'm not dating."

"Proactive."

"Are you going to deny that you were going to ask?"

A growl grows in his throat, and he trails a finger down the front of my sundress through my cleavage before he pinches one nipple and then the other.

"I don't give a fuck if you do."

"Then why ask?"

"Only asked if you were married. That's the only union I respect. The rest only means you're open season."

He hitches my sundress around my hips and pushes me forward, my breasts pressing into the counter. Large, coarse hands smooth over my ass cheeks, cupping and grazing them before he parts them.

He slides my panties down my hips and to my thighs.

"What are you doing?" I moan as he slides a finger inside of me.

"What does it feel like I'm doing, Camila?"

"Seems to me like you're taking liberty with something that doesn't belong to you," I purr as he slides another finger inside me.

He chuckles, and the air fills with the sound of my panties ripping.

Spinning around, I ask, "Nazár, what the fuck!"

He spins me back around just as quickly and pushes me against the counter again.

"Not taking liberty with anything. I'm just indulging you in what you want and what I need."

He plunges two fingers inside me, and all protests slip from my mind as my eyes close again, and I rest my cheek against the cold counter. With one hand, he rubs my nub, and with the other, he continues to pump in and out of me, increasing the pace as the sloshing sound of my juices being stirred fills the kitchen.

"Nazár, I can't," I murmur just as I'm about to come.

He leans forward, his back resting against mine and his erection pressing into my thigh.

"You can and you will, mi amor. Give me everything, Princesa. Every drip, every drop, every ounce of you," he says.

My hips jut back as he continues thrusting his fingers inside of me. I don't feel the pain of my breasts pressed against the counter, the pinch of my eyelids closed tightly, or the numbness creeping into my fingers as I grip the counter tightly.

I simply spread my legs wider, allowing him to insert another finger inside me, wishing it were his dick.

"Oh God!" I cry out as he inserts yet another finger inside me; before I know it, he's filled me with four thick digits.

My orgasm takes over every sound, thought, scent, and awareness I should lay claim to. A gasp creeps from my throat. I lie with my face and tits pressed into the counter, my mouth agape until I hear a sucking noise.

Standing, I turn around to see Nazár sucking my juices from his fingers, and the fire in his eyes looks as if he wants to consume me. Before I can fix my dress, he lifts me onto the counter, spreads my legs, and pushes me back.

The wineglasses shatter to the floor, but he doesn't seem to care. With my feet on the counter, legs propped up, I find my hips arching into the air as Nazár shifts his hands under my ass to lift me slightly.

With his head buried between my thighs, Nazár sucks, licks, and compels more juices from my pussy. I had no idea that I had anything remaining. Pleasure and tension are at war in my body, and I'm powerless against both.

The pleasure he brings as he eats my pussy like he's just worked a hard, long day and he's a starving man leaves me breathless. The need to feel him inside me, stroking and digging, increases the want.

His hands and forearms wrap tightly around my thighs, and I know he'll leave marks there. The scruffiness of his growing beard tickles and scratches, but it feels so damn good. The grunts and growls he releases are satisfying, knowing I'm the cause of his sounding like that.

His sucking tongue and lips on my pussy lips, paired with his burrowing nose and finger against my nub, drives me insane. My pleasure is heightened when he slides a finger inside my ass and begins to thrust and slowly circle there.

My heart tightens in my chest, and I can barely breathe. It's as if Nazár senses this because he picks up the speed and intensity of his tongue, lips, nose, and fingers, driving me to higher planes.

He wraps long, tapered, coarse fingers around my neck and squeezes. I call his name in a loud, keening screech I don't recognize.

"Nazár! Fuck!"

He steals my breath and gives it back to me in one swoop, restricting and releasing my airway. His fingers, tongue, and lips overwhelm me until I can't take anymore. He hums against my pussy before he sucks it. His fingers pulse inside me as he returns to humming—the pace and intensity of his sucking increase. I hold my breath, waiting for the ecstasy to end, for the climax to be ridden out, and Nazár squeezes again and then releases.

I shudder and shudder . . . until I pass out.

15

NAZÁR

Being with Camila is easy. It's the first time I've been with a woman in a long while, and I don't feel the pressure to be anything more than just in the moment. I want to open up to her in many ways, but I don't think I'm ready.

Opening my heart to a woman entails loving her and giving parts of myself that I no longer think exist. Losing Bella destroyed parts of me that I can never recover. It's easier to lock parts of me away and settle for what I know I do well with a woman. Fuck her.

And that's what I'm doing.

When Camila regained consciousness after passing out on my kitchen counter, I carried her into a guest room and lay her on the bed.

"Where is this? Your bedroom?"

"No. A guest room. Are you sure you're going to be fine?" I ask, changing the subject.

She turns her head sideways on the pillow and smiles at me. "Yeah."

"Guess you'll tell me that's never happened to you."

"And you'd be right. God, I'm so embarrassed," she says, throwing her arms over her face.

Pushing up on one elbow, I tug her arms from her face.

"Don't be. All you did was boost an aging man's ego," I tease, winking at her.

"Aging man? Is that your way of calling yourself old?"

Chuckling, I say, "Not old where it matters."

"Clearly not," she says, shaking her head and closing her eyes again. "How old are you?"

"Thirty-six. And you're twenty-nine, right?"

Her eyes widen in surprise. "You've been doing your homework on me."

"Saw it on the copy of your passport we have on file."

"You make a habit of looking at your guests' IDs?"

"When I don't know them."

"Do you make it a habit of eating your female guests on your kitchen counter?"

I lean over her and brush my lips against hers. "Don't tell anyone," I tease. "And this incident . . . We'll keep this between ourselves."

"I would hope so!" she exclaims in astonishment.

Smirking, I reply, "Your secret's safe with me. Besides, I won't be the one who will kiss and tell."

"You say that as if you think I might."

"It's a known fact that women gossip."

"Not all women and men can be worse than women."

"Well, I wouldn't know since those aren't circles I travel in."

She stares at me, her eyes glowing.

"What?"

"Just . . . wondering."

"About what?"

"If you're scared now."

"Scared?" I ask, lifting an eyebrow. That's not a feeling that I relate to.

"Of having sex with me."

"Why would I be scared?"

"Well, seeing as how I just passed the hell out on your counter after you ate me out, I can't imagine that you'd be in a rush to do anything more to me than that."

My lips brush hers again, and my finger traces the lines of her eyebrows and nose down to her jaw. Her eyes follow mine, and I can see the question in them. She wants me to take her now. Dipping my head between her neck and shoulder, I lick along the space, rubbing my hands down her arms.

"You have no idea what I'm in a rush to do to you. That incident only stoked my curiosity."

Camila opens her legs, making room for me between her thighs. I hover over her, not wanting to let my weight press down onto her, but when she wraps her arms around me, she pulls me closer, eliminating any space between us.

Her body is hot like a branding iron and welcoming like a small town. She wraps her arms and legs around me, lifting her head slightly to meet my lips.

"You're not ready for me," I say against her lips.

"I'm so ready, Nazár."

"You're ready for sex . . . but not for me."

Rather than pursue an argument, I roll off her and remove my boxers. I watch as her eyes go wide.

"What?"

"Of all the things that I expected, Jacob's ladder wasn't one of them."

"Are you afraid now?"

"Never. This just upped the ante," Camila giggles.

I wink and pull the nightstand drawer open. Removing a condom, I hand it to her to open. Her tiny hands hold me, stroking over the intricate rungs pierced through my dick. She fingers the rounded bars at the end of each rung before running her fingers over the skin covering the shaft of the piercing.

"Like it?"

"Think I'm loving it," she says, rolling the condom down my length and holding it firmly before she looks up to meet my eyes.

With my erection so close to her lips, I want to pull the condom off and strangle her with my dick, but I don't.

I pull her up and turn her around to face the bed. She plants her hands on the bed, and I use my feet to shift her legs further apart, spread wide for me. My hands roam over the curves of her body, appreciating every dip, valley, and hill.

My eyes drop to her high, fat ass, and I can't help but revel in the fact that she has an ass made for spanking. As hard as it is, I don't take her downstairs to the dungeon. I quell the need building inside me; instead, I plunge inside her.

The cry that rips from her throat isn't gentle, soft, or ladylike. It's nothing short of earth-shattering. Her fingers coil tightly around the cover, snatching it back and shoving it into her mouth.

Smacking her ass, I grunt, "I want you on your toes."

She does as I ask, allowing me to dig deeper into her. My movements aren't cautious or considerate. I'm a greedy bastard, and I've warned her that she's biting off more than she can chew. While I know she isn't ready for the full-course meal that consists of me, I'm ready to satiate her appetite.

My thrusts are merciless as I grab her hair and jerk her head back while my other hand holds tight to her hip. She's wet and tight, and what I wouldn't give to ride her bareback. That will come in time.

It takes everything in me to restrain the aggression, the tension, the need to see her at my feet, to watch her soak up the pain I can inflict upon her body. Yet, I know she feels all that in my barely controlled thrusts.

She slips to her knees several times, and I pull her back up by her hair, thrusting deeper and harder into her until she's thrusting back, giving me herself just the way that I want.

Her breathing is ragged when I finally pull out of her and lift her onto the bed. It's the first time that I see tears coating her eyelashes.

"Are you okay?" I whisper as worry floods me.

I knew that I shouldn't make a move on her so soon. Knew I should have fucking held back.

She smirks at me as if she can read my thoughts. Spreading her legs and arms wide, she replies, "Give me all of you. Don't hold anything back, Nazár."

I shift onto my knees and dig deep inside her, enjoying the connection of our bodies with a bit of space between us far too much for my comfort.

When her hands run up and down my back, easing my guilt and frustration, I know I must get far from this woman. Yet, I can't. She feels like where I need to be.

My lips trace a line along her jaw until I push up slightly to run my fingers over her nipples, even while thrusting inside her. Camila lifts her hips, welcoming every pump that I have to offer.

"Don't be shy," she says, lifting her tits and offering them to me.

Licking my lips, I reply, "Never been accused of that."

Leaning in, I bite her nipple, and her eyes widen as tears emerge. Twisting her nipple in my teeth, my arousal grows harder as I swivel my cock inside her, loving the gasping noises she's making and how redness surrounds her chocolate nipples.

My finger grazes her pussy lips even while I'm still inside, and her eyes drift closed, forgetting about the pain I'm inflicting.

Arching her hips up until her ass no longer touches the bed, she wraps tightly around me before she starts swiveling her pelvis, working her pussy all around me, claiming me, sucking everything out of me.

I finally release her breast, firmly placing my palm in the middle of her chest and shoving her back onto the bed. Holding her in place, I pummel her until she's on the verge of another orgasm. Only then do I pull back just a bit to turn her onto her side.

I enter her again. Pummeling and slamming into her, I work her body over until she's trying to pull her leg free from my grip. I refuse to release her, preferring instead to watch her come. Seeing her juices coating my condom-clad dick makes me lose my last bit of restraint.

Like a runner racing for the finish line, I pick up my speed and keep my pace steady and strong until I've released everything I'd been holding back.

"I'm sore," she murmurs after a few moments, clasping her hand between her thighs and gripping her forearm with her other hand.

I wrap my hands around her, lifting her petite frame from the mattress on the opposite side of the bed and pulling her closer to me.

Allowing myself to do something I haven't done in years, I nuzzle my lips against her neck. It's not a pleasure that I allow myself because it's too easy to be pulled into a woman's web. That's something that I can't afford to do because I know they can't handle me. Not all of me in my raw and primitive state.

She turns over in my arms, resting her cheek on the palm of her hand.

"Why did you hold back?"

"You think I did?"

"I know you did. I felt a few times where you pulled back just as you were on the border of losing control. There's this raw, pent-up aggression inside you, and I felt it a few times. Just when I thought you would release, you drew back. Why is that?"

"I don't think you can handle it."

"Why, because of my size?"

I close my eyes, inhaling deeply, and don't say a word. How can I tell her who I really am and the damage I have the potential to inflict on another with my unrelenting demands impervious to the feelings of those around me? Not just physically but mentally.

"Camila, I'm not simply rough or aggressive in the bedroom. It's a way of life for me. I have a way of being unrelenting and excessive in my demands, and when it starts in the bedroom, it leaks out into other areas of life."

"And?"

"And it can be damaging . . . life-changing."

"Don't you think everyone has the power to say no or realize when they've reached their limit?"

"Not always. Not when a woman is intent on pleasing a man and not wanting to disappoint him."

"Then she must know her limitations and balance that with pleasing him. If she can't do that, maybe it's not the relationship for her."

I shift uncomfortably when she says "relationship." We're lying together intimately, her head resting on my chest, my arm crooked about her, holding onto her possessively while my other arm is propped under my head. It's easy to get the wrong impression about what this is we're doing.

"Maybe," I concede. "Either way, I have to take self-responsibility."

She shifts onto her elbow and looks down at me. "I think you're doing just fine, Nazár. You're doing just fine."

Camila climbs on top of me and bends down, kissing me softly with gentle brushes of her lips and sweet, slow pecks. My arms wrap around her, forcing her to lie on me as she bends her knees, crushing her to my body.

She feels good in this space, her weight resting comfortably on me, and our lips entangled in a sweet kiss, growing hotter by the moment. Camila begins to rock into me, pressing her heat against my rigid cock that seems never to be satisfied.

My hands shift down to curve into the crook of her ass, pulling her harder into me as I claim her lips, refusing to allow this moment to end, though I know that I need to be stronger than this. If I'm not, one or both of us will crash and burn to our detriment. I will hurt her. There's no doubt in my mind about that.

Fuck! Camila's a stranger to me. Why does she have me wanting and yearning for more than I know that I deserve? Why does she have me thinking thoughts that haven't appealed to me in years?

I want to lift her into my arms and carry her into my bedroom. Only if I do that, I won't stop there. I'll go beyond the bedroom and take her into my private lair.

I've never shared my bedroom with another woman since my wife passed all those years ago. I'm not about to start now. That's a level of intimacy that I'm not ready for.

"Why doesn't a woman like you have a man?"

"A woman like me?"

"Yes. Beautiful, sensual, sexy, smart . . . good."

"You think that I'm a good woman?"

"I know you are. Yet, I sense you haven't always felt that way about yourself."

"I haven't found the right man, Nazár."

"What's the right man?"

"The one who won't judge my promiscuous past. A man who appreciates that I love hot sex as much as a good conversation and gets my blood roaring. Whether he's pushing my limits in the bedroom or . . ."

She stops and looks away as though uncertain what more she should say. I cup her chin and turn her face back to me.

"Or what, Camila?"

"Nothing."

"Tell me," I rasp.

"Or being comfortable with where I am . . ."

"Where are you?"

"I'm trying to figure myself out. I'm just someone trying different things to know what makes me tick, what makes me happy, and what I won't tolerate. Still trying to learn who I am ... so ..."

"So, that means you can't have someone helping you figure that out?"

"I need someone who will accept and love me as I am. Perfectly flawed."

My thumb rubs the seam of her lips, and she sucks it into her hot mouth. My eyes grow heavy, and I grumble, "Don't start shit you can't finish."

"What makes you think that I can't?"

"You said you're sore."

Smiling, she says sleepily, "Yeah, you did give me a pretty good banging."

"But good, huh?"

"Notable."

"Remarkable?"

"Rare."

"Special?"

"Definitely that and ... noteworthy."

"Noteworthy," I say in a disappointed tone.

She taps her chin and pretends to think. "Extraordinary."

"Unheard of?"

"Exceptional."

"Exceptional?"

"Unprecedented."

Smiling, I flip her onto her back and say, "I can live with that one."

She leans up slightly to kiss me and says, "Good," before she lays her head back on the pillow. I pull her into my arms and kiss her forehead, holding her close. Within ten minutes, I hear soft, gentle whispers of her breaths, and I know she's asleep.

16

ANYSSA/CAMILA

ANYSSA'S THIRTY–BEFORE–THIRTY LIST

- ☑ Make love in a stairwell
- ☑ Hike the Rocky Mountains
- ☑ Ride an elephant
- ☑ Dance in the rain
- ☑ International road trip
- ☑ Learn an art
- ☑ Ride in a hot air balloon
- ☑ Go backpacking
- ☑ Make love to a stranger
- ☐ Perform on a stage
- ☑ Tattoo on my ass
- ☑ Scale a summit
- ☑ Learn a foreign language
- ☑ Swim at night, where you can see the stars
- ☑ Snorkel
- ☑ Parasail
- ☑ Make love on a train
- ☐ Take a cooking class in a foreign country
- ☑ Learn to ski
- ☐ Stand under a waterfall
- ☑ Swim with the dolphins

☑ Sing a karaoke duet with a stranger
☑ Ride a gondola in Venice
☑ Travel the world
☑ Send a message in a bottle
☐ View a sunrise from a place where you can see the horizon
☐ Do something along the lines of exhibitionism
☐ Find my father
☐ Try kinky sex
☐ Fall helplessly in love

ANNY'S ANNALS

Aloha!

Hey, it's me again . . .

I walked on the beach a few nights ago when I couldn't sleep. Not recording and writing has me all worked up. I know that season three of Romance Abroad *will start filming in six weeks, and I'll be so busy I won't have time to think about boredom. I'll be too busy managing stress.*

Earlier that day, I had a phone call with my producers, Sarah and Emmett, to pitch an idea about doing a five-segment special show on weddings abroad. The idea is to send out an online call to brides- and grooms-to-be who have a wedding destination in mind to apply to be on the show.

We will interview the selected participants and their respective families and friends. It will allow us to tell their story of how they met, their hopes and dreams for a partner, their future families, and the journey to their special day. We would attend the wedding and the reception, capturing it all, and then air the segment about a year later on their anniversary. In that segment, we would include a follow-up interview with the married couple to see how they're doing.

Of course, Emmett saw all the pitfalls, which is his job. He was worried about if someone left their partner standing at the altar, or if they decided to elope, or if someone stood up at the wedding condemning them, or far worse, if a year from then, they were no longer together.

He said that any of those things, plus another list of ten that I won't dare get into because that's who Emmett is, could ruin the image of wedded bliss and romance we're attempting to portray. Sarah, the more logical of the two, is also a romantic at heart. She suggested that we would have contracts in place like we do for any of the guests at our show. All wedding guests would have to sign a statement that would sign away their rights to interrupt, alter, or inhibit the wedding in any form.

Sarah agreed that there might be barriers but that we could meet with our lawyers and creative team to review any issues that might arise and develop resolutions to them.

I'm excited that Sarah was on board with my idea, and though Emmett remained the dubious one of the two, he was coming around by the end of the phone call.

Of course, after the call, my thoughts turned to Nazár. Nazár is always not too far from my mind these days. That led me to walk on the beach, which led me to run into him.

Naked as a jaybird and as fine as a Greek god!

Michelangelo's statue of David would have blushed to see that man in all his glory. Nazár wasn't even erect when he walked out of the water, but damn, he was bigger than any man I've been with. There was no shame in him.

His golden, tan skin was finely lined with hair along his arms, legs, and chest. His dick was covered with dark hair at the base. After he challenged me, we swam together, sat in the sand, and talked for a long time.

When I began to yawn, he walked me back to the hotel again, and I got the best night's sleep ever.

Yesterday, we had dinner in the vineyard, which turned into drinks at his place, which turned into dessert, but the only thing eaten was me!

Believe it or not, he ate me out on his counter after he fucked me with his fingers. When he ate me out, I fucking passed out! I've heard of that happening before, but I thought people were just talking shit. And it wasn't from his dick, but his tongue!

Can you believe that shit? I fucking Passed. Out!

I woke up early this morning and started to walk back, but he wasn't hearing it. I told him I didn't want anyone to know I spent the night with him, and I think he admired my discretion.

He walked me back to the hotel early this morning. It was romantic, and he left me at the hotel's side door with a kiss.

Before he disappeared, he asked about my plans for the day. I told him about snorkeling and was disappointed he would not be on that trip. I shared with him that I'd be touring the formal gardens, and he also said he wouldn't be there because he had a business meeting at that time.

I hoped he would surprise me and pop up anyway, but he didn't. Once I could accept that he wasn't coming and put both ideas out of my head, I enjoyed snorkeling this morning and the garden tour this afternoon.

He did tell me that he had a surprise for me. What that entails, I have no idea.

Well, someone's knocking rather urgently at my door. Somehow, I doubt that it's him, though. There doesn't seem to be any urgency where he's concerned.

Until next time, Anny!

Nys

"Just a moment!" I call out as I put my journal and ink pen away. Popping off the bed, I glance into the mirror and pull my fingers through my tangled curls before I walk through my suite to the door.

Peering out the peephole, I see one of the workers from the lobby holding a stack of boxes.

Frowning, I unlock the door and pull it open.

"Hello, Jamesina."

"Hi, Ms. Martinez. These boxes were delivered for you today."

"I didn't order anything," I say, staring at the boxes and back up again into her brown, freckled face.

Her red-tinted lips turn up into a beautiful smile.

"I know, but I was told that I needed to make sure you received these," she says, holding out the boxes.

I accept the boxes and mumble, "Thank you," as Jamesina says, "You're welcome. Enjoy."

Setting the boxes on the arm of the chair, I close and lock the door again. Enjoy what? I wonder.

Grabbing the biggest box up like a little kid on Christmas morning, I sit in the middle of the living area floor and rip the gold wrapping paper apart.

When I open it, there's a little white linen card with handwriting scrawled across the front. Before I can read the card, I run my fingers across his signature at the bottom.

Pulling the card to my nose, I inhale deeply, basking in his unique scent of amber, tobacco, and black currant. Closing my eyes, I hold it against my chest and think about the other night and last night when he returned me to the hotel.

It's been a while since I've walked on a beach with a man and just talked. We walked so closely that our shoulders brushed from time to time. At one point, when I tripped, he grabbed my elbow and righted me, linking his fingers with mine.

We strolled hand in hand for the remainder of the walk. Our conversation was peppered with subtle glances, innuendos, and cocky smirks. All those gestures are promising and let me know that, if given the chance, he could break me.

I finally read the card.

Hello, Princesa,

Meet me tonight at the gazebo in the garden at seven for dinner. Wear this, and you'll get your first lesson in stress management. Wear only what I have provided and not a thing more.

Nazár

I remove a black silk dress from the butter-yellow tissue paper. Running my hands along the dress, I can already tell it's expensive.

What the hell?

I pick up my phone and notice it's five eleven. I have just under two hours to get ready.

The second box is much smaller than the first and is the size of a shoe box. When I open it, I find that my assessment is correct. I can't help but wonder how he knows my dress and shoe sizes as I stare at the silver strappy sandals.

The third box contains three smaller boxes inside. All three are pearls: earrings, necklace, and bracelet.

Panic fills my chest, along with nervous butterflies in my belly. The shrill ringing of my actual phone in my hand only adds to the agitation. I glance at the phone and see my mother's smiling face. I can't help but answer.

"Nys."

"Hey, Mommy."

"I haven't heard from you on this last trip. Where in the world are you, anyway?"

"Mommy, I told you I couldn't disclose my location. I'm doing research, and I signed an NDA."

"What?"

"Mommy," I whine.

"Anyssa, I need to know where my child is. It doesn't feel good knowing that you're somewhere in the world that I have no clue about. What if something were to happen to you?"

"Mommy, I can't do the negative energy right now."

"You're right, sweetie. I'm sorry, but, Nys, try to see my side. Are you in the country? Can you at least tell me that?"

"No, Mommy. I'm not."

She sighs loudly over the phone, and I get up from the floor, grab the dress, and leave the other packages behind.

"I'm in Africa."

"Africa? Didn't you visit there two years ago?"

"I did, Mommy, and I'm back on a special project."

"In the same country as last time?"

"No, Mommy, and that's all I will say. Trust me when I tell you that I'm safe. I'm probably safer than you are at home. The place that I'm in is very secure and protected by armed guards and—"

"Anyssa! Are you in prison?" she whispers.

And just like that, all my fears are dispelled, causing me to laugh at her. "No, Mommy. I'm not in trouble, but I am having a wonderful time exploring new ideas and getting to know other sides of myself. I know you want to know more, but I can't tell."

"Is it going to be on your channel or the show?"

"Nope. Look, I have to go, Mommy. I have an appointment that I need to get ready for, and I'm already running late," I say, glancing at the alarm clock on the nightstand.

I lay the dress across the bed and remove my shorts and tank top that I've worn all day.

"Nys?"

"Yes, Mommy?"

"Be careful."

"Always."

"I love you."

"I love you too, Mommy, and you be safe. I promise to call you tomorrow, okay?"

"Sure."

She clicks off the phone, and I sit on the side of the bed. I click into my mother's contact information on my phone and run my fingers along the planes of her face. She is my world, the only person I truly have, and I'm all she has.

We look a little alike, but she's told me I look mostly like my father. I've never seen him. She didn't so much as keep a picture of him around. When I was old enough to learn the truth about him, it broke my heart that my mother had been running from him when she was pregnant with me, always looking over her shoulder and always living in fear.

She no longer has to do that because she has me now. If I ever meet him, there will be many things I want to say to him. Probably the most important is why. Why would you do the thing to someone else's child that you wouldn't want to be done to your own? Why place that fear in a woman's life that she could never truly know peace?

I hated him for a long time, but after my twenty-first birthday, I began to feel sorry for him. What kind of horrible, self-loathing person did you have to be to run off a pregnant woman? I wondered what he had gone through and why he was so weak. It was his loss that he didn't have Mommy and me in his life.

"Damn," I mumble, remembering I'm supposed to be getting ready for dinner with Nazár. Hopping off the bed, I run into the bathroom to shower and shave. An hour and a half later, I'm showered, shaved, smelling great, and I've pressed out my naturally curly hair.

A glimpse in the mirror and the nervous butterflies in my belly turn into ones of excitement. The black silk maxi dress is fitted, hugging every curve of my body, outlining my hips and ass provocatively.

It's an off-the-shoulder dress, and the sleeve straps hang off my shoulders parallel to my breasts, which are boosted and show ample cleavage. I can't help but smile at myself because while I'm not an arrogant woman, I know that I look good and sexy as hell.

I'm sure he can't help but want to have me all to himself when Nazár sees me tonight. There's no way he'll be able to keep his hands to himself, and maybe that's precisely what he wanted. I suspect he was holding back when we had sex yesterday. I want the full Nazár Rivas experience.

I grab my purse, phone, and key card and slip out of my hotel suite since I only have ten minutes to go downstairs to the garden.

17

NAZÁR

She's as beautiful as I knew she would be. After I'd walked her to her hotel this morning, I was determined that I wouldn't see her again. I'd given up on that thought two hours after she left when I found myself fisting my cock to relieve myself at just the thought of her.

Camila says she wants all of me, but I know she's biting off more than she can chew. Alternatively, I don't have much time to ease Princesa into my way of life, so tonight, I'll warm her up to the idea. Though I've been dropping clues, and she continuously tells me she's open to whatever I'm into, I must be certain.

The dress clings to every curve she has, and while leaving little to the imagination, it's just as sensual as provocative on her curves. My only misgiving is that she's straightened her hair. While it is beautiful on her, I prefer her with her natural curls. They give her a more angelic look, and I have been yearning to feel my fingers entangled in her hair while choking her with my other hand.

I don't share this with her. Instead, I say, "You look lovely, Princesa."

"Thank you, Nazár. You clean up rather well yourself. Are we eating here on the grounds?"

"No. We're going to my home. Will that be a problem?"

"Not at all. Are we walking?" Princesa asks, looking down at her feet in the heels I'd sent her.

"No, your chariot awaits, my lady," I say, taking her hand and turning the corner to the side of the hotel.

Seldom does anyone come to this side of the hotel, so I'm not worried about anyone other than staff seeing us. They have all signed an NDA as part of the terms and conditions of their employment. I pay my staff a handsome salary to maintain discretion, from the cleaning staff to management, and I'm well rewarded for my efforts.

"Wow, you meant it, huh?"

I smile as I take her hand and help her into her seat. Then I turn back and walk to a colorful flower display that lines the walkway. Picking an orange and a purple one, I head back to the rented horse and hop up beside her.

"They're beautiful," she whispers as I tuck them behind her ear.

"Yet, not quite as lovely as you," I say.

After we're settled in, the driver glances over his shoulder. With a brusque nod from me, he turns around again, and we begin to move forward down a cobblestone trail marked "No Trespassing."

"You have many of those around?" she asks, pointing at the sign.

"Wherever it may lead to or encroach upon my personal property," I reply as the horse makes its way down a path.

"I hope you didn't already have plans for the evening, Princesa."

"I didn't have any at all," she says, gracing me with the most beautiful smile that I've seen in a long time.

We enjoy the ride in silence, both aware that our driver may be listening to our conversation as the horse and carriage navigate the path parallel to the gardens and behind the resort leading to my house.

"I wasn't expecting all this when you said that you have a surprise for me," she says, waving at her dress and pearls.

"Why not? I wanted you to understand that this evening is a special occasion for us."

"Special in what way? I don't think that you can get more special than by opening a premium bottle of wine that you've held for three decades," she says.

"It's just wine."

"An expensive bottle."

"And you don't think that you're worth it?"

She turns her head away from me and stares into the clearing that overlooks the ocean as we turn up the hill toward my house.

"Princesa," I say, cupping her chin and turning her face toward me. "I would like to embark on a journey to know you better. And I want you to get to know me. That's not an easy thing to do."

"You realize I only have two weeks remaining here on the island?"

"I do. Which is why I don't want to waste another moment."

"Why me?"

"Why not you? You intrigue me. You're beautiful, and we have a common love."

"That being?"

"Our vineyards."

"Yes, we do," she says, smiling at me.

"I'm sure you always have companions at the resort that intrigue you."

"It has been a while since that has happened. Besides, you're among the few people I allow around me."

"Are you saying that you're a hermit?"

"I'm not a hermit, but I am deliberate about who I let into my world and when."

"Have you been hurt?"

"Haven't we all?"

"It's just odd that a businessman who runs a resort and lives only a short distance from it would be as detached from those around him as you appear to be."

"The last few years of my life have been difficult, Camila. Those that I thought I could trust turned out to be deceptive. And I've suffered plenty of losses. It's not often that I trust someone to come into my world. Do I have sexual relationships? Yes, but even with those, I am careful who I approach and how far I become involved with them."

"And is that what you're seeking from me? A sexual relationship, Nazár?"

"I am exploring something with you. What it is, I do not know at this point. Only time will tell."

"That's a bit cryptic, Nazár, especially considering we don't have much time."

"Time is irrelevant, Princesa. If I am nothing else, I am an honest man, Camila. You will find that with me; what you see is what you get."

She casts her gaze to the ground before mumbling, "Somehow, I find that hard to believe."

Just as my house comes into view, I cup her chin and say, "I will never lie to you. Will I place all my cards on the table up front? No. It is not an advisable move in a card game or the game of life. Yet, if you ask me anything, I will answer you honestly."

"That's all that I can ask."

"Will you promise to answer me truthfully when I ask you questions?"

A smile graces her lips. She inhales and says, "Of course."

"Then that is good enough for me," I say, helping her to climb down from the carriage.

I give her the tour of my home that I didn't give her yesterday. I'd only shown her the living space, the lanai, the kitchen, and one of the guest bedrooms. When we're finished, we settle under the palm trees on the other side of the infinity pool.

Nigel approaches with a serving cart and places our plates on the candlelit table before disappearing again.

"Do you eat out here often?"

"Not often enough. I usually take my meals inside or on the lanai."

"Well, thank you for sharing it with me," she says.

We both grow silent when we begin eating our meal of lamb chops cooked in red wine and rosemary, risotto, oven-roasted Mexican carrots, Brussels sprouts, blistered shishito peppers, and yeast rolls.

There's a lemon cake for dessert.

"If I ate like this every day, I would gain a hundred pounds," she gushes, closing her eyes and enjoying her meal.

I love a woman who isn't afraid to eat.

"Nigel would appreciate that you enjoy his cooking. I'll be sure to give your compliments to the chef."

"Please do. This is delicious."

Once our meal is finished, I grab the bottle of wine, and we walk a little further away from the house to a ledge overlooking the ocean.

"Everyone should be so lucky to have views like this," she says.

"Yes, they should," I reply, staring at her neckline and lips as she speaks.

Camila turns to me, smiles, and says, "You're not even looking at the view."

"Oh yes, I am. It may not be the one you're looking at, but it's the only one that matters to me."

"Do you always know just the right thing to say?"

Pulling her into my arms, I look down at her and answer, "No. I just say how I feel."

Her lips part slightly, and I know she wants me to kiss her, and I will, just not at this second. I remove my suit jacket and spread it on the ledge for her.

"Have a seat. In a couple of minutes, you will begin to witness one of the unknown wonders of the world."

She does as I ask and says, "What wonder would that be?"

Pressing a sweet kiss to her forehead, I say, "Patience, Princesa. Hand me your glass."

I refill her wineglass with red wine before refilling my own.

"Look at that," I say, holding my glass toward the Indian Ocean.

I've seen the spectacular view a million times or more, but never through fresh eyes.

"Nazár! This is spectacular!" she exclaims, watching the radiant hues of reds, yellows, oranges, and purples descend over the horizon.

"That's one of the unknown wonders," I say several minutes later when the sun finally sets.

She turns and smiles brilliantly at me. "Thank you for sharing that with me."

I lean in, cup her chin, and brush my lips against hers. "You're welcome, Princesa. It's only a small price to pay for everything you will share with me."

She pulls back and stares into my eyes with her mouth slightly open.

"Don't make promises that you cannot keep, Nazár. You're making promises as though I'll be around for a while, and we both know that's not true. Besides, a man like you will surely tire easily of one woman."

Not wanting to discuss feelings or expectations, I dive into her mouth again, taking advantage of it being open. She's sweet and tart like the red wine and the cake and a bit gamey like the lamb chops, and I love it all. It only fuels my appetite for her and my struggle to maintain control.

She hums into the kiss, a slight vibration coming from deep in her throat, which hardens my cock. My thumb rests on the pulse in the base of her neck, my fingers sweeping across the fine hairs at the back of her neck.

Her hands come up and rest on the side of my face before one of them moves around to sweep through my hair. She tugs and pulls, lying back on the rock. It can't be comfortable for her, but she does not complain.

Dare I get my hopes up?

I hover over her, brushing the tips of her nipples, pinching them as she arches closer toward me. My free hand moves to her hip, brushing, caressing, and gently grabbing the silk of her dress, pulling it up as I rub.

When I pull back from the kiss, I ask, "Are you uncomfortable on the rock, Princesa?"

"I am comfortable wherever you would have me, Nazár."

"Are you open to me taking you on the rock, Princesa?"

"I am whatever you need me to be, Nazár. I simply want to please you."

Fuck! My dick jerks in my pants and grows impossibly hard.

Sliding my hand from her hip, I snatch her dress further up and rub her thigh and hip. Hope blossoms in my heart. My fingers rub across her swollen nub, and a smile bursts in my heart.

She's obedient. I asked her only to wear what I sent her, and she obeyed. She's not wearing a bra or panties, just the dress I sent, the shoes, and the jewelry.

"Good girl. I love obedience more than anything else, Princesa."

Her eyes gleam, and she smiles bashfully at me. Her innocence is provocative. It has me wanting to do all sorts of things to soil her. None of which compares to what we did yesterday.

I kneel between her legs, spreading them wider to accommodate me.

"You're so beautiful, love."

She smiles proudly at me, but her eyelids are heavy with lust.

My thumb caresses her clit, slowly sliding inside to stroke her interior front wall. She arches her hip, and I know the rock must be digging into her back, but she still doesn't complain. Instead, it appears as though there's pure bliss on her face.

I scissor my fingers inside her until she looks like she might come. Only then do I remove my fingers, kneel, and take my first swipe at her.

Fuck yeah! She's so delectable and juicy. She's like a ripe Georgia peach waiting to be plucked, devoured, and sucked until she is no more.

I have no problem satiating my hunger for her or consuming the nectar of her juices.

I look up at her when she starts moaning and arching her back.

"Promise me you won't pass out."

She giggles. "Where's the fun in that? Besides, I think you choked me out." She winks, and relief swells inside of me.

The wind picks up off the ocean and sweeps across us, bringing precious relief from the day's heat. Seagulls cry out overhead, and the palm and flamboyant trees sway in the breeze.

As beautiful as all those things are, none are more lovely than the picture of Camila before me, with her pussy glistening as she coats my lips, nose, and chin with her essence.

I take, and I take until she's crying and clutching my hair, legs locked around my neck, and banging her fist against the rock.

She is mine.

18

ANYSSA/CAMILA

ANYSSA'S THIRTY–BEFORE–THIRTY LIST

☑ Make love in a stairwell
☑ Hike the Rocky Mountains
☑ Ride an elephant
☑ Dance in the rain
☑ International road trip
☑ Learn an art
☑ Ride in a hot air balloon
☑ Go backpacking
☑ Make love to a stranger
☐ Perform on a stage
☑ Tattoo on my ass
☑ Scale a summit
☑ Learn a foreign language
☑ Swim at night, where you can see the stars
☑ Snorkel
☑ Parasail
☑ Make love on a train
☑ ~~Take a cooking class in a foreign country.~~ Get eaten out on a ledge while looking down onto the ocean!!!
☑ Learn to ski
☐ Stand under a waterfall

- ☑ Swim with the dolphins
- ☑ Sing a karaoke duet with a stranger
- ☑ Ride a gondola in Venice
- ☑ Travel the world
- ☑ Send a message in a bottle
- ☐ View a sunrise from a place where you can see the horizon
- ☐ Do something along the lines of exhibitionism
- ☐ Find my father
- ☐ Try kinky sex
- ☐ Fall helplessly in love

ANNY'S ANNALS

Aloha!

Hey, it's me again . . .

Remember when I told you there was a knock at my door yesterday and I had to go? Well, it was a staff member with three boxes. You'll never guess what they were and who they were from.

Nazár sent me a silk dress, a pair of sandals, matching pearl earrings, a necklace, and a bracelet. He invited me to dinner at his place and told me to wear only what he sent.

It was very suggestive, and I heeded his command. It made for a very appetizing dinner, and I was rewarded nicely. Tee hee!

Last night was the stuff that dreams are made of. After dinner, we had an engaging conversation. He's a sweet and gentle man, but he's much more.

We watched the sunset, and I have seen the sunset from so many locations worldwide, but none are comparable to the one I watched last night. I don't know if it was the company I was in or just what, but it was astounding. When I thanked him for sharing it with me, he kissed me.

That kiss led to so much more because if the meal wasn't sufficient for him, he made me his encore for the night. Lying on a ledge overlooking the Indian Ocean, Nazár sucked and licked and consumed my pussy like it was the last fruit on earth.

When we'd finished, he helped me sit up again, and we talked a little longer. When I yawned, he helped me stand and walked me back down the beach to the resort again.

We walked with my sandals in his free hand and his other holding mine. I asked him questions about BDSM, and he answered. That segued somehow into politics and his businesses. I didn't talk much about myself; I knew it was for the best.

He left me at my hotel door with the sweetest kiss tinged with the essence of me.

His home was breathtaking, with high ceilings and large glass openings that looked out onto the infinity pool and ocean. The open floor plan living room looks right into a state-of-the-art commercial kitchen. His dining and living areas flow into the outdoor terrace and barbeque area near the pool.

There's a beautiful lanai, as well, that I can tell he spends a lot of time in from the slippers under a wicker rocker and the number of worn books scattered leisurely on the low glass coffee table. The championship golf course and ocean views from every room in the five-bedroom, five-bathroom home make it a magnificent house.

Why does a single man need eighty-seven-hundred square feet? He even had staff quarters!

There's something that's bothering me, though. Nazár shared that he's lost people close to him and found that the ones he thought he could trust were deceptive. He kept talking about honesty and how much it meant and said he would never lie to me.

Then he asked me to promise him to do the same.

What the hell am I supposed to do, Anny? I want to tell him the truth, I really do, but I can't. I've signed that NDA with Camila, which prohibits me from doing it.

I can't even call anyone to talk to them about this. As much as I want to call Camila, I don't want to stress her when she's worried about her dad, and I don't want to alert her to what could be a figment of my imagination.

Anny, I wish you could talk back to me and give me sound advice. I can't even call my friends or Mommy for advice.

What am I going to do?

Until next time, Anny!

Nys 💋

I place my journal away and lock it up before I pull my phone out and call my mother first, and then I'll call Kayla.

"Hi, Mommy."

"Hi, baby. How's everything going?"

"It's good."

"Did your appointment go well yesterday evening?"

I blush, thinking about how Nazár used his mouth, tongue, and fingers on me and what I hope he'll do to me tonight.

"It did, Mommy. What about you? What are you doing?"

"Delores called and invited me to dinner tonight with her and her husband and a friend."

"Ohhh . . . A blind date?" I ask.

Laughing, she says, "No. Nothing like that. Just four church members getting together to enjoy a meal."

"Church member, huh? Does this church member attend your church?"

"No. He does not, but he does attend church."

"Besides the point."

"Girl, you're making this into something that it's not."

"Mommy?"

"Yes, baby."

"You do know that I wouldn't have a problem with you dating."

"What makes you say that?"

"You placed your entire life on hold to care for me, never having any relationships and keeping people at a distance. I'm grown now and out of the house. I just want you to find happiness."

"I am happy, baby."

"I know you are, but there's nothing wrong with a little companionship."

"Nys, that has nothing to do with you, and you know it."

"Yeah, but you used me as your excuse originally. It's time to live, Mommy. It's okay to be cautious but not give up on living because some asshole did what he did to you."

"Watch your mouth, little girl."

"Sorry, but—"

"No. I understand. I'll be fine. Let me go before I'm late."

"Look, last night it was me rushing you off the phone, and tonight it's the opposite," I tease.

"Girl, goodbye."

She hangs up without waiting to hear me say goodbye.

I chew on my bottom lip before dialing Kayla. This call won't be as easy as the one to my mother.

The phone rings continuously, and she answers it just before it goes to voicemail.

"Hullo!" she greets, sounding out of breath.

"Hey. Is this a good time to talk?"

"Yeah."

"You sound like you had to dive for the phone. All out of breath and panting. Are you—"

"No! Before you go down that alley, don't say it. All it will do is make me horny, and God knows it's been far too long since I've had sex."

"Sounds like you need to do something about that."

"I'm a bit more selective than you . . . So there's that."

I roll my eyes. I am so over my friends judging me. So what if I'm a free spirit? So what if I love having sex and enjoy having my body pleasured and using it to pleasure others? I'm a grown-ass woman. I'm careful, and I always use protection. I haven't even been down on a man in forever, not since my last relationship.

"Get out of your feelings. I can hear your internal gears clicking. No judgment here. I'm simply stating that I'm more selective than you are, which can also be a downfall."

"Then what were you doing?"

"Working out."

"Trying to get rid of all the tension? There's a better way to do that, you know? Sex could serve a dual purpose. Help you get rid of the tension *and* be a wonderful workout."

"Again, I'm selective. When the right one comes along, he might as well hang it up because I'll be riding his dick day and night until he gets a sprain!"

I crack up, laughing at her silliness.

"So, what's up with you, Nys?"

"I can't give you all the details of the trip that I'm on, but you know how I told you about using an alter ego?"

"Yeah."

"Well, I've met this amazing guy. He's gorgeous, intelligent, thoughtful, sexy as hell, and—"

"You've screwed him?"

"That's beside the point."

"Then what *is* the point, Nys?"

"I think he thinks I'm fragile and is overly cautious with me. I want him to let loose."

"Don't overthink it. Maybe he's trying to get to know you before he shows his true colors."

"No, I don't think it's that at all. He's not the relationship type. He's a very sexual being. The man invited me to a romantic dinner yesterday by the ocean out in his backyard. We talked and had a great time together. He led me to a spot where we had the perfect view of the sun setting over the ocean, and then he kissed me when I thanked him for sharing the view with me."

"Aww, that's sweet."

"Yeah. Then he ate me out, spread out on the ledge by the ocean, Kayla. It was the best thing that's ever happened to me in terms of romance anyway."

"So, what's the problem?"

"The problem is he shared a few things with me last night. Nothing too personal, but he told me about how he's lost some loved ones because of deception. He said that he would never lie to me and that I only needed to ask if I wanted to know anything about him. Then he made me promise the same."

"Shit!"

"Exactly."

"Well, you've only got two more weeks. Enjoy your time and leave there with your secret intact. You won't see him again after this."

"I know," I groan. "That's the problem. I *want* to see him again, but I can't see him after this without revealing my identity. Besides, if he found out who I was, I'd get kicked out of the resort."

"Is he security?"

"No."

"Management?"

"Yeah," I lie. "Anyway, I'm enjoying being around him and not ready to go."

"That's a first. You usually get tired of the guys after a week and are ready for the next destination."

"I know, but this time is different."

"You think it has anything to do with him being careful with you during sex? Maybe it's the chase, and him holding back has piqued your curiosity about the IQ of his dick."

Laughing, I say, "Shut up!"

"Hey, you're the one that came up with the term DIQ!" she roars with laughter too.

I'd told her once a long time ago that I could tell how good a man could be to a woman by his DIQ, dick intelligence quotient. If he knew how to work the dick too damn good, like making you forget your name and Social Security number, he probably wasn't about shit.

If he was confident in his game and could put you to sleep, but you still remembered your name the next day, even if your legs were shaky and your back was weak, he was a good man. He was the one you could marry and take home to Mama.

Then there were the ones who talked a good game, but they either had a big one or a little one but didn't know jack shit about how to work the magic stick. You're lying there on your back while he's patting himself on the back and priding himself on how good he is to you, and you're trying not to fall asleep or making a mental shopping list. That's the crazy-assed stalker types from which your ass needed to run as fast as possible.

"I think it's deeper than wondering about his DIQ, though, Kayla. I've met plenty of men, old and young, intelligent and average intelligence, rich and poor. None of them have stirred within me what this man has."

"All without testing the joystick?" she asks in disbelief.

"I tested it but haven't had the full ride."

"Sugar bear . . . It's too soon to be love."

"I know, and it isn't that. Trust me, it's not. It's just that he has potential."

"Thought you said he wasn't interested in relationships."

"He's not, but I . . . I don't want to walk away without figuring out what this powerful hold he has on me is. I mean, I don't even know the guy."

"You know enough, Nys. And you're a pretty good judge of character."

"I am."

"Then just take the next few weeks and see where it leads. As for your identity, you need to pray about that. I don't want to see you hurt, so please, be careful."

"There's something else."

"What?"

"He's . . . He's into BDSM."

"Is that where he's holding back?"

"Mm-hmm."

"Lord! Heaven help her now!"

I don't think anyone can. I've made up my mind that I want Nazár.

19

ANYSSA/CAMILA

After my phone calls, I headed to the lobby and asked them to get a message to Mr. Rivas that a guest would be waiting for him tonight in Noir at BoDSMe. The young man I passed the message to smiled but kept his opinions to himself. The staff prides themselves on discretion, so I'm not worried that my secret will get out.

I eat dinner downstairs in the bar with Felice and a few other guests, trying to quell my nerves for the evening. We share stories about our travels, talk about affairs we've had in the past, and discuss our common interests. No one talks about their lives at home, and I guess I can understand that. After all, this place is an escape that lets you shed your problems and find sanctuary in pleasure. At least for a time, anyway.

When it's almost time for me to head to BoDSMe, I wish everyone a good night.

"Hey, can I speak with you for a moment?" Felice asks, catching up with me as I approach the elevator.

"Sure. What's up?" I ask, stepping away from the opening doors as people pour into the lobby to grab something to eat or head out.

"I'm not saying this from a place of jealousy or anything. I like you, Camila, and the easy friendship and camaraderie we've developed here."

"So do I, Felice," I say, smiling, although warning bells go off inside my head.

"I've noticed that Nazár has taken a special interest in you."

"You've noticed?"

"Yes. He seldom comes around the hotel or mingles with guests. Every now and then, he does when a particular group of friends he's known for a long time visit. But he's usually more standoffish with people like you who have been referred, and he doesn't know."

"I didn't realize that."

"Yeah, he's been different since you've been here. That could be a good thing."

"Or . . ." I prompt uneasily, ready for her to get to her point.

"Or it could be a bad thing. For you. Not for him. Never for him."

"Look, I don't know that he's taken a special interest in me. He's nice, we have great conversation, and that's about it."

"That's who he is. It always starts that way, but . . . Nazár likes a particularly kinky kind of sex. While I'm not saying you're a prude, I remember your initial reaction to the nude beach when you arrived."

"And I've gotten over that. What are you trying to say, Felice?" I ask, my impatience growing.

"Don't get too wrapped up in him. Enjoy Nazár when you're here, but just know he'll be on to the next woman when you leave, whether it's here or somewhere else. He's not the settling type, Camila. You're very sweet, and you're young. I don't want to see you get hurt chasing a fantasy."

"Fantasy?" I laugh.

"Yeah. He's nothing more than that."

Smiling, I pat her shoulder and say, "Thanks for the warning."

I head into the open elevators and turn to face her with a smile and a wave. She smiles too, but it doesn't reach her eyes.

I'm no fool. I know better than to fall for a man like Nazár. But calling him a fantasy? He's more than that . . . Isn't he?

What if she's right?

I second-guess my decision to meet him while I shower, dress, and walk to BoDSMe.

"Welcome to BoDSMe," Jennifer, a petite, dark-skinned woman with short, curly hair I haven't met before, greets.

"Thank you."

"May I see your key card, please?" she asks.

I wait as she checks my card against her system and says, "Noir is reserved for you. When you need to open the locked cabinets in the room, use this same key card."

"Thank you," I say.

"Enjoy your evening, Ms. Martinez."

"Thank you, Jennifer," I reply, walking to the rear of the building.

The wall to the left is mirrored, and I can't help but glance and check out myself. My leather knee-length skirt fits me like a glove and laces in the back with a zipper from top to bottom.

The leather halter top exposes my back and stops underneath my breasts, baring my belly and the skirt hanging low on my hips. It's sexy and provocative. My black, red-bottom pumps set the outfit off just right.

I wear no jewelry, and my pressed-out hair is combed away from my face. Mascara and red lipstick are the only concessions I make to makeup.

Nerves rattle in my belly, and Felice's words haunt my thoughts. I inhale deeply and rest my hand on the doorknob. Pushing my anxieties aside, I don't allow myself to focus on Felice's words or the nervousness that Nazár often invokes in me.

I'm a cultured, experienced woman who has had many lovers. I'm comfortable in my body, confident about my sexuality and my boldness, and very astute in my perception of others. There is nothing that I have to be afraid of.

Still, I inhale deeply and hold it for a count of five before slowly releasing it. Repeating the cycle twice to curb my anxieties, I finally open the door. Disappointment floods me when I see no one inside.

I'd hoped he would beat me here because I was unsure what to do. I just know that I want to experience BDSM with him, and I want him to know that.

Yet, I don't allow myself to dwell on the disappointment, but instead, allow my curiosity to swell in me and lead my actions. I'm here to learn, and regardless of whether Nazár is here, it doesn't stop that.

I walk to the tall cabinet in the corner and slide the key card against the card reader. A soft snick lets me know the cabinet is unlocked, and I look through the supplies to see what may be useful. I lift a black paddle and smooth my hand across three silver, raised nubs on the back, wondering what it would feel like on my ass.

"Do you even know what you're getting yourself into?"

Startled, I jump, dropping the paddle to the floor and spinning around to face Nazár.

"You scared me."

There should be a law against anyone looking as good as he does. He's wearing a charcoal bespoke suit, a dove-grey tie, and leather lace-up shoes. His long, dark hair is combed back from his forehead, with one errant lock falling over.

He closes the door behind him and locks it before he stuffs his hands into his pockets, slowly walking in my direction. Nazár's scent is beguiling, curling around my nostrils like a snake being charmed and dragging me close to him.

I don't even realize that I take steps toward him, but I do until he says, "Stop."

I don't move another inch, though a foot of space lies between us.

"Why are you here, Princesa?"

"I told you I wanted to learn more about your world."

"You can have me in your bed, darling, without entering my world."

Boldly, I lift my head and say, "I want *all* of you. The good, the bad, and the dark."

He runs a finger over my lips, leans close to my ear, and whispers, "Be careful what you wish for."

A sharp pain runs through my earlobe and into my ear when he pulls back. *Did he just bite me? I think he bit me.*

My hand goes up to touch my earlobe, but he grabs it, tightening his hand around my wrist and jerking me forward to close the remaining space between us.

"What is it that you *really* want, Princesa?"

I've been thinking about this all night. I questioned my sanity dozens of times, but I know I'm not wrong.

"I want to feel, Nazár."

"Feel what?"

"I want to feel alive. I want to feel what it means to be the sole object of someone's affection and attention, almost to the point of obsession. I want to be controlled and guided, but I want to know what it means to submit to your demands. Nazár, I want to feel what you feel."

"Why?"

"Maybe you can't understand my answer, but I'll tell you in the only way I know how. I've been drawn to you for some incomprehensible reason since I came to this island. The first night I saw you standing under the tree outside my room, I couldn't see you completely, but I could see your outline and traces of your features. Do you find me attractive, Nazár?"

"Of course, but there are plenty of attractive women walking through here daily. What makes you worth more than a good fuck?"

"Perhaps you should be asking yourself that question. You're stalking me around this resort just as much as I'm stalking you. We both know that our connection is strong. I know that you feel it. It runs deeper than our primal instincts, and I'm interested in exploring it."

His finger traces the pulse point at the base of my neck, and he licks his lips, his eyes on me the entire time.

"I can make love to you and have your pussy dripping wet, a never-ending waterfall. Send you back home with memories of a great vacation," he says, sliding a finger down my cleavage.

"Or . . . I can subdue you, take you to the brink of hell, and bring you back again. If you choose to walk down that dark path, there's no going back until I say so. You're under my command and my power. I'm the only one that you answer to. When I call, you come. Alternatively, when I speak . . . you come . . ." he slides a hand between my thighs and pinches my pussy lips hard.

"And you never . . . *ever* wear any panties. Your hair," he says, tugging it so hard tears spring to my eyes, "I prefer it curly."

"Is that all?" I ask smartly.

"And when you get smart with me, you will pay a high price. I have no compassion. My only desire is your pain and my pleasure, but you will learn to derive pleasure from pleasing me in those two areas. The most important thing for you to remember . . . There's no walking away from me until I release you. These things are nonnegotiable. Is that understood?"

Am I a glutton for punishment, or what? Am I psychologically impacted so profoundly by the abusive relationship between my parents that I *want* to walk in their shoes? I'm sure a psychiatrist would have a field day with me.

"You do realize that I leave in two weeks, Nazár?"

"You heard my terms. Pick your poison. Do you agree?"

"I agree."

"When we are in public, you may call me Nazár, but when we are alone, you will call me Dominio."

"Dominio," I say softly, trying it out. It feels right, perfect on my lips, as though he were born into that name, and I was designed to be here at this moment, calling or screaming his name.

"Spanish for dominance."

Nazár runs a hand down my bare shoulder and kisses it.

"You left a note for me that it was urgent for you to see me about a business matter. What was so urgent?"

"This. I wanted to see you tonight. To be with you," I say softly.

He pauses with his lips on my shoulder before he cups my chin and jerks my head sideways to look into his eyes. There's fire and anger there. A sneer comes over his lips, and I feel the anger radiating off him in waves.

He bites my shoulder, and tears smart my eyes.

"And you never need to lie to me. Is that understood?"

"Yes."

"Yes, what?"

"Yes, I understand."

"That's not what I want to hear, Princesa. What do you call me?"

"Dominio?"

"Is that a question? Are you hard to teach, a difficult student? I have no time for games, Princesa."

"I won't play any games, Dominio, and I won't lie to you."

My stomach clenches as I think about the lie I'm already telling him.

"I will never do anything to jeopardize your safety. You should tell me if anything we do during our intimate moments becomes more than you can bear. You need to create a safe word."

"A safe word?"

"Yes. A word that tells me that you've reached your limits. Then and only then will I back off."

"Travel."

"That's your safe word?"

He sounds doubtful, but it's the closest that I've come to being honest with him about who I am.

"Yes."

"Camila, if I'm to have you the way I want you, I won't continue sneaking you in and out of doors and meeting you in back alleys."

"We haven't done that."

"That's exactly what we do when we meet behind the hotel, and I have to have dinner with you away from prying eyes."

"I thought you wanted to maintain discretion."

"I do. That's why if we do this ... You come to stay with me."

"Stay with you?" I ask, doubt creeping in.

"Yes, in my guest home on my property. That eliminates the risk of being discovered, and I can have you at my beck and call whenever I want to. No barriers."

What in the hell am I doing? The thought of being that close to Nazár and him having me whenever he wants thrills me. I can't believe I'm giving up my independence, something I treasure, and I say, "Okay."

"One more thing."

"Yes?"

"You don't call me. You come to me when *I'm* ready for you."

He turns and walks to the door, opens it, and leaves me standing there as he closes it firmly behind him.

What the entire fuck did I just get myself into?

20

NAZÁR

"Why do you need this, Nazár?" Leona asks, holding the phone out to me.

"You don't question me, Leona. That's not your position in my life," I say, taking the phone from her hand.

I step off the lanai into the bright afternoon sun.

"Izad, how is the family?"

"We've just returned from vacation, and I think we have a sixth baby on the way."

Laughing, I say, "You weren't supposed to be making babies, just love."

I can hear the shrug in his voice when he says, "That's part of the territory. It seems like my wife becomes pregnant whenever I look at her."

"So, are congratulations in order?"

"We won't know just yet, but it's safe to say that I put in the work, so I'm sure congratulations will be in order a few weeks from now."

"I'll be sure to send my finest bottle of rum and some Colombian cigars."

"I should have told you that I was already successful," he says, chuckling.

"Well, whether you did the deed or not, I'll send them to you. A congratulatory present either way. You either have another one on the way or dodged a bullet."

"You should not be so cynical, my friend."

"If you'd lived my life, you would understand."

"Did you forget what I do for a living? I have seen a lot, so I do understand. Eventually, you have to move on and choose to be happy."

"Which brings me to the point of my call today."

"What can I do for you, my friend?"

"I need you to investigate someone. I want a thorough background check of their financials, criminal records, family history, and mental and physical health. I need to know who their neighbors are, where they've traveled, and who they've spent time with over the last three months."

"The executive package?"

"Yes."

"You know the drill. Email me the name and any pictures you may have of the person. What's your desired turnaround time?"

I think back on Camila's words the day before yesterday. She said she had two weeks, and I've spent two days ignoring her, holed up here in my home.

"Your assistant told me you were backed up from that two-week vacation. Five days should be fine if that works for you. Given your backlog, I know it's a short turnaround time, but you know I'll reward you handsomely for it."

"It works perfectly well for me. If I encounter any situations, I will inform you immediately."

"Great. I'll send 50 percent, plus expenses, to your account today and the rest when you turn in the results."

"Sounds good, my friend. As always, it's a pleasure doing business with you."

"And you too, Izad. Try not to slip in another baby between now and then, huh?"

Laughing, he replies, "I can't make any guarantees."

We end the call, and I turn around to face a scowling Leona with arms crossed over her chest.

"What?"

"I can't believe you."

"What?"

"Are you having Camila Martincz investigated?"

"Why?"

"Because you already do a preliminary background check before they're allowed to come to the resort. You just ordered a full-scale investigation of her. What are you up to, Nazário Sebastian Rivas?"

"Nothing," I mumble, turning my lips down as I walk back onto the lanai and pluck a handful of grapes from the ones in the bowl.

I pop a few in my mouth and settle into my chair, watching her watch me. We're in a stare-off, and this isn't unusual for us.

"You can be so damn stubborn and foolish when you want to be! You're going to run her away."

"If she's meant to be here, Leona, she isn't going anywhere."

"And if she leaves because she found out you snooped into her background?"

"Then she wasn't destined to be here," I say, picking up my glass of rum and sipping.

"Why can't you just learn to trust people?"

"You know that I don't open my life to just anyone. It will be five years since Bella passed away in a couple of months. With all the speculation around her death, I don't want intruders trying to sneak into my life. At this point, anyone I meet will fall under the same strict scrutiny that she is. For all I know, she could be some reporter trying to get close to me to sniff out a story."

"You're supercilious."

"Leona, it's not my own self-importance that I'm inflating. Bella was an A-list actress before her downfall. People loved her, and though she wasn't getting all the stellar parts she once did, they still loved her. They were reminded of that love after her passing. People love to celebrate the anniversaries of tragic incidents more than anything."

I lean forward and grab another cluster of grapes as Leona tries to snatch them out of my reach.

"Are you saying that people are naturally dismal?"

I grip the edge of the bowl tightly and snatch it back in my direction. She releases it and stands straight, rolling her eyes.

"They are naturally drawn to adversity and calamitous events. Rather than judging me, Leona, I need you, Gary, and Jules to look for anything that seems out of the norm."

With my free hand, I plop grapes into my mouth and gesture to a chair behind Leona, which she grudgingly takes.

"I'm not judging you, Nazár. And if you're so skeptical about Ms. Martinez's motives, why are you spending so much time with her?"

"To weed out her true intentions," I lie.

"You don't need to spend time with her to do that. Lately, all your free time has been spent creeping around the grounds with her."

"I don't creep. This is *my* fucking property!" I snarl.

"Well, that's exactly what you do when you take her through back doors and bring her in and out under cover of night. If you don't want her in your life, don't play games with her emotions or have your way with her in your home . . . on a certain ledge, I might add."

"You've been spying again, Leona? I will have to give Gary some pointers for keeping you preoccupied. Clearly, you're missing me."

"No! If you'd forgotten, the guest house has a perfect view of that side of the property. I saw you when I returned to drop off the groceries you'd requested."

Smirking, I pop more grapes into my mouth before leaning forward and grabbing a mango from the same bowl.

Camila's not a patient woman, and she's taking things into her own hands. I have a lesson or two to teach her. It doesn't matter to me that she's leaving in a couple of weeks. She must learn that *I'm* the one in charge, *not* her.

I'm the one who gives the commands, and she's the one who obeys. I tell her when, where, and how we meet.

To her, this is a game; for me, this is a lifestyle. I prefer a submissive woman because it's easier for me to protect her. When I fail to protect a woman, especially a self-destructive one like Bella, it causes me to feel defenseless and useless. Remembering that season in my life has the power to plunge me into depression.

I know that my mood swings can be a lot to handle, and the only way to determine if a woman can handle me in my entirety is to see how she submits in our intimate life.

Thus far, I haven't had luck in that field.

The only thing I'm sure of is that I won't put more pressure on a woman than she can bear. If it becomes intolerable for her, then she's not who I need in my life.

I am who I am, and I'm not changing for anyone. Neither do I want a woman to change for me. I just have to find the woman who is mine. The one who wants to belong to me, no questions asked.

"Seriously, Nazár, you could give the wrong impression if you become intimate with her and bring her into your home. Maybe tread lightly with Camila. She seems extremely impressionable; if she falls, she'll fall hard and won't easily recover."

"Good."

"That's cruel."

"No. It's good that she's easily impressionable. That means she's easier to train."

"She's *not* your pet, Nazár!"

"Leona, I need one more thing before you can retire for the evening."

Sniffing, she remembers her place and stands with her hands primly crossed in front of her crotch. Slowly, I let my eyes drop down to the area her hands cover, and I smirk, biting my bottom lip.

Very intentionally, I allow my gaze to trail up again, slowly over the contours of her breasts that rise heavily with desire, before moving to her lips as I lick my own and stop at her eyes.

"Call the hotel and give them the instructions I gave you earlier. Then send a car for Ms. Martinez. I think that I need a little relief."

"You bastard," Leona hisses before she turns on her heel and leaves the room.

She's right. I am that. Leona is still attracted to me, though she's moved on. We respectfully keep our distance from each other. She keeps hers because she knows she cannot meet my demands and doesn't like failing. I keep mine for those same reasons and out of respect for her relationship.

☑ ☑ ☑

"I thought you were out of town," Camila says, stepping from the car.

I take her hand in mine to help her up onto the sidewalk. Leaning into the car, I ask Errol, the driver, "Would you please take Ms. Martinez's bags to the guest house?"

"Yes, sir, Mr. Rivas."

I tap the car's hood, turn around, still holding Camila's hand, and lead her back into my home.

"Have you eaten?"

"Not since lunch," she says softly.

"Good. I will enjoy feeding you," I reply with a smile.

"Were you out of town?"

"No."

"Busy with work?"

"No."

"Oh . . . I thought I would have heard from you by now, especially with how you left me the other night."

I can hear the tension in her voice, and I stop in the foyer, turning her around to look at me.

"Princesa, *I* set the rules, and *you* obey. Are we going to have a rough time with that before I go any further?"

I tilt her chin slightly.

"No, Dominio."

I smile.

"Good girl. We will eat, and then I will take you to the guest house, where you will stay for the remainder of your visit."

She nods. "Where can I wash my hands?"

"Follow me," I say, leading her down the hallway on the opposite side of the house.

Pushing the third door open, I say, "You may wash and get dressed here."

"Dressed?"

"Yes. Your attire is laid out on the bed for you, along with your shoes in the box there," I say, pointing at an orange and crème box.

"When you're finished, meet me on the lanai. We'll be serving ourselves. Everyone has the night off."

She looks happy about that, and I close the door and head back to the lanai to ponder my thoughts a bit longer.

It's been a while since I've developed feelings for any woman. I keep them all at a distance as they only serve one purpose for me: relief. Aside from that, I've treated them well and taken good care of them, but I have no further use for them. Yoni was correct, but I didn't want to give her the wrong impression.

She compared her boyfriend to me, and I didn't want her to be put off by my thoughts, which may not be the same as his.

Camila Martinez intrigues me in a way that a woman never has, not even my late wife. Not only does she intrigue me, but she makes me want her badly. It's been hell keeping my dick in my pants the last couple of nights. I'm not sure how long I'll be able to do so tonight, especially with what I purchased for her to wear.

The only thing that will keep my desire at bay is inflicting punishment on her. Seeing her take the pain that I love to dish out will turn me on, but it will also serve as a deterrent.

I think back to Leona chiding me about getting Camila investigated. My logical side knows I must do this for my peace of mind. If we connect how I believe we can, I need to know everything about her. It's the only way that I can let her in completely.

Yet, another side of me wants to wade deeper into that water with no questions asked. That side of me responds when Camila steps out onto the lanai with me.

She's wearing a transparent mesh three-piece set. The bra barely covers her nipples and wraps in a bandage style in the front with three slim bands across her back. The garter belt is a series of leather straps that hook up to thigh-high stockings.

A chain attached to the front of the garter belt travels in two directions, each attaching to the handcuffs on her wrists. The heels she's wearing tonight are incredibly high, but she can walk in them, as I suspected.

"You're beautiful, Princesa," I say, reaching for her hand.

She comes to me and, with a little pressure on her shoulders, kneels before me.

"This, mi amor, is how I love looking at you. You're beautiful resting on your knees at my cock, ready to serve me whenever I want. Seeing you in this position makes my cock as hard as a rock. I would love to shove my dick down your throat right now and watch you choke on it. Would you like that, Princesa?"

"Yes, Dominio," she says, bowing her head.

"Princesa, you may look me in the eyes and speak to me whenever you want unless I punish you. And trust me, when you're punished, you *will* know it. There will be no doubt in your mind. Are you comfortable?"

Smiling nervously, she says, "It will take some getting used to, but I like this."

"Can you handle it, Princesa?"

"Yes."

"How does it make you feel?"

"Sexy. Powerful. The way your eyes lit up when I walked into this room made me feel in control, desired, and beautiful."

"You're all those things, Princesa. But remember, even when I'm exacting strict commands from you, you're still powerful. What makes you even more powerful is when you agree to give that control to me over your body and your will."

She smiles so beautifully at me that I want to reward her, but I won't. I explain the expectations of our relationship. I explain what she can expect and inquire about what she wants. We spent an hour negotiating the terms of our relationship and the boundaries. I explained hard and soft limits, and we agreed on hers.

"What do you have planned for tonight?" she asks when we finish.

"Be patient, Princesa. Be patient. If you're a good girl and can withstand my plans, you will get a reward," I say, removing the lids from our plates.

Tonight's meal is cedar-planked salmon, lobster ravioli, risotto, steamed broccoli, and fresh garlic bread. We'll finish it off with coconut flan.

"Would you like wine, rum, or water, Princesa?"

"How about I serve you, Dominio?"

"You're a fast learner. Please, go ahead."

I watch her breasts jiggle while she prepares our drinks at the minibar and then returns to me, kneeling before me and holding my glass.

Tonight, the furniture has been removed from the lanai; the only remaining are palm tree mats for sitting. Soft jazz music is piped into the space from overhead speakers, and when she's finished preparing our drinks, I move to sit beside her.

"Let me feed you, mi amor."

She smiles, pleased that I want to serve her.

I take my time feeding her and enjoying how she engages with every bite, showing how sumptuous the food is with sultry moans and licking her lips.

And when I'm finished feeding her, she does the same for me. I shake my head when she forks a piece of salmon for me.

"Take it off the fork and feed it to me."

She does as I ask, and when her fingers meet my lips, I hold her wrist, slowly sucking the meat from her fingertips. When I've consumed it all, still holding her wrist, I lick her fingers clean.

Returning to her index finger, I slowly suck it suggestively until she moans and squirms, and I can smell her heat.

"What do you want, Princesa?"

"You."

It's the one thing I've known since seeing her on the balcony that night. She wanted me. It was in the sway of her hips, the way she pressed against that railing, and the smile on her lips. Every time we've been in contact with each other since, no matter the words on her lips, the desire was in her eyes, and I could always . . . *always* smell her heat.

My hand grips the back of her neck, and she inhales, holding her breath. Quickly, I loop my fingers in her hair, jerking her head backward. I see the tears smarting her eyes, but she doesn't utter a sound.

Leaning forward, my mouth closes over hers, and I suck on her lips until she opens for me. Princesa welcomes my tongue, my growl, and my ownership of her mouth as I take control of her tongue and the kiss, leading her where she dares not go.

She's sweet, warm, and hungry for what I have to offer her. When I release her, she stares breathlessly at me.

"Follow me," I order, walking into the house from the lanai.

We take the hallway to my suite on the opposite side of the house from all the other rooms. I close and lock the door, although I know everyone has left for the evening.

"Your room is different but nice," she says.

I never showed her my bedroom when I gave her a tour of my home.

I look casually at the modern furnishings and try to see the black walls and black leather furniture with strategic spotlighting through her eyes. The luxury art pieces displayed on an illuminated shelf are my only concession to color in an otherwise monochromatic bedroom. Even the fireplace is tiled with black tourmaline, and the minibar is crafted from black onyx and framed in black leather.

"Thank you," I reply, placing my hand over an invisible black plate on the wall to the left of my art shelf.

The shelf begins to slide sideways, and I hear a little gasp behind me, which causes me to smirk just a little.

I step inside the space and turn to face Camila in the bedroom, staring in amazement.

"Don't be afraid of the dark, Princesa."

She finally closes her mouth, looks over her shoulder as if considering running, and then back at me.

"I promise. It will hurt just a little unless you want more."

She inhales, and I see the moment she makes up her mind. She releases her breath, straightens her shoulders and head, and a tiny smile dances on her lips.

I hold my hand out . . . welcoming her into my lair.

21

ANYSSA/CAMILA

ANYSSA'S THIRTY-BEFORE-THIRTY LIST

☑ Make love in a stairwell
☑ Hike the Rocky Mountains
☑ Ride an elephant
☑ Dance in the rain
☑ International road trip
☑ Learn an art
☑ Ride in a hot air balloon
☑ Go backpacking
☑ Make love to a stranger
☐ Perform on a stage
☑ Tattoo on my ass
☑ Scale a summit
☑ Learn a foreign language
☑ Swim at night, where you can see the stars
☑ Snorkel
☑ Parasail
☑ Make love on a train
☑ ~~Take a cooking class in a foreign country.~~ Get eaten out on a ledge while looking down onto the ocean!!!
☑ Learn to ski
☐ Stand under a waterfall

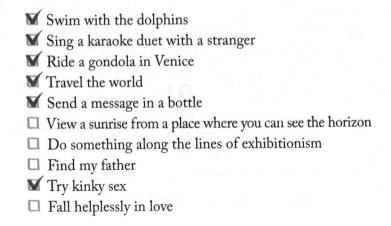

- ☑ Swim with the dolphins
- ☑ Sing a karaoke duet with a stranger
- ☑ Ride a gondola in Venice
- ☑ Travel the world
- ☑ Send a message in a bottle
- ☐ View a sunrise from a place where you can see the horizon
- ☐ Do something along the lines of exhibitionism
- ☐ Find my father
- ☑ Try kinky sex
- ☐ Fall helplessly in love

Black and blue. Sexy. Elegant. Yet reminiscent of bruises. Black velvet damask wallpaper covers the walls, and recessed fluorescent lighting gives off a dim bluish-white light throughout the room.

A low, black, metal four-poster bed is centered in the room. Chains and cuffs hang from each post of the bed, and black, sheer curtains are pulled back around each post. Underneath the bed is a cage with a black floor pad, and above the bed is a helical chandelier suspended by heavy cables.

A black metal and leather X is at the end of the bed.

"What's this?" I ask, stroking my hands over the metal and leather, looking at the handcuffs at the top and the bottom of the X.

"St. Andrew's Cross."

"A cross? In a room like this? Or should I say, dungeon?"

A small lobby led to steep stairs when we stepped behind the art shelf. We took the stairs down into what looked like a dungeon to me, but one that he'd transformed into this sexual lair.

Nazár steps behind me, wrapping an arm around my waist and his other around my midsection under my breasts in a hug.

"If you're good, Princesa, you would be restrained to the cross facing the front so I can tease and pleasure you. However, if you're a naughty girl, I will restrain you with your back to me so you can be punished."

A shiver runs down me, and he releases a low, husky chuckle that shoots straight to my core.

"Do you like this room?"

I glance around and notice there are no windows, and there's only one way out: the way that I entered, up the stairs, and behind his art shelf. That door is now closed and probably locked, as well.

As I face the bed, to my right is a wall of mirrors across from the bed, but next to the entrance is a cabinet. I'm sure Nazár holds his "supplies" in there. To my left is a table similar to the one at BoDSMe, probably for wax play, and a stool sits on the other side.

Everything in the room is black except for the lighting, which gives a blue hue when reflecting off the black objects. Even the floor is made from African blackwood.

"It's a beautiful room, Dominio," I say, testing the mattress by sitting on it and bouncing.

"As are you, Camila, mi amor. So beautiful and so sexy."

A part of me desires to hear him call my real name the way he says her name. I want to hear the thick Spanish accent as he says Anyssa lovingly and tenderly.

"Undress me, Princesa," he grumbles, holding his hand out and beckoning me to him.

My fingers slowly release the buttons of his white dress shirt as I inhale the rum on his breath and the aftershave coating his face. I want to kiss and lick him, but I don't dare move beyond what he permits me to do.

When his shirt hangs open, my eyes dance across the silken hairs on his chest.

"May I touch your chest, Dominio?" I ask.

"You may touch my chest."

My hands run across his chest, swirling through the silky hairs, and they're just as soft as I thought they would be. I look up at him; fire is swirling in his eyes, and his nostrils are flaring.

Slowly, I drag my hand down to his washboard abs, hovering just above the waistband of his pants. His eyes grow dim, and his breath deepens as I dance dangerously close to the precipice of destruction.

Unbuttoning his pants, my left hand returns to his chest. My right hand unzips his pants as the left continues to dance further south until my fingers touch the beginnings of the silky hairs at the top of his crotch.

Just as my fingers run for the border, he grabs my wrist tightly in one of his hands and says, "I don't like disobedience, Princesa."

My chest heaves silently, and my fingers itch to go where they've never gone before. I jerk my hand in his grasp, but only so slightly. Unfortunately for me, he doesn't miss the subtle movement.

Nazár rolls the cross away from the bed and to the other side of the room near the wall of mirrors.

"Step up," he instructs in an irritated voice. I step onto the stand at the bottom of the cross.

I hold my arms up, knowing what comes next, and a tingle runs through me as he pulls the handcuffs down from the top using a pulley system. Excitement floods my core as he secures my wrists and ankles to the cross.

Alarm fills me when he pushes me against the cross, pulls a belt from the center of the cross, and secures my waist to the cross.

"What is your safe word, Princesa?"

"Travel."

"You'd do well to remember that," he says, walking to the cabinet to my left.

I watch in fascination as he unlocks it and takes his time assessing the tools in his arsenal. I'm surprised that the tools in this cabinet far surpass the ones in BoDSMe, and I'm interested in what he might choose.

He walks away with the flogger, and I'm relieved.

"Do you think this is a game, Princesa?"

"No, Dominio."

"I don't want to waste your time. After all, you were the one who reminded me you only have two weeks. So don't you fucking waste my time," he says, and the first lash slices across my ass.

I bite my bottom lip clenching below at the sweet sting of pain on my ass cheeks.

"Scream as loud as you want, Princesa. This room is soundproof. No one can hear your screams. The sexy part about that is there's no one on these grounds except you and me."

This time, he hits harder than before, and the sting brings tears to my eyes, but I don't utter a word. The lashes move up to my shoulders, and my head jerks back as I shift my head so my hair covers my shoulders, but Nazár is quick. He grabs my hair, yanking my head sideways. He whips my shoulders, the backs of my thighs, and my ass in swift, successive movements.

Aside from the sting, I love the flogger's popping sound when it hits my flesh.

"Does this turn you on, Princesa?" he asks, stepping closer and whispering.

"Yes," I whimper.

"If you fucking come, I will make you wish that you'd never lain eyes on me," he threatens.

It's hard to clench my legs closed, but not so hard to clench my core. I will my pussy not to release a single drop, but the betrayer that she is, she doesn't listen. I feel a pearl of dew moisten my pussy lips, and I desperately want to release it.

Who knew that this type of behavior would arouse me?

When he finishes, he clicks a locking mechanism on either side of the cross and slowly begins to bend the cross forward until I'm bent in half with my ass jutting out.

Once again, he returns to the cabinet, and this time, it's harder for me to angle my head to see the tool he's selecting. He doesn't hide it for long because I feel the sting of the paddle on my ass.

"Dominio!" I cry out at the hard whack that he brings across my behind the second time.

"Did I give you permission to speak?"

"You said that I wasn't restricted."

Chuckling, he shakes his head and says, "And she has a smart mouth. You will pay for your sarcasm and disobedience, Princesa."

Is he serious? I didn't disobey; I stayed within the rules.

The next time he spanks me, I realize those other spankings were mild and tame. It isn't the force of the impact that takes my breath away, but what's behind it.

At once, vibrations shoot through my body with the stinging awareness of pins and needles that electrify every possible nerve ending throughout me. Unfortunately, no numbing accompanies these sensations, so I feel every impression.

He does this several more times, and each time my mouth opens to say his name, it's shocked straight out of me.

"Do you remember your safe word?" he asks, straightening the cross and bringing me upright.

I'm only slightly dizzy, but my body is trembling, and my ass is sore.

I manage to nod as the trembling in my body slows.

"Good," he says, kissing my shoulders and the back of my neck.

The tension eases from my body at his sweet and attentive touches from his lips and hand. A tickling sensation erases the relaxing feel and begins to take over as I wonder what he's doing to my body.

"Dominio," I giggle.

The giggle is swallowed by a feeling of pain instantaneously as though the same toy he used to tickle is now being used to torture me.

It feels like claws are dragging down my back, across my ass, and then the backs of my thighs. The same object he's using to bring me pleasure, he's also using to inflict pain on me, and it feels as if my body is all over the place.

He spanks my ass while the feathery tickle crosses over the backs of my legs. My entire body clenches into a tight muscle, and I hold my breath, overwhelmed by the confusing sensations. I'm unsure if I love it or hate it.

"How do you feel, mi amor?"

"I don't know," I reply honestly.

"You didn't use your safe word."

"No, I didn't. At times, it felt good and then, not so good."

"Did it hurt?"

"Yes, it felt like claws dragging up my body and the electrical spanking you gave. I've never experienced anything so . . . electrifying?"

He chuckles and says, "I'm proud, Princesa, that you held up under pressure. How does your body feel?"

"It hurts, but I'm good," I reply softly.

"I want you, Princesa. I want you so badly."

"You can have me, Dominio."

He grabs my chin, jerking my head sideways, and says, "You don't make the calls. *I* do."

My eyes graze over his and down to his lips. I want to kiss him, but he releases me and steps back.

"You will get me, but not how you want me."

"All I want is you, Dominio."

He removes his belt from his pants, and I wonder if he will spank me with it, but he doesn't. Nazár lays it on his bed, steps out of his pants, and puts them on the bed.

I watch carefully with my heart in my throat as he removes his boxers. He's ready for me, and I want to ride him until his dick falls off. Knowing that I make him this way excites me.

Nazár's dick is huge and swollen with purple veins and a dark-red, bulbous, angry-tipped head.

It weeps and looks like it might explode if it gets a smidgen harder.

"Are you about to take me?"

"Yes, Princesa. I am."

Why am I second-guessing my smart mouth that landed me in this situation?

This time, he goes to the cabinet behind me, and I hear him open and close a drawer before he returns to me.

"Is this ass virginal?"

My heart rushes to my throat. "It is, and it's too tiny to do whatever you're thinking, Dominio."

"Are you employing your safe word, Princesa?" he asks, pausing.

My gut clenches, but my resolve is iron-clad. I said that I wanted the pain. I told him I wanted what he wanted, and he told me that if I walked down this path, there would be no going back.

Well, here I am.

"No, Dominio. I'm not employing my safe word," I manage to grit out.

"What reservations are you having?" he asks, stroking his dick.

"I can't imagine that big-ass pierced dick fitting in my tiny hole."

Laughing, he says, "You have a very *generous* ass, Princesa."

"Ass . . . as in cheeks. Not my asshole. That is a tiny, miniature, minuscule, almost nonexistent thing."

He laughs again and says, "Are you employing your safe word?"

"Not using it."

"Good."

His hand slaps my ass harder than he did with the flogger or the paddle. The sound echoes around the room, and it's dark except for the bluish-white light.

He slaps my ass again before he begins to rub my ass cheeks in opposing circles, getting me to relax. My pussy clenches when I feel his tongue licking around my ass.

His lips and tongue give me a workout back there that makes me come harder than any other man's dick ever has. The entire time he's eating my ass, his fingers pulsate and scissor inside my va-jay-jay.

My legs shake as I release, and a mewling cry erupts from my throat. Nazár kisses my ass cheeks, smacks me on the ass, and says, "That's my good girl."

Now that I finally let my guard down, he dribbles cold liquid in my crack and moves my ass in opposing circles.

His fingers slide inside my pussy again.

"Are you thirsty, Princesa?"

"No. I'm not."

"Are you sure?"

"I'm sure. Let's get it over with."

"No. Not with that attitude, Princesa. Your role is to please, submit to, and give me power and authority over your body. Are you ready to get spanked again?"

As much as I want to say yes, I can't help but think about the vibrations, throbbing, and sensations accompanying that electrical spanking.

"No, Dominio. I'm not ready to be spanked."

"Good," he says, clicking the locking mechanism again and bending me forward on the cross. My ass is tilted at an angle that leaves me completely exposed. I feel as if no part of me is hiding from Nazár.

After he pours the lube, he starts the work.

First, the stretching and the pulling, and then comes him massaging it all in. His finger rubs my swollen clitoris as he presses himself against my ass. I feel the pressure but don't give in, choosing to stay clenched against a pain I cannot fathom.

"Princesa, you will submit to me. You will give me what I need, or I will take what I need. Otherwise, use your safe word. Do not ever . . . play with me. Understood?"

"Yes," I breathe softly.

I brace myself, inviting and welcoming the pain as I jut my ass out further.

My head rocks back and forth as I hold tight to the leather pillow at the top of the cross. Nazár presses his way into my ass.

"I love that you're a virgin in this area and that I'm your first. I promise you'll never forget me, Princesa."

"With or without anal penetration, I will never forget you, Nazár," I say.

We didn't need to take it to this step. Yet, I want to prove that I can handle whatever he can dish out.

I'm a patient woman. I genuinely want what he wants.

22

NAZÁR

She'll be leaving me soon. That's all I can think about. That and ways to convince her to stay because I'm not ready for our time to end. I've even considered buying her property and transforming it into a lucrative resort, but I don't think she'll agree.

Camila isn't afraid of impact play, anal penetration, or anything else that I throw her way. Her breasts jut upward, and a moan slips from her partially open lips. I lean down and pull her lips into mine, sucking her breath away. Her eyes flit to mine, and I keep my mouth over hers, stealing her breath and not allowing her to have any oxygen.

Slowly, I release, and when I step back, she coughs as she tries to refill her lungs with fresh oxygen. When she's calm again, I resume my activity, dribbling orange candle wax over her thighs and hips, mingling with the white, purple, and blue already drizzled there.

"How does that feel, mi amor?"

"It burned at first, but the higher you lifted the candle, the more it felt good. It almost tickled," she shares.

I exchange the orange for a yellow candle and repeat the pattern on her left side, creating the same swaying line until I reach her breasts. Reaching across the table, I grab the orange candle again and make large looping circles around her breasts, holding a candle in each hand, coloring her left breast orange and the right one yellow.

"Mm. Feels so good," she purrs, flicking her nipples with the edge of her nails.

Slowly, I lower the candles closer to her body as I watch the yellow and orange wax drip onto her nipples. Camila grips the edge of the table, her body turning rigid at the pain. She bites her bottom lip, causing the color from her lip to dissipate.

"You're so beautiful, mi amor," I say, dragging a finger through her slickness.

When I'm satisfied that she's on the brink of pain and my cock is harder than before, I step away, placing the candles on the table.

"Turn over, Princesa."

She does as I ask, and I grab the ball gag.

"I don't want to hear your screams, and yet, I know you won't be able to hold them in," I say, securing the leather collar at the back of her neck and fitting the ball inside her open and waiting mouth.

When I'm finished, I pull the blindfold over her eyes. Then I move to my cabinet and grab the supplies I'll need.

I found Camila on the beach today, playing volleyball in the fucking nude. I nearly lost my damn mind when I saw her like that. However, I had to restrain myself from allowing everyone else to see my jealousy, but with one glance at me, she knew that I was angry.

I haven't spoken with her about it since she returned to my place. She'll know soon enough. In the few days she's been staying at the guest cottage, she's been punished a few times. I think she loves the pain and looks forward to my punishments.

Her body is an eclectic art piece with reds, oranges, purples, blues, and whites. I run my fingers over her body, basking in the wax's smooth yet rough surface.

I remove the gag temporarily and ask, "Do you trust me, Princesa?"

"I do."

"I am about to remove the wax, but you must be very still."

"Will it hurt?"

"Only if you move. I have a knife, and that's what I'm going to use to remove the wax from your body," I say, replacing the ball gag.

I drag the back of the knife along the backs of her thighs.

Chill bumps rise along her skin, but she remains still. Only soft whooshes of breath can be heard. Slowly, I pull the knife across the wax on the backs of her thighs, removing the remnants of wax there. I'm so proud of how obedient she is. She's remarkably still as I remove the candle wax from her ass, hips, back, shoulders, belly, breasts, and legs.

When I'm finished, I drag the knife across the bottom of her feet. Camila clenches the sides of the table and inhales deeply, holding her breath. Shaking the remnants of the wax from the knife, I press it against the inside of her thigh, dragging it along her pussy, and coating the blade with her juices.

I pull the blindfold up so that she can watch me. I place the knife in my mouth, sucking it clean. I hear a tiny gasp erupting from her before she starts moaning.

Placing the knife on her belly, I slowly drag it back up to her breasts, tracing slow circles around her nipples with the tip of my blade.

"Mmm," she moans around the ball gag when I smack her pussy lips with my free hand.

She arches up, and I know she wants more. Now, I exchange the knife for a feather.

Slowly, I drag the feather down her body, and she struggles to maintain control.

"Be still," I growl as I drag the feather between her legs, up her midsection, and along her neck. We engage in soft play for a while. When I know she's had enough, I help her off the table and tie her to the St. Andrew's Cross with her back to me, securing the blindfold in place again.

Once she's cuffed, I pull out the crop with the rubber edge. With one hand, I drag the feather up and down her body and spank her with the other. Alternating between tickling and spanking makes her skin extremely sensitive and keeps her nerve endings alert.

When I know she's ripe for the pain, I apply plastic clips along her back and hear her first whimper. Leaning in, I pull the ball gag back and ask, "Safe word?"

"No!" she hisses, pressing her face against the cross.

I replace the ball gag and exchange the crop and tickler for two floggers. With alternating hands, I whip her shoulders, thighs, and ass. Her moans of pleasure and pain are my delight. My cock grows harder the more we play, and I continue until her skin turns red.

Only then do I use the floggers to whip the pins off her body, hitting her harder and harder until the clips fall off slowly, one by one.

Uncuffing her and removing the ball gag and blindfold, I ask, "How are you?"

"Ready for you," she whispers.

I see the tears streaking her eyes.

"Are you sure?"

"Yes, Dominio."

"Do you know why you're being punished?"

"Punishment feels so good, though."

"Do you know why you're being punished?" I repeat in a harsh tone.

Her gaze meets mine, and I see a bit of defiance there.

"Of course I do. You were pissed when you saw me playing ball with the others on the beach."

"Nude!"

She glances away. I lead her to a chair in the corner where she sits, and I hand her a pair of fishnet leggings that only cover up to her thighs.

After she pulls them on, I tie her legs to the chair. She's spread eagle before me, and I kneel in front of her, pulling open the storage bin of the chair. I remove a vibrator, a bullet vibrator, and a butt plug.

She shifts comfortably in the chair for me to insert the butt plug inside her. Then she reaches for the bullet vibrator, and I allow her to place it inside herself while I grab the vibrator and turn it on.

"You will feel all the pleasure I bring you, Princesa. But you will not release any of it. I will take you to the edge and make your body feel pleasure, but you cannot give in to it. No matter how badly you want to come, you're not allowed to fucking come. Is that understood?"

"Yes, Dominio."

"Good girl," I say, grabbing the handle of the bullet vibrator. I twist it inside her, watching her head drop back and her eyes close as she releases a moan of pleasure. I place the vibrator against her clit and pump the vibrating bullet in and out of her pussy with my other hand.

"Please, Dominio. It feels so good," she moans.

"That's what I want, mi amor."

I remove both and kiss her pussy lips, sucking at them until her hips arch upward.

"Please! Just fuck me," she begs.

I replace the vibrator and the vibrating bullet inside of her, fucking her until tears are flowing down her face.

"I can't take anymore, baby, please," she begs.

Pressing my finger against her clit I rub it in hard, fast circles and meet her gaze. "I am not your fucking baby."

She holds her breath as I pump the vibrating bullet in and out of her.

"Dominio, please!"

Slowly, I pull the butt plug out and then push it back in until my movements increase, using it to fuck her in the ass at the same time I'm using the vibrating bullet to pleasure her pussy.

"I . . . I . . . can't . . . take anymore!" she cries.

"You can, Princesa, and you *will*."

Tossing the vibrating bullet aside, I use my fingers and the vibrator to pump inside her for several seconds before sitting back and allowing her to sit there with her legs spread.

She moves her hand between her legs, and I growl, "Did I give you fucking permission to touch yourself?"

"No," she cries, removing her hand.

I see how she's buckling and wishes her legs could close, but she can't.

"You will pay for showing off what belongs to me."

"I'm sorry, Dominio."

"*Te arrepentirás mucho.* You will be very sorry," I repeat in English.

I apply the vibrating bullet to her clit, and she moans and purrs.

"Do. Not. Come," I warn.

She's so fucking beautiful spread before me with her glistening pink pussy and those beautiful thick lips.

"I can't take it."

"You *can* take it, Princesa. You're stronger than you know."

I smack her pussy hard with my palm, and she arches as much as the bindings will allow her. Her eyes close in bliss, but the tears return when I rub the vibrator generously against her clit and pussy.

When I feel she's had enough, I walk beside her, unzip my pants, and tell her, "You will pleasure me."

Her eyes dart up to meet mine, and then she shifts her gaze sideways.

"Is there a problem, Princesa?"

"No," she replies, grabbing my cock in her hands.

Her lips are wet and warm, her mouth hot and deep. She takes me inside her mouth, working around my piercing, and sucks me raw and hard. Fuck!

I've wanted to feel her mouth on me almost from the night I saw her on that balcony. Not once have I asked her, nor has she ever suggested it, but it was so worth the wait.

"Suck me off, Princesa," I order.

Her hands hold me tight, pulling me in deeper and returning to the tip again. When I can take no more, I grab the back of her head and pump her mouth hard and vigorously as if I were inside her.

She hums around my cock, and spit dribbles down her chin, down my dick, and her eyes begin to water.

"Use your free hand to fuck your ass with the butt plug," I tell her.

Camila shifts in her seat, grabs the butt plug, pulls it out slowly, and pushes it back while holding my dick with her other hand and working me over with her mouth. My cock grows harder in her mouth, watching her fuck her own ass, and I'm so close to releasing my seed down her throat that I don't think I can hold off much longer.

She sucks me harder until I pull out and hold my dick long enough to regain control. I untie her bindings and walk her to the bed, wrapping her lower legs and thighs together in elastic bindings. When she's on her knees with her ass and feet in the air, I use the butt plug to fuck her, and with my free hand, I stroke my dick.

"Dominio, it feels so good," she moans.

I smack her ass, enjoying the redness that develops and her soft, sensual moans. Moving toward the top of the bed, I turn her face toward me and rub my dick against her lips. She licks all around the head and sucks it back into her mouth.

When I finally pull back because I can take no more, I flip her onto her back, release the bindings, and straddle her. Again, she takes my dick into her mouth and sucks until I'm on edge. Pulling back, I release my come around her neck, decorating her with a pearl necklace.

"Good girl," I say, kissing her lips.

When I stand and pull her up, she asks, "And me?"

"And you will not have an orgasm until tomorrow. You wanted inside of my world . . . So welcome to Dominio's Den."

23

ANYSSA/CAMILA

"**H**ow did you get into kink?"

"I've never had a fascination with vanilla sex, but taking it to the limits that I do now isn't something I've always done either. Even with you, I'm cautious."

"I keep telling you that you don't need to be. I can handle it."

"I believe you," he says, stroking my head.

We're upstairs in his bedroom now. My body is sore and tired. When we first left the dungeon, Nazár gave me a full-body massage, rubbing a mixture of jojoba, sweet almond, and shea moisture virgin coconut body oils all over me.

As part of my aftercare, he makes sure to give me massages and hold me close afterward, reaffirming our connection.

"Princesa, I do not take pain and pleasure for granted. I won't push your boundaries too far because this is all new to you. I won't take it there until I'm comfortable that you're ready for the next level. Sometimes, subs think they know their limits when they're new to this world, but they truly don't. Some push too far, and others are afraid to push far enough."

"You're worried that I'm pushing too far?"

"Yes."

"Have you had a bad experience before?"

His eyes close, and he remains quiet for so long that I'm certain he's fallen asleep. I rub his chest and kiss it before lying back in his arms and snuggling into his side.

"I misjudged a woman before. Thought she could take everything that I had to dish out. Equated her strength with mine, but nothing could have been further from the truth."

"Your wife?"

He nods.

"She was into this world?"

"No. I wasn't either at the time. I pushed her in other ways, tested her boundaries, and thought she could handle it. My pressure for her to rise to the challenge of being a wife, submitting to me, and understanding that I had her best interest at heart is what ultimately broke her."

"How so?"

"Bella was a people pleaser, and what others thought of her was always important to her. The success she enjoyed in the film industry was her identity, or so she thought. I knew she had more to offer the world than what they saw. But I also knew that she needed to learn to follow me completely to get the best out of her. When she didn't, when the pressure from the outside world came on her to give them what they wanted over what I wanted, I added more pressure instead of being her comfort and reassurance. Made unfair demands of her."

"Such as?"

"Start a family, spend more time at home, be the gracious host I needed her to be at my business luncheons and dinners."

"And what was her reply?"

"She tried but said she wasn't ready to have a child yet. She still hadn't reached a certain pinnacle in her career that she was striving for. She started coming home late for business dinners she was supposed to prepare or have catered. Then she started being out of town in New York, Los Angeles, or London, more often, shooting films."

"And how did you handle that?"

"Not well. I would show up at sites demanding that she remember her vows to me. Expressing how important our marriage was before the outside world. She said I was embarrassing her and then . . ."

I wait for him to go on. I refuse to pressure him because discussing this is painful for him. As Nazár talks, his eyes are closed as though he's reliving past pain.

"Then one day, she finally did get pregnant. It was the happiest day of my life, but it seemed like her saddest day."

"Why?"

"She said that her career would have to go on hold and that once the baby came, I would apply more pressure for her to be home than before. She said she knew I wouldn't accept her traveling around the world with an infant at home, nor would I tolerate the baby traveling."

"And she was right, I'm guessing."

He nods.

"Anyway, I told her we would work it out and make room for her career and our family. Five months into the pregnancy, she miscarried. I blamed it all on her because she was shooting a film in Spain."

My heart clenches in my chest because I have no idea what he must be going through between losing his child and wife and his guilt. That could not have been an easy time for either of them.

It seems his marriage was already under pressure before the miscarriage. I can only imagine those had to be dark days afterward.

"You didn't want her over there?"

"No. We argued before she went, and she assured me she would be okay. When I got the news, I rushed to her side, but she couldn't even face me. She knew I blamed her, and it was impossible to convince her otherwise. It was in my eyes, my actions, and my words. When she recovered and returned home, she shut me out and sank into depression. We moved to Mauritius shortly after.

"I didn't realize she'd picked up a nasty little drinking habit while on set and at the lavish parties she attended. It started before we met, and she hid it well. Even after the marriage, she did a great job hiding it, and I thought she only drank on special occasions, parties, or dinner parties. Part of that was my fault because I traveled so much. We both did. The issue didn't show itself until she was stuck at home with no contracts coming in."

"Did you get her help?"

"I tried in the beginning, and she refused. After a year, she finally gave in, but there was so much damage in our marriage. We both blamed each other for everything: movie deals not coming through, land negotiations failing, and our careers suffering because we were stuck in a rut and couldn't see our way out. That's when I came up with the idea of turning this place into a resort."

"Seems like everything you touch turns to gold if the history galley you have on-site at the rum distillery is to be believed."

"Well, it did before our challenges came. Things finally picked up again."

"Did it make things better for you all?"

"No."

He doesn't say anything, and I rub the stubble on his face at a loss for words to comfort him. I wonder how often he's told this story.

"In time, I found that she was having an affair with one of the men on the construction site."

"Well, damn, that was bold of him."

Shaking his head, he says, "She manipulated him into it. He was let go, and I pushed her to check into rehab, and she still refused. About a year later, she became ill when the construction was over halfway complete. She was hospitalized and diagnosed with liver cancer."

"Oh no."

My heart goes out to him, thinking about what a scary time that must have been for them. I can hear in his voice the love he had for his wife. Despite their trials, it's evident that he loved her.

"She, uh . . . She was strong. Kept a smile on her face because, by then, she'd overcome the depression. I was scared she'd sink back into it."

"She fought through, though. For you and her."

He inhales deeply and then exhales loudly through his nose. I can tell that wasn't the case at all.

"She was still drinking. Though she'd promised me that she would quit after the diagnosis, she hadn't. I left town on a business trip and returned two days earlier than expected. The business meeting hadn't gone as planned, and things went downhill. I returned home, wanting to hide away from the world for a while, and found her passed out drunk in the living room.

"I woke her up, but she was incoherent, so I carried her to our bedroom. When she woke the next day, I confronted her with the bottles of rum and vodka that I'd found lying beside her, along with the hidden bottles of tequila, brandy, and scotch throughout the house."

"How long had you been out of town?"

"About three days, but I found out she'd had that stuff hidden here all along. It didn't just pop up while I was gone."

"Maybe she was beyond caring at that point. Sometimes, people get so depressed with a diagnosis, especially a terminal illness, that they don't care. They want the pain and the sadness to just end."

"Maybe. I'll never know."

"Unfortunately, there are some things we won't have answers to. We simply must find peace in it and move forward in our healing. One day, on the other side, you'll find the answers you need, Nazár. I think for the time you had her, you shared a beautiful love. Now, you have this place as a legacy of that love."

"Didn't protect her enough. From my family or the world," he grumbles.

"Your family?"

"They never thought she was good enough. My parents looked down on her, and my brothers thought she was 'easy.'"

I remain silent at that.

"In the end, I'm the one that drove her to her death."

A chill runs up my spine. I look up at him.

"You couldn't have, Nazár. You loved her . . . and from the way you sound, you still love her, or what you had with her."

He clears his throat and says, "A part of me always will love her, just like a part of me will always have regrets. I felt like her place was here on the island, making a home for us, not out in the world."

"Maybe you were right, Nazár. It seems that the world's pressures, not you, started her drinking. You said she'd been doing it before you met. The world crushed her spirit, and drinking was how she coped."

Nazár kisses the top of my head and squeezes me into him.

"We argued that night."

"What night?"

"The night she died. It was the same night I'd confronted her earlier about her drinking. I overheard her making plans on the phone with friends to go out to a new club that night. They were going for drinks and dancing. One of her single friends mentioned the cute guys that could be there and the trouble they could get in. I overheard her say that what I didn't know would never hurt me. She showered, dressed, and prepared to leave before I finally approached her."

"Did she deny it?"

"She told me I was making a big deal out of nothing."

"Were you?"

"No. I knew she'd do exactly what they wanted her to. She always had, and she always would. I told her that she couldn't leave and that the marriage was over if she did. She said she was sick of being stuck between the house and the hospital, and for once, she felt good and wanted to enjoy the short life she had remaining."

"That must have been hard for her and you."

He nods.

"She left against my wishes, and I ran out of the house after her. I'll never forget that it was raining that night. I ran after her, begging her not to leave, and when she got into her little sports car I'd bought her the year before for her birthday, she sped past me, kicking up rain and mud. I stood outside in the driveway and watched her go."

"Then it wasn't your fault, Nazár. The wet roads, slippery conditions . . ."

"And arguing with her husband."

"Not your fault. That didn't lead to the accident."

"It could have. She must have been so upset that she couldn't see clearly," Nazár says, releasing me and sitting up in bed.

I rub soft circles on his back, and he pulls his knees up to his chest, resting his chin on them and staring into space.

"Even if you never spoke up, something could have happened. We sometimes assume the role of God when we think it's up to us how something happened. In theory, it sounds good, but in reality, nothing is further from the truth. We have no control over fate or destiny. If it was going to happen, Nazár, there wasn't shit you could do about it. So, you can sit on this island, lord over the resort, and think you hold all power in your hands, but you don't. If you're not careful to come down off that high horse, you'll get a mighty swift kick in the ass on the way down."

He glances over his shoulder at me.

"You can be upset with me, Nazár. I don't say this to piss you off but to let you know that you're unfairly taking yourself through misery because you think you created a situation beyond your power. Shame on them if someone hasn't told you that by now."

He runs his fingers through his hair, still staring at me, before he says, "I never shared all of that with anyone before now. Not even Leona or Gary. They know we argued and how she died, but not everything I've told you."

Pressing my lips together, I rub his back a little firmer and say, "Thank you for trusting me with your pain."

His eyes drift over me in a soft caress, and he reaches back and cups my face. I sit up and kiss him slowly, caressing his face, willing him to heal from the pain of his past.

When we pull apart, he smiles slowly at me. "Camila Martinez, you're the most perfect and best thing that has come along in a long time."

Hearing that, my stomach tightens, and I think I'm going to be sick.

24

ANYSSA/CAMILA

ANYSSA'S THIRTY−BEFORE−THIRTY LIST

☑ Make love in a stairwell
☑ Hike the Rocky Mountains
☑ Ride an elephant
☑ Dance in the rain
☑ International road trip
☑ Learn an art
☑ Ride in a hot air balloon
☑ Go backpacking
☑ Make love to a stranger
☐ Perform on a stage
☑ Tattoo on my ass
☑ Scale a summit
☑ Learn a foreign language
☑ Swim at night, where you can see the stars
☑ Snorkel
☑ Parasail
☑ Make love on a train
☑ ~~Take a cooking class in a foreign country.~~ Get eaten out on a ledge while looking down onto the ocean!!!
☑ Learn to ski

- ☑ Stand under a waterfall
- ☑ Swim with the dolphins
- ☑ Sing a karaoke duet with a stranger
- ☑ Ride a gondola in Venice
- ☑ Travel the world
- ☑ Send a message in a bottle
- ☐ View a sunrise from a place where you can see the horizon
- ☐ Do something along the lines of exhibitionism
- ☐ Find my father
- ☑ Try kinky sex
- ☐ Fall helplessly in love

"I'm tired," I complain, wiping the sweat from my brow as we approach a set of steep stairs.

"Not much longer. It's just down these stairs," Nazár says. "Hold tightly to the railing, and be careful."

We've been hiking all morning, and he said it would end at a place of beauty that he wanted me to see. I see rocks all around but hear water somewhere, like a rushing river.

Halfway down the stairs, I see it.

"Come on. We can walk around this path so you can get a better view," Nazár says, reaching for my hand.

I take his hand and step off the steps onto a concrete platform protected by a tall, wooden railing.

"Why does it feel like we're in a large bowl hidden away from the world by magnificent trees?" I ask as I inhale the fresh scent of the rushing water falling over the edge of the natural rock formations.

"Because you are," he says, shoving his hands into his front pockets.

"This place is beautiful," I say as we approach the water.

He smiles and winks at me. "It's called Wild River Falls. Worth the hike?" he shouts.

I nod. This place is still on the resort but deep at the back of his private property. I haven't seen any "No Trespassing" signs yet, and many other people are here.

"I'm surprised you let people visit."

"How could I not?"

"Take a picture of me under the waterfall," I shout, remembering item number twenty on my Thirty-Before-Thirty List.

He pulls his phone from his shorts pocket and gestures for me to get into place. I walk behind Wild River Falls and pose for him to take a picture of me. He takes several just as some other people wander along.

Surprising me, he stops one of the men and asks, "Would you please take a picture of us?"

"Sure," the guy replies as Nazár hands him his phone.

I'm speechless, to be honest. I know he has a strict no-picture-taking policy, but I wonder if that just means on the resort. As I look around, I surmise it must be because other people also take pictures.

The man hands Nazár's phone back to him. Nazár shows me the pictures to ensure I like them.

"Beautiful," I say.

I purchased a prepaid cell phone for this trip as part of my cover. That's the number that I give Nazár to text me. When they come through, I immediately text them to my real number as we walk away from the waterfall.

He holds my hand, and I bask in the tenderness of that gesture. There are so many parts to this multifaceted man. While I don't want to hurt Camila, I owe Nazár the truth.

We're getting too close, and I cannot continue to hide it, even if it means breaking my promise to Camila.

"Nazár," I say.

"Yes, baby."

"We need to talk when we get back. There's something that I want to share with you."

Nazár smiles, but his eyebrows dip in a frown.

"Sure," he replies, dragging a finger across my lips.

The rest of the day is spent touring the grounds I haven't seen in the last two weeks.

"I'm tired. I feel like I've been working hard all day rather than being on vacation," I say as we return to his property.

"I can do something to make you feel better," he flirts, kissing my lips.

"Nazár!" Leona calls to him as we step out of the car.

He turns toward her. "Yes, Leona?"

"You completely forgot about your one o'clock meeting. Your guest has arrived, and I've been trying to reach you for over an hour," she says.

Glancing at his watch, Nazár frowns. "Damn, I'd forgotten all about that."

Turning to me, he says, "How about you nap, and I'll have something ready for you to eat when you wake up?"

"How about I grab a sandwich now, shower, and then nap in that order?"

"I'll get Nigel to whip you up something real quick. Shower and *then* eat."

"Okay," I say, resting my hands against his chest as he pulls me into his embrace. We share a slow, heated kiss before we pull apart.

"Keep tasting like that, and you won't get any sleep," he warns.

I bite my bottom lip, giggle, and turn toward the guest cottage. I glance over my shoulder once to see him and Leona moving up the walk with purposeful, long strides, their heads bowed together, discussing something.

I can't help but wonder what that's all about and who the meeting is with.

When I'm locked safely inside, I pull my actual phone from a locked bag and check my messages. I have two missed calls from Camila, one from Kayla, one from my mom, and one from Logan.

"I hope her dad is okay," I mutter, deciding to call Camila first.

The phone rings four times, and Camila answers just when I think it's going to voicemail.

"Hey," she says, sounding sleepy.

"Hey, yourself. Did I wake you?" I ask, glancing at the clock.

"I'm fine," she mumbles.

It's one thirty in the afternoon here, and when I do the quick calculations, I realize it's midnight there.

"I'm sorry. I forgot about the eleven-hour time difference. Call me when you get up."

"No, it's okay. I've been waiting for your call. Fell asleep waiting for it, actually."

"Yeah, I did see that I had a couple of missed calls from you. Is everything okay?"

"Yeah. When are you coming back to the States?"

"I should be back next Friday," I say as sorrow at leaving Nazár pours through me.

How could I already be missing a man that I barely know? Yet, there hasn't been a day gone by that we haven't spent together since I moved into his guest cottage.

"Think you can make it happen before then?"

"Umm . . . What's going on?"

"I have something that I need to share with you. Something important, but . . . I can't talk about it over the phone," she says, yawning.

"Is it related to Belle Baie?"

"No. Nothing like that."

I can't imagine what else she would have to tell me if it isn't related to the resort.

"Let me finish this trip, and I promise I'll see about getting my return flight changed to Sonoma instead of Atlanta."

"Okay."

"Camila, is everything okay?"

I hear her inhaling deeply, and then she says, "Yes, Anyssa. Everything is just fine."

"And your dad? How did his other surgery go?"

"It was touch and go for a while, but he made it through."

I can hear what she *isn't* saying, and I don't want to press her for details because it could make her emotional.

"Glad to hear that. I just returned from a hike and was about to shower and nap."

"Okay. Enjoy."

"Thanks. You go back to sleep and get some rest yourself."

"M'kay," she mutters sleepily.

After ending the call, I undress, shower, and find a sandwich and chips waiting for me in the dining area.

I finish my food and then head to my room for a nap.

☑ ☑ ☑

I wake up and turn over in bed. Stretching, I'm surprised to find Nazár standing in the doorway watching me.

"Hey, is everything okay?" I ask, sitting up, disturbed by the scowl on his face.

Nazár runs his fingers through his long, dark hair, pulling it back from his forehead before he stands up straight.

"Business."

"Meeting didn't go so well?"

"It was fine. It's other things."

Swinging my legs over the side of the bed, I pat the space beside me. "Come here."

He takes long strides into the room and sits beside me. My fingers loop through his curls, and I straighten them individually before they loop into a swirl once more. I massage his scalp with my fingers and straddle him.

"What's wrong, Dominio?" I ask, calling him his dominant name to ease the tension and get him in the mood for play.

Pressing his forehead against mine, he bites my bottom lip and runs his fingers up my tank top, scratching my back. His kiss is rough and forceful, nipping and biting my tongue and lip. I feel the blood rise to the surface of the bruised and perhaps broken skin.

Nazár rips my tank from my body, leaving nothing but the little cotton shorts that I have on me. Lowering his head, he bites a nipple with his teeth, gnawing at it, and I cup my hands against the back of his head, pulling him closer.

"Oh, Dominio," I moan as desire swirls in my belly and nestles into a pool in my pussy.

Still biting and tugging on my nipple, his hand slips inside my shorts, and he roughly forces several fingers inside me, shoving and scissoring, pumping rough and hard. There is nothing gentle about his ministrations today, and I can't help but wonder what happened. What has put him on edge?

"Hey, are you okay?" I ask, turning his head to look at me.

He nods and then turns his gaze from me and looks between my legs instead.

I lift just a little and give him more room inside of me, and his fingers pump as my desire throbs and swells. My arms wrap around him as I bask in the pain of the second nipple that he's biting. My hips jerk forward hungrily, accepting the pleasure he brings.

It won't be long before I release; I guess he senses it too. Nazár flips me onto my back and shoves my shorts aside. I see the desire in his eyes when he confirms that I'm wearing no panties per his instructions. I haven't worn any since we've been together.

With my legs pulled into the air and my ankles fisted in one of his hands, he uses his other hand to slap my pussy several times before he forces three fingers and then four inside again. He scissors them furiously, pulling them out and shoving them in again.

I want him, and there's no way that I'll be satisfied until he's inside of me, but it's not me, but him who's in control. I watch greedily as he pulls his hand from inside me, shoves his running shorts down, and fists his dick.

It's angry, looking much like its owner. The same purple veins throbbing in his forehead now throb in his dick. It's swollen and bruised red like the coloring on his face, which is slick with sweat, and he hasn't even begun.

Roughly, Nazár pushes himself inside of me. Though I feel like I'm tearing down there, the feeling is so good, making me want more of him. It makes me wish that this would never have to end and that it could always be this way.

Hot. Rough. Deep.

There's no lovemaking, no sex, and no kink. This is pure fucking with no apologies.

His anger betrays itself in the swivel of his hips, the thrust of his pelvis, the ramming of his dick tearing at my inner walls. It's evident in his tight grip on my ankles that I know will be bruised because they're already sore.

It's demonstrated in how his lips are pulled back over his teeth in an angry snarl, the fire in his heated gaze, and the flaring of his broad nostrils.

The sweat dripping from his brow and chest are even angry, singeing me as each drip falls to my body.

Yet, what can I do but take it? After all, I want this as much as he does. Something about how he's fucking me right now is tearing at my insides, bruising my heart. It's like I know that he's severing our connection, but why now?

I still have six days remaining, and we can enjoy our time. Yet, in his gaze, he's already breaking away from me. Nazár's already regarding me as a casual fuck, a random stranger that he could care less about. As if, after this, he'll never see me again.

And then I know. I don't know how I know, but I know that he's found out about me. He's punishing me most cruelly. There's no connection. He's just fucking me like some random woman.

A slap across the ass stings and is quickly followed up by several more, and I know I'll be sore for days to come. He's showing me no mercy, not even checking to ensure I'm okay because he's beyond caring.

He's in a mental space I've never experienced with him. Another slap to my ass, and he growls and picks up his pace as his dick slams inside me, knocking the wind from my lungs and every coherent thought from my mind.

I try to open my legs wider to brace for him, but I can't break his grip on my ankles or part my legs to force him out or lock him in.

"Dominio!" I cry out.

That angers him more as his punishing thrusts become more brutal and aggressive. When he finally releases my ankles and legs from the air, it's only to shove them apart and position himself between my thighs. I welcome him, wrapping my legs and arms around him, but he breaks the grip, placing a barrier between us by not quite lying on me but neither lifting up completely.

"Safe word?"

I shake my head no.

I can't push him out. If this is the last time that we'll be together, I want to remember what it feels like when he's filling me up and what he smells like when he's doused in sweat, arousal . . . and anger.

With his hand on my neck, Nazár gently applies pressure as he increases the intensity and pace of his movements. The faster he moves, the more pressure he applies until I cannot breathe.

My hands lift to pry his hands from my neck, but he doesn't budge. I close my eyes, allowing harmony to take over as I enjoy the pain of a harsh fuck paired with breath play that excites me.

The lightheadedness and dizziness begin to take over, clouding my vision and thoughts. I float on the feeling and wait for him to let up. Panic takes over when he doesn't release as he usually does after several seconds.

My eyes fly open, and I reach out to him, slapping his hand until he releases. My head spins as I choke and regain my breath. Nazár is on me again, covering my mouth with his and then kissing me.

I melt under his attention, wanting our bodies to meld together. Lifting my leg to wrap around him, I'm surprised when he slaps my thigh, pressing it away from him and onto the bed.

Through all this, he never loses his momentum or rhythm. The headboard slams into the wall, and I thought this bed frame was relatively stable. My hiccuping cries rival the sound of the slam, but I still don't use my safe word even in all this.

My pussy is sore, and if that weren't enough, Nazár pulls out of me and flips me onto my belly. Using his knee, he spreads my legs apart and grabs my arms, wrapping his large hand around my wrists.

"I want you up on your knees with your ass spread open, Princesa."

Maybe we're okay after all. At least, I hope so.

I do as he says, and he releases my hands momentarily. Long enough to spread my cheeks apart and guide himself inside of my asshole. He resumes the grip on my wrists, pulling me toward him and shoving me forward again as he fucks me anally like there's no tomorrow.

My face presses into the pillow, and I bury my screams. The pain that soars through me as he thrashes inside my ass and the breath play is a heady combination. Despite his brutal punishment, I can't help that I come.

Only it isn't pleasing to Nazár because he pulls back and begins to spank my ass with his hand. Not once, not twice, not even three times, but repeatedly. His hits are harder than usual as he grunts, "I never gave you permission to come! You're a disobedient little slut!" he growls, lifting my hips again and then entering me once more.

This time, he pumps a few times until he empties himself inside my ass. He slumps over me for a few seconds but quickly stands up, pulling up his shorts and underwear before sitting on the bed again.

I lay on the bed, on my back, watching him. He's distanced himself from me with his shoulders hunched over as he stares at the floor.

Finally, Nazár pulls his fingers through his hair and sighs loudly.

"Hey," I say, reaching out to touch his shoulder, but he pulls away.

The action is subtle, but I don't miss it.

"Is there anything that I can do to make you feel better? It seems like something's off between us," I say.

"Yes, something's very off, Anyssa," he replies gruffly.

I sit up on the bed with my heart hammering in my chest. Yet, it doesn't feel how I hoped it would upon hearing him say it the first time. He spits it out in disgust as a condemnation of my sins.

"So, you know who I am."

"Why did you lie to me, Anyssa?"

"I never meant to lie to you, Nazár. Not you as a person."

"I thought what we shared was real and wasn't scripted. Why would you do that to me?" he asks, turning to stare at me.

The pain in his eyes is evident as a thousand questions float in them.

I feel him blocking me out already and putting the walls in place. It's the least that I deserve for being torn between my promise to Camila and my obligation to him.

"Honestly, Nazár, I never expected things to jump off between us. I came here as a favor to a friend of mine, the real Camila Martinez. My only desire was to find someone to love me along the way."

"So, I was a game to you? Just another segment of your TV shows?"

"No! Never that! When I first saw you, hell, when we first met, I had no idea who you were! I only knew I was attracted to you and wanted to get to know you. I had no idea you were the owner of this resort. Not until the day that we toured the vineyards."

"Why didn't you tell me the truth then?"

"Because I'd already signed the NDA with Camila and was locked into that. It wasn't something that I could break."

"Yet, you could overlook the NDA you signed upon coming here?"

"No, I haven't done anything like that. Your NDA said nothing about my identity or pretending to be someone else or anything. We honestly meant no harm. It was just a way to ensure that she didn't lose out on all her money, destroy her friends' reputation who referred her to you, and make sure that she could come again in the future."

"She should have come herself."

"She couldn't. Her father was having emergency surgery, and she wasn't sure if he would make it through, but she didn't want to lose everything that she'd invested in this trip either. We thought it was a good plan and never meant to harm anyone. I swear, Nazár. I never meant any disrespect."

"The photos! I should have known when I caught you taking those photos in the vineyard."

"That was the only time that I did that. It was for my personal collection. Selfies of me on vacation. Nothing that I planned to share with anyone. I still haven't shared them, Nazár. Look, I know this is all screwed up, but I never could have expected our connection. I didn't foresee this coming."

"But yet, you were here looking for love. What if it had been another man? Would you have screwed him over too?" he asks, standing and walking to the door.

"Nazár, I'm sorry. It's screwed up, I will admit it. I had every intention of coming clean with you this afternoon. That's what I was mentioning when we were at the waterfalls."

"I don't believe you."

"I was. What else would I have had to talk to you about?" I ask, walking to stand directly in front of him.

"I don't know."

"Please forgive me, Nazár. We can work through this. I'm the same woman you met and have spent these few weeks with. Just a different name, but everything else is the same."

"How can it be when I don't know you? Your career and interests aren't real. How can I believe any of the rest of it was?"

"Just please give me a chance, Nazár," I ask with tears clogging my throat.

Shaking his head, he rests his hands on my shoulders and stares into my eyes. "When I first learned about your lie, I tried taking a minute to get over it. I tried telling myself that it wasn't as big of a deal as I was making it. You haven't pried into anything about my wife. I willingly shared those things with you and you never asked or got too deep into it. That alone makes me want to believe you."

"Because I didn't care about that. I just wanted to get to know *you*, Nazár."

"But I'm very particular about my guests. I hand select each one of them exclusively. You've been running around my property and my home with free rein. I've let you into my home, Anyssa, without a second thought. I caught you taking pictures of my estate, you lied about your identity, and I have no idea who you are."

"I don't know what's real and what's not right now."

"My feelings for you are real, Nazár. That's something that you can believe," I insist.

Nazár drops his hands from my shoulders and closes his eyes. When he opens them again, I see the steely resolve there.

"There's a lot for me to think about, Anyssa, and I need the time and space to do it. Until I get clarity and the answers that I need, you must go."

As much as it hurts, I understand his decision, and I have no reason to try to fight him on it. I'm wrong, and that's the end of it.

"So, is this goodbye for now or goodbye for good?" I ask over the wobble in my voice.

He doesn't meet my gaze. He simply says, "Get dressed. A car will be here to pick you up in thirty minutes."

"Where will I go, Nazár?"

"Wherever you want to go. Anywhere but here."

"Nazár, please don't push me out completely," I plead as tears pool in my eyes.

He leans down and presses a soft kiss to my lips. "Goodbye, Princesa."

"I'm so sorry, Nazár," I apologize as the tears spill.

Sadness fills his eyes. "Leona will be here to help you pack."

He turns and heads out of the room. I grab a T-shirt and pull it on as I rush into the living room behind him. Leona is waiting on the porch when Nazár pulls the door open.

"Ms. Kelley," Leona says gently with a sympathetic smile as Nazár jogs down the steps to a waiting car.

I watch Nazár climb into the chauffeured car.

"Nazár!" I call, running down the steps after him.

He looks at me with sorrow-filled eyes one final time before he closes the door, and the car pulls away.

I turn my tear-stained face to Leona, and she pulls me into her arms. "I'm sorry, sweetheart."

She turns me around, helps me inside the house, and closes the door.

"What happened?" I whisper, dropping down onto the couch.

"There have been some leaks online about the resort. Pictures. Details. Things that are forbidden."

"And he thinks that I—"

"Yes, he does. Not at first. We weren't certain who leaked the details, but it wasn't until a couple of things happened that he knew."

"What things?"

My head throbs, and I'm suddenly exhausted as if I hadn't just napped.

"The business meeting that he forgot about earlier was with an investigator friend of his. Before Nazár invited you to stay at the cottage, he asked his friend, Izad, to look deeper into you. He wanted to make sure that you weren't a reporter nosing your way into his life."

"He had me *investigated*?"

"Yes, but Izad had just returned from vacation and had an impressive backlog of requests. So he told Nazár he would get to it as soon as possible. A couple of days ago, Nikolaus Galanis, one of the resort guests, bumped into Nazár. He mentioned that he was glad you were no longer at the resort because it made him uncomfortable, fearing that he might see himself on your show.

"Nazár was uncertain what the man meant. The man mentioned your YouTube channel, your show on the Travel Channel, and your travel magazine affiliations. Understandably, Nazár was confused, but he still gave you the benefit of the doubt even after seeing those things himself."

"Because he didn't expect Camila Martinez to have travel magazine affiliations, let alone host a Travel Channel show."

"Precisely. So, he had me call his investigator friend. Izad called first thing this morning, wanting to meet with Nazár in person. Izad presented a full report that appeared to show everything was on the up and up until he gave the pictures of Camila Martinez to Nazár, who said that wasn't you.

"His friend assured him those were pictures of Camila Martinez, and Nazár showed him pictures of the two of you at the waterfall this morning. I'm not sure how he pulled the information so fast, but he gave Nazár a comprehensive report on who you are during that meeting."

"Oh my God. I can see how this all looks far worse than it actually is with those leaked photos. I've wanted to tell him the truth."

"Perhaps you should have long before now."

Pressing my fingertips against my temples, I massage them and ask the question bugging me.

"Well, if he knows who I am, it's easy to prove that I wasn't the one who posted any information about the resort. He can look up all my social media accounts, my YouTube channel, my travel articles, and see that I haven't written anything about it."

"We looked for any videos posted while you were here. We found a video on YouTube of you in the shower at the hotel. A questionable photo of your assets with a lioness peering through a paw."

I pull my hand over my face as I recall the day I took that video, never thinking anyone would figure it out.

"Why didn't he just come to me and ask? That's the only thing that I posted."

"Yet, your NDA says nothing should be posted. He also mentioned that he found you taking pictures in the vineyard. You do understand the impossible position you placed him in. This time of the year is naturally hard for Nazár."

"Why?"

"The fifth anniversary of his wife's passing is coming up. People are curious, looking for reasons to spark the rumors again. Unfortunately, my dear, you have given them the fuel to light that fire."

Sickness washes over me on his behalf. He'd never mentioned that.

She remains quiet, and I finally say, "Maybe I'll just wait for him to cool off, and then I can completely explain everything when he returns."

Leona shakes her head. "You don't know Nazár Rivas as well as you think. He's a very stubborn man."

"But maybe—"

Shaking her head again, she says, "No. He's going to the airport to catch an early flight to Switzerland. He was supposed to leave in a few days, but he pushed up the time. His bags were already packed and loaded into the car before he came here to see you."

"What's in Switzerland?"

"A business arrangement and a friend."

Just how she says "a friend" shatters my heart.

"Come on. Errol will be here to pick you up soon."

"I haven't made arrangements to fly home yet," I mutter.

"Nazár has arranged for you to stay at the Four Seasons Resort Mauritius at Anahita. He will cover the costs of your stay for one week. The balance of what has been paid for this resort will be returned to you."

Anxiety creeps through me when I think about how I've ruined this for Camila. Not to mention that she probably will never speak to me again. I talked to her several hours ago, and all seemed well.

How the hell am I going to break this to her?

My mind is muddled as I pack my bags.

25

NAZÁR

Red, leather-clad hips rock from side to side. The leather thong disappears inside her ass, and it jiggles with each stomp she makes across the stage in her thigh-high, stiletto, black, patent-leather boots.

She faces her audience as the red tassels jiggle from her tits. A ringing sounds off from the bells hidden by the tassels. Shantel cracks the black whip in the air, causing the man and the woman kneeling before her to bow.

She moves behind them, the whip slicing through the air just before she brings it down over their asses. The impact of the speed and intensity with which she cracked the whip leaves a red welt on both, and the woman spreads her legs wider, giving the audience a glimpse of her uncovered cunt.

The man rocks forward slightly, and the women in the audience cheer and whistle in appreciation as his dick swings back and forth.

Shantel looks out at the audience, finds me, smirks, and licks her lips before she turns back and has the woman kiss her boots. The woman stands and reaches back down for the man, helping him to stand and leading him to St. Andrew's Cross in the middle of the stage.

The man is cuffed to the cross, and the woman begins to flog him with two floggers before she hands them over to Shantel. Shantel hands her a cane, and the woman expertly maneuvers it across the man's shoulders and ass. His fists clench slightly when the woman hits harder than before, but his body is motionless otherwise.

After a few minutes, the man and woman exchange positions, and he paddles her before he switches to knife play. My mind drifts back to the evening when I removed the wax from Princesa with the knife and how obedient she'd been.

Was this her angle all along? Getting close to me to get a story for the fifth anniversary of Bella's passing?

There's no way that I could have misjudged her so greatly, was there? I guess I had. The facts don't lie.

She probably even lied about being a virgin to BDSM. She'd taken to it too quickly. It all makes sense now; her safe word was "travel." She'd given me a hint of who she was then.

I had missed it. How many other clues had I missed or ignored along the way? Just to think, I'd told her things about Bella that I'd told no one else. Not even Leona and Gary.

I got too comfortable with Princesa. I'd moved meetings around to spend more time with her, acclimating her to my wants and needs and getting to know what mattered to her. And she'd only wanted to get close because she was a reporter. I'd let the enemy in unknowingly.

When I look up again, I notice the show is ending. Shantel has released her partners, and they're both kneeling before her. She cups the backs of their asses individually, slashes them with the floggers across their asses, and walks in front of them.

First, she cups the man's head and kisses him, then does the same to the woman. Lifting the tassels on her tits, she leans forward, and the man and the woman suck her nipples, and the audience applauds.

I leave my seat and walk backstage to wait for her by her door, marked, "Madam Shantel." My wait is less than five minutes when she comes running back to me in those dangerously high boots.

"Nazár! I am so excited to see you," she says, leaning up and kissing my lips.

I pat her ass and smile at her. "Seems you've got your hands full these days," I say as she unlocks her dressing room door and tugs me in.

"Always ready for you. My place or yours?" she asks, grabbing a coat and tossing it on.

Shantel rarely bothers to change into clothes when I come to her shows, and we leave together.

"Whatever is most convenient for you."

"Your hotel is closer, no?"

I nod.

"It's a plan, then."

She grabs her purse and chats happily as we leave the building for my chauffeured car. People stop her along the way to tell her she did a great show or to simply hug her.

The drive to my hotel is less than five minutes, and we're in my suite in no time. I will probably have her clothes sent for since she seldom wears any when we're together.

"What brings you here sooner?"

"Business plans changed," I lie.

"Would it have anything to do with the story about your resort and the pictures released?" she asks, pouring me a whiskey at the bar.

"It would have everything to do with that."

"I have never been to the resort, but I knew it would be beautiful. It surpassed my expectations. Why did you post now?"

I accept the glass she hands me and mumble, "Someone broke the NDA clause. It felt better to get a story out there to accompany the leaked pictures."

"Your lawyers are on this?" Mila says before taking a sip from her glass.

"They are."

They are all over it and ready to pursue charges against and sue Anyssa, but I'm not sure that's what I want. On the other hand, why the fuck not? I'm usually relentless in my pursuit of vengeance. There's no reason this time should be any different.

Except it is.

"You look stressed. Why don't you let me help you unwind after a long flight, Nazár?"

I've been here for twenty-four hours now. I didn't notify Shantel when I arrived, but I've had time to unwind. Still, I don't stop her when she takes the drink from my hand and finishes it before setting it next to her empty glass.

Climbing on my lap to straddle me, she wraps her arms around my neck, and her creamy thighs close me in. I feel the heat emanating from her core. Botox-infused lips kiss my neck and jaw and finally land on my lips.

"I've missed you, Nazár," Shantel says in a singsongy voice, dragging her lips to my earlobe and sucking it.

Her long, pink nails drag through my hair, scratching my scalp, and I'm reminded of how Princesa did the same thing yesterday. Sex with her then was extremely rough because I was angry.

I had no idea who I'd been sleeping with and allowing into my home. I had no idea who the stranger in my cottage was, the woman who'd shared my bed, my dungeon, and was infiltrating my heart.

I'd gone over to kick her out, but she'd still been asleep. Doubt, anger, and desire ran through me as I watched her sleep. She must have sensed my presence because she woke up within a few minutes. There was no way that I could send her away without feeling her one last time.

And so, I had. I'd fucked her so raw and so hard before I kicked her out of my home and out of my heart.

Shantel removes the tassels from her tits and pulls my head down to taste them. I think about how two other people did the same thing I was doing not even two hours ago, and I pull back.

She bites her bottom lip and slides off my lap, kneeling before me. My stomach turns at the thought of being with another woman who isn't Princesa. But I have to. I have to fuck her out of my mind and my heart.

Sourness has been a constant companion since yesterday morning. I knew from the moment Nikolaus Galanis told me about Princesa that something was wrong, but I chose not to confront her. Instead, I continued to drown myself in her presence until Izad could return the results of his investigation.

It felt good to have a woman in my arms, in my home, and in my heart once more. I didn't want to let that feeling go.

How she and I immediately connected had been too good to be true. I've always trusted my instincts, and the one time that I chose to trust my . . . can't say my heart, but it wasn't my dick either. I'm not sure what about her made me move the way I did, but it failed me.

The only way to get past this betrayal is to immerse myself in the one thing that drives me: kink and pain.

Flying to Switzerland was a no-brainer. Shantel was excited to hear that I would be here earlier than scheduled.

"Dominio," she purrs, kneeling before me with her hands on my zipper. "I am your stress reliever."

My hands wrap in her long, dark hair to pull her closer.

Her hands are on my cock, and her mouth surrounds me, but I feel nothing inside. I'm empty. Shantel knows how to please me and can withstand the pain I dish out. Does she love it? No. But she tolerates it well without complaint. That's more than I can say for most of them.

I close my eyes, trying to drown out my problems and indulge in Shantel sucking me off, but all I can see is Camila when I close my eyes. Or is it Anyssa?

Fuck! Why did Princesa lie to me?

I release Shantel's hair, pushing her away.

"What's the problem, Dominio?"

"I'm not in the mood."

"*He* is in the mood," she purrs, closing her mouth over me and sucking hard.

I close my eyes again, but I still can't concentrate. Shantel looks up at me compassionately.

She licks the head of my dick and then tucks it away, zipping me up. Standing before me with her glistening pussy and proud, naked breasts, she places her hands on her hips.

"I'm sorry . . . It's not you."

"Oh, I know that it's not me. I am a beautiful woman with a wet pussy waiting to fuck you, and your cock is ready, but you cannot get your mind on me. Must be some woman, no?"

I smile at her and pull her onto the couch beside me in my hotel suite.

"Why are women such beautiful manipulators, Shantel?"

"It is what we were born to do. It's a gift to get a man to cater to us and give us whatever we desire whenever we get a whim."

"There must be some beautiful, nonmanipulative women out there, right?" I ask, pressing my fingers to my temple.

She chuckles, runs her hand down my chest, and says, "Sure. Just like there are men who can resist dripping-wet pussies."

I wrap my arm around her and pull her into my embrace. She leans into me, and we sit on the couch and drink as I reminisce over the last couple of weeks.

I was just considering letting my guard down and letting Princesa into my world. I pretty much had. Over the last four days, my social media manager had brought to my attention pictures posted online that were linked to our resort.

Pictures of the vineyard, the formal gardens, the hotel itself from a distance, and even the nude beach. Luckily it was late enough in the evening and far enough away that you couldn't make out the faces of the people there, but it was enough to be damning.

People spent a small fortune to get the discretion that my resort offered. Thank God there were no pictures of the spa or BoDSMe.

I couldn't imagine who would do such a thing because all the guests had been here several times before. Not once has anything like this occurred. Princesa flashed in my mind because she was a first-time guest, but I waved it away.

I've always been a great judge of character and have never once been wrong. Could I have been so blinded by my feelings for her that I'd misjudged her so greatly?

Here, I sit with a beautiful woman I know and am comfortable with. She's ready to do anything that pleases me, but I can't get my mind off a scandalous, lying, manipulating woman.

What the hell is wrong with me?

26

ANYSSA

ANYSSA'S THIRTY-BEFORE-THIRTY LIST

☑ Make love in a stairwell
☑ Hike the Rocky Mountains
☑ Ride an elephant
☑ Dance in the rain
☑ International road trip
☑ Learn an art
☑ Ride in a hot air balloon
☑ Go backpacking
☑ Make love to a stranger
☐ Perform on a stage
☑ Tattoo on my ass
☑ Scale a summit
☑ Learn a foreign language
☑ Swim at night, where you can see the stars
☑ Snorkel
☑ Parasail
☑ Make love on a train
☑ ~~Take a cooking class in a foreign country.~~ Get eaten out on a ledge while looking down onto the ocean!!!
☑ Learn to ski
☑ Stand under a waterfall

☑ Swim with the dolphins
☑ Sing a karaoke duet with a stranger
☑ Ride a gondola in Venice
☑ Travel the world
☑ Send a message in a bottle
☑ View a sunrise from a place where you can see the horizon
☐ Do something along the lines of exhibitionism
☐ Find my father
☑ Try kinky sex
☐ Fall helplessly in love

"**W**ell, what are you going to do now?" I ask, wrapping my hands around the steaming mug of coffee.

"What else can I do?"

"His lawyers may contact you, wanting you to say I stole your identity. Otherwise, they may try to sue you for breach of contract or some shit like that," I mumble, dropping my chin on my folded hands over the coffee mug.

Camila reaches her hand out and places it on top of mine. "Sweetheart, that's the least of my concerns now."

I arrived in town an hour ago, and Camila met me at the airport. On the ride to her place, I told her everything that happened and just finished my story.

She's not behaving the way that I expected her to. No angry words, threatening legal action, cursing, angry tears—none of that.

Tears fill her eyes, but I don't think they're linked to what I'm going through.

"What are your concerns then?"

She sighs and looks away, resting her chin in her palm. "I don't know how to break this to you except to do it."

She reaches for an envelope on the other side of the table and slides it toward me.

"What's this?" I ask, eyeing the envelope suspiciously.

Maybe she is suing me after all.

"Open it."

I pull it toward me with the tip of one nail before glancing at her again. She nods encouragingly, and I undo the metal clasp, keeping the envelope closed. I slide a slip of paper from the envelope, and a few pictures fall out.

Confusion crawls through me as I look at the pictures. It's a family. There's a man, a little girl, and a woman. In a couple of them, the woman is curved into the crook of the man's arm, but she isn't looking at the camera. Her gaze is cast down, like her mouth. She seems unhappy, but I can't tell since I can't see her well.

The little girl has two long pigtails, and she's smiling. Interestingly enough, she looks like me. The man is deceptively handsome and clearly of some Spanish descent. Cuban? Dominican? He looks proud, but there's something about him that I can't put my finger on, which makes me uneasy.

I look up at Camila, who watches me closely before my eyes drift to the woman again. Shaking my head, I go to the final picture. It's similar to the last one, except the little girl is a bit older in this one. The man has a cigar dangling from his mouth, and the woman looks slightly rounder than in the last picture, as though she may be at the beginning stages of pregnancy and is just putting on weight.

That isn't what strikes me. The thing that steals my breath like a slash from Nazár's flogger, only not as pleasant, is that I *know* the woman.

It's my mother.

My hands shake, and my bottom lip trembles.

"What's . . . What's this?"

"Read the birth certificate, honey," Camila encourages.

Shaking my head, I shove it back at her. "No."

"You need to read it, Anyssa."

Tears fill my eyes, blurring my vision as she shoves it back to me and places a firm hand on my wrist when I try to stand.

"No more running. Please, read it."

I slowly sit down, and my eyes drop to the birth certificate. It's Camila's. The parents are Christopher Martinez and Annalise Rebecca Kelley-Martinez, my mother's name, except without Martinez.

"Did you know? When we met in Curaçao, did you know?" I demand.

Slowly, she shakes her head as tears pool in her eyes. "No. I swear I didn't."

"She never . . . I never knew his name," I say slowly, accepting what I can no longer deny.

"It's why our resemblance to each other is so striking."

"How did you find out?" I ask, looking up at her and then at the last picture.

My fingers trace my father's features, then my mother's younger ones, and drop to her belly.

"She was pregnant with you in that picture. She left three weeks after it was taken, and we never found her."

I hear the hiccup in Camila's voice, and for the first time, I think about how hard it must have been for her not having her mother all these years. It had to be devastating, knowing your mother was out there and had left you behind.

Tears fill her eyes, but a smile lights her lips. "When I came home, I talked to Dad about the trip before the surgery. When I showed him the pictures I took, some of them with you, he said you looked like my mother."

"We get that all the time."

Camila nods. "My stepmother, Orenthia, was good friends with our mother before she left."

"Yet, she married our father?" I ask in disbelief, with a hint of bitterness in my voice.

Camila squeezes my hand. "That didn't happen until three years later. She initially spent so much time with me, watching me while Daddy worked in the vineyard, ran errands, or just needed time off. She was the only mother figure I knew. Before long, she moved into the house, and we became a family. It may not be ideal, Nys, but it worked for us. It was what I needed."

"While my mother had to suffer raising me alone because he couldn't keep his hands to himself!" I hiss, standing up from the table.

"Nys, I never knew. Not until now. When I showed him the pictures, he knew that it was you. He said he knew Mom was pregnant. She'd been trying to hide it, but she'd confided in Orenthia. That's when he started looking for her but never found her. He said he deserved her leaving him, even if he was initially angry. The vineyard was struggling, and finances weren't what they should have been. His temper got worse the more he drank. He went from saying cruel things to hitting her. He knew he was too far gone."

"You don't think it was pressure for her too?"

"I'm not excusing it, Anyssa. Just saying what he's told me. I had no idea why she had left all those years ago. For the longest, I was angry with her, hurt, and confused. Mom never told me why my real mom left, either. She said it was better if we didn't discuss it."

"Leading you to believe it was Mommy's fault? That she just didn't love her child enough."

Camila nods sorrowfully. "Yes. In time, I got over the anger, but it hurt. It took some time to forgive her, and then . . . When they told me the truth, I was angry at them—Dad and Mom."

"You call her Mom?" I ask, feeling as if she betrayed our mother.

"She was all I had, Nys. All I know."

I know she's right. I can't imagine what it might feel like to know that your mother walked out and left you behind.

"Did you know about me?" she asks.

"Not really. I've seen a picture of you as a toddler, but she always led me to believe it was a cousin. Someone she loved like her own child but couldn't take with her. Whenever she pulled out your picture, I would ask about you, and she'd tell me you were a pretty, courageous, and smart little girl. She'd tell me stories of things you did and said, and she would always cry. Sometimes, she would hide in her room and stare at your picture. She would fall asleep holding it with tears in her eyes."

Camila looks away, and I see the tears fill her eyes.

"Sorry."

Shaking her head, she says, "It's okay."

I walk around to her side of the table and wrap my arms around her where she sits. "No, it's not."

Camila, my older sister, cries in my arms, and I softly rest my chin on her head, crying into her hair.

☑ ☑ ☑

I never dreamed of being alone when I crossed this item off my checklist. Yet, watching the beautiful sunrise over the horizon gives me peace.

I shouldn't be up this early, but I can't sleep. Not when my world has turned upside down. Finding out that the woman I've been pretending to be is my older sister and that maybe fate had us meeting at that resort in Curaçao is mind-boggling.

Then there's the fact that the man I was falling in love with kicked me out of his resort and banned me from his life altogether . . . I've tried reaching out to him in every possible way to no avail.

It hurts. My chest aches, knowing I won't see him again. Last night, after Camila had helped me settle in the guest room, I showered and went to bed. The only thing that I did was cry for hours.

I must have fallen asleep at some point because my eyes were swollen when I woke up again, and it was completely dark outside. Camila's house was quiet, so I went outside to sit on her veranda.

I searched the internet for a glimpse of what was happening in his life. I shouldn't have been surprised not to find much. Aside from some articles once again speculating whether he had a hand in his wife's death, there was nothing.

The accusations were outrageous and sickening, ranging from statements that she was having an affair that he'd found out about and had chased her off the road purposely to he'd walked in on her and her lover during sex. That one claimed that he'd murdered them both and placed her in the car, driving it to the cliff and then sending it over. Some even said that she'd committed suicide after finding out that she was pregnant with her lover's baby.

Knowing what I knew of Nazár, I now understood his firm stance on his values. The stories were ridiculous, even some of them alleging that he was the one having an affair with another man, and she'd walked in on them, so he'd chased after her, planning to keep his secret, and had chased her to her death.

Reading that, I'd become physically ill, run into the bathroom off the hallway, and vomited the little I had eaten earlier. Then washing my face with cold water and tossing on some clothes,

I returned outside and kept walking until I came to this spot on Camila's property. You can see where the sky meets the earth and how majestic it is as the sun rises over it.

Awe fills me, and I inhale the earthy scent of the fresh morning dew intermingling with the wild smell of the grass around me. I hug myself, staring at the sun until tears fall.

I don't know whether they're from me staring for so long or because I'm missing him so badly. I suspect it's the latter, but I know there's nothing more I can do about it.

I must let go and move on. I fell helplessly and irrevocably in love with a man I only met a few weeks ago, but my soul knows him well.

27

ANYSSA

ANYSSA'S THIRTY—BEFORE—THIRTY LIST

- ☑ Make love in a stairwell
- ☑ Hike the Rocky Mountains
- ☑ Ride an elephant
- ☑ Dance in the rain
- ☑ International road trip
- ☑ Learn an art
- ☑ Ride in a hot air balloon
- ☑ Go backpacking
- ☑ Make love to a stranger
- ☐ Perform on a stage
- ☑ Tattoo on my ass
- ☑ Scale a summit
- ☑ Learn a foreign language
- ☑ Swim at night, where you can see the stars
- ☑ Snorkel
- ☑ Parasail
- ☑ Make love on a train
- ☑ ~~Take a cooking class in a foreign country.~~ Get eaten out on a ledge while looking down onto the ocean!!!
- ☑ Learn to ski
- ☑ Stand under a waterfall

☑ Swim with the dolphins
☑ Sing a karaoke duet with a stranger
☑ Ride a gondola in Venice
☑ Travel the world
☑ Send a message in a bottle
☑ View a sunrise from a place where you can see the horizon
☐ Do something along the lines of exhibitionism
☑ Find my father
☑ Try kinky sex
☐ Fall helplessly in love

I couldn't remain behind in California any longer. As much as Camila wanted me to visit our father in the hospital, my heart wasn't ready for it. My mind still struggled with accepting the facts of our relationship.

First, I need to have a conversation with my mother and then bask in the familiarity of home. Then I might consider returning to California for a visit.

There's so much unforgiveness abounding in my soul.

While I have to forgive my father for the pain that he took my mother through, I also have to forgive her for not telling me the complete truth.

She'd lied to me about my sister, telling me it was a cousin. I couldn't understand how she could leave a child behind, knowing that the child could possibly be in harm's way.

Although I tried to downplay my mother's behavior to Camila, I could see the hurt in her eyes. Not only could I see the hurt in her eyes from being rejected, but I could also see that she was trying to pretend it didn't hurt her so much. That was more for my benefit than hers, I suspect.

I need to know why Mommy chose to do what she did. This wasn't a conversation you had over the phone. So, I remained in California for another day to get to know Camila better. She'd given me a tour of her property and the vineyards.

She warmly introduced me to her staff on the property, but when her stepmother announced that she would visit her soon, I knew it was time for me to go. I'd booked a flight back home with little warning to Camila.

I explained that I needed to talk to Mommy in person about this. It wasn't something suitable for a phone conversation.

She'd understood why when I explained and hadn't hassled me about it. Instead, she'd asked me to reconsider returning. I promised her that I would and would also see if Mommy might consider visiting or allowing Camila to come for a visit.

I have been back home for two days, and today was the first time I had called Mommy. I needed time to process everything that had happened on this last trip, including Nazár.

Finally, I decided to push him to the back of my mind while I dealt with family matters. When I called Mommy to invite her to dinner this evening, she said she would come after she finished some program they were having at church.

In the meantime, I needed to be around someone who would keep me grounded. Being alone for too long allowed my thoughts to meander down roads they had no business journeying.

I was happy when I called Kayla and discovered she was free for the afternoon. She'd come by with a bottle of wine and a box of turtles for us to demolish while we caught up on each other's lives.

The chocolates were finished long ago, as was her brief update on her life. Nothing much had changed for her, so my life events had dominated the last hour of conversation.

"So, what are you going to do?" Kayla asks, reaching for my right hand with her left one.

We're sitting side by side on my couch with our feet propped on the table. Our heads are leaned back on the sofa, and we both hold a glass of wine loosely in our fingers.

"Honestly, I don't know. It depends on what Mommy says. She's avoided this topic for so long, and forcing her to deal with it now is almost cruel."

Squeezing my hand clasped in hers, Kayla says, "And almost just as cruel for her not to answer your questions, especially when you're so close to getting the closure you've always sought."

"Do you think I'm being selfish?" I ask, rocking my head sideways to stare at my best friend.

"Hell no! You didn't do this to them, Nys."

"Mommy didn't do it either."

"Not that I'm blaming her for any of this because domestic violence in any form is inexcusable. But she did make the choice not to talk to you about him. She chose never to reveal what lay behind the hurt. She chose not to answer the many questions you've had through the years, Nys. That was very much in her control."

"I know, but she was hurting."

"And I understand that. I'm sure she was scared too, but again, just because you want these answers doesn't make you selfish. Too many years have passed, and there's no way that he can hurt her now. Your parents are older, and it seems like he's knocking at death's door."

I chuckle softly and point my finger at her. "That was not funny."

Smirking, she replies, "I wasn't the one laughing, though, was I?"

"No," I say solemnly as the smile drops from my lips.

"You need to confront him to get closure. And peace," she adds as an afterthought.

"Do I, though?"

"Mm-hmm. You don't want to wander through life with a bag of what-ifs. Your ass will be weighed down with shoulder pain and back pain."

I laugh again. "Maybe."

"Forgiveness is a wonderful thing. And though you may not feel like it, at the end of our lives, we all deserve to know that we've been forgiven by someone we've wronged. Give him that gift, Nys."

We unlock our fingers, and I pull the wineglass to my lips again, pondering her words.

As I sip from my glass, Kayla says, "You know this shit sounds like a Lifetime movie, right?"

Laughing, I pull the glass away and shake my head. "Nope, not even Lifetime worthy. This is more like a women's fiction novel."

"You're right about that. Too much hot sex involved to be a Lifetime movie, but definitely more than a women's fiction novel," she says before pulling the wineglass to her lips.

My head bobs lightly, and I close my eyes. "Yeah, maybe more like an erotic romance novel?"

She licks the droplets of wine from her lips, points a finger at me, and nods. "Mm, good one. Speaking of which, what's happening with you and ol' boy?"

"Nothing is going on. I told you, he's blocked me out completely."

"Well, you're the one who wanted to play games," she points out.

Nodding, I say, "I had a valid reason."

"How did Camila take that?"

"Very well, considering. But her mind is on other things. I didn't get the impression she was even concerned about the possibility of being banned from the island. With her father's health deteriorating and finally finding my mother and me, she doesn't have time to worry about visiting Belle Baie in the future."

"That's a shitload of stuff she has to deal with."

"Yeah, it is."

"Are you two going to build a relationship or keep in contact now that you know you're sisters?"

"Absolutely. You ever feel like you've been plodding along in life, but you know that you're operating at less than full capacity?"

Kayla nods.

"And then, did you ever feel like the real reason you weren't operating at full capacity was because a vital part of you was missing?"

"I can't say that I've had that experience."

"Well, that's what this feels like. The missing part of me is finally surfacing after all these years, and the water is subsiding so I can get a clearer picture."

"Is that picture a beautiful self-portrait or a caricature drawing of what should be muddled by the lens of life's sorrows?"

Shrugging, I reply, "Only time will tell."

☑ ☑ ☑

"Pass me that cayenne pepper, girl," Mommy says, reaching her hand out as she stirs the meat sauce for our spaghetti.

"Mommy, light on the cayenne. Remember your heartburn."

"Girl, you love this stuff."

"I know that I do."

"And so do I."

"Right, but it doesn't love you back, Mommy."

"Mm," she says, dropping a teaspoonful of cayenne into the meat sauce.

Her ass knows she's going to pay for that later. I just shrug and return the canister to its space in the cabinet.

"You want some wine?" I ask, pulling two fresh glasses down.

"Mm-mm. From the looks of that empty bottle on the living room table, it doesn't look like you need any more wine. And why did you let Kayla go home? She should've stayed here until—"

"Mommy! Mommy!" I interrupt her in a whiny voice. "She didn't drive home. She caught an Uber. Her car's still outside, and I'll take it to her tomorrow, so please quit playing judge and jury."

"Not judging. I just love Kayla, and I don't want her hurt."

"Well, she won't be. Won't be catching any DUIs either because she's being safe."

"Okay, that's all I want."

She returns to stirring the sauce and then replaces the lid on the pan. Turning to me with her hands on her hips, Mommy lifts an eyebrow.

"What?"

"I know that you didn't invite me over here for me to cook dinner."

"You're right. You were supposed to come and eat, but you took over in the kitchen."

"That's because you always wait until the last minute to cook. It should have been ready when I arrived."

Smirking, I say, "You got me. I love your cooking. Besides, you're right. That's not why I invited you."

"Then why? We Kelley women do not keep secrets from each other."

"Ohhwhoowhoo! You might wanna revise that statement, Mommy."

"Girl, what are you talking about?"

Taking her hand, I lead her into the living room, and we sit on the couch. Turning, with my knee resting on the couch cushion and my other foot planted firmly on the floor, I stare into my mother's eyes.

"Mommy, I met a lady in Curaçao. She's beautiful, smart, and funny. We had a conversation which led me on this last trip that I just went on."

"Which I still have no idea where that was."

"I know. That's not my point. My point is that she contacted me before I returned from my trip and begged me to visit her. I didn't understand what was so urgent, but I flew there before I returned home."

"Flew where?"

"California. Sonoma."

My mother's eyes widen, and she seems to stop breathing, but I press on.

"She wanted to show me something. She had a little envelope with some pictures and her birth certificate in it. Mommy, the woman's name is Camila Martinez."

The blood drains from my mother's beautiful brown face, making her look ashen and tired. Tears pool in her eyes before she drops her head into her hands.

I scoot closer on the couch to her and wrap my arms around her. My mother sobs for an interminably long time before I finally speak again.

"Camila says that she is my sister. And on her birth certificate, I saw your name. I also saw you in several pictures with her when she was younger . . . and my father."

"Anny," my mother moans.

The hurt in her cry is so deep and so painful that I feel it in the depths of my soul.

"I'm so sorry, baby," she continues. "Oh my God. My sweet Cami. My sweet, sweet Cami," she cries. "Oh God!"

We rock like that, and she continues crying and repeating those statements. I don't stop her. I suspect that she needs to get this out of her soul.

Mommy never openly grieved for the loss of my sister. It was always something that she hid away from me.

If I happened to walk into her room in the middle of a crying session, she would quickly tuck the photo away, wipe her tears, put a smile on her face, and insist that she was okay.

This time, when she sits up and wipes her face, she turns to look at me. My mommy has aged several years in just a few minutes.

"I'm so sorry that I didn't tell you."

"I saw that picture, and you always said she was my cousin."

"I couldn't bear to tell you the truth, Anny. There would have been so many questions that I couldn't answer."

"Couldn't or wouldn't?" I challenge.

"How is she doing? Is she healthy? Is she happy? Does she have her own family now? What did she say about me?"

Her questions come like torpedoes firing one after the other.

I take my mother's hands in mine to offer her comfort. "She's doing well. She's running the vineyard now and looking for ways to expand it. It's been very successful. Whether she's happy or not, I don't know. She seems to be from all appearances. When I spent time with her in Curaçao, she was very reserved but polished, mature, and friendly when necessary. She holds a deep commitment to family and making sure that she upholds her responsibilities, even at the detriment of what's important to her," I say, thinking about how she had to give up the trip to Belle Baie in exchange for being there with our father during his surgery.

"So, she does have a family?" she asks with open wonder, still wiping the tears from her face.

"No. Not like that. She's not married, and she doesn't have any kids. I meant family as it relates to her father and . . . stepmother." I struggle with saying "our father" to Mommy because I don't know how she will take it. I also don't know how to tell her he married her former best friend.

"So, he remarried."

"Yes."

"Good for him," she says.

There's a tiny hint of bitterness in her tone, and I wonder if she's mad that he went on with his life while she didn't.

"Did you meet him?" she asks after several seconds.

Inhaling deeply, I shake my head. "No. I wasn't ready for that. I needed time to process everything that I'd been told. Besides, I needed to speak with you first."

"Anny, I'm sorry for lying to you. When you were little, it was necessary to protect you. If you knew the truth, I was scared you might say something to a teacher or classmate at school. You always had a gift of gab. It wasn't surprising to me when you said you wanted to become a reporter," she says, cupping my face.

I smile, and she continues. "I didn't want you telling the wrong person. God forbid it somehow got back to Chris, and he found us. He would have taken you away from me, and I have no idea what he would have done to me. Physically. Though taking you would have been the worst thing."

"All the way in Georgia? I doubt that news would have traveled back to California."

"It wasn't a risk that I could take, baby. I was terrified."

I nod, trying to understand, but I've never walked a mile in her shoes.

"What about when I got older? When I became an adult and you would shut me down whenever I asked you questions about him?"

"It was ingrained in me to be that way by then. I was angry that you would even *want* to meet him. So that selfish part of me that wanted to punish him for hurting me didn't want him to be a part of your life. That was how I punished him."

"You also punished Camila and me by keeping us from each other."

"I told myself that. It still wasn't powerful enough to overcome my fear and my bitterness toward your father for what he had done. Anyssa, I am so sorry for what I did wrong. I could never apologize enough. When I ran, my only thought was protecting you. That he wouldn't take you from me the way he'd planned to do with Camila."

Seeing her pain etched so deeply and feeling the raw, heavily burdened guilt that she carries, I know that I have to forgive her. I cannot be angry at her for her choice to leave me in the dark about my family. She's suffered enough by carrying this weight around.

"Mommy, Camila wants to see you."

Those words start a fresh round of tears for Mommy and for me.

28

ANYSSA

He's so frail lying in that hospital bed. Orenthia sits at his side with tear-filled eyes. I can tell that she loves him. Maybe he did become a different person than the one that my mother knew, but I can't help but fault the man who broke our family apart. The one who caused decades of heartache and wasn't there to pick up the pieces, not only in my mother's and my life but also in Camila's.

His physical and mental abuse caused Mommy to run from him, leaving her child behind. She's flown into Sonoma after many reassurances that my father couldn't hurt her. Even with those reassurances, it took a few days to convince her to do so.

Camila was okay with visiting her in Atlanta but said it would be awhile before she could get away. The man known as my father, Christopher Martinez, is dying. Camila wants to be around to say her goodbyes. She knew him as a loving father, and he took good care of her despite his faults.

Orenthia looks up, sees me, and waves me in. I've visited him three times in the last few days, but he is always asleep, or maybe he's pretending.

I watch as she leans over his bed, kisses his forehead, and then walks to the door.

Opening it, she hugs me and kisses my cheek like she's always known me. She calls me "Chris's baby girl."

"He's waiting for you," she says now, squeezing my hand before stepping out of the room.

I turn and watch as she closes the door behind her. I'm rooted in the same spot for the longest, unsure how to put one foot in front of the other. Then I hear a warbly voice that I don't recognize.

"Hija, you did not come this far not to have your say," he rasps.

Turning around and taking one step and then the other is the hardest thing I've ever done, aside from letting that damn car take me away from Belle Baie and the love of my life.

His round, brown face is weathered and aged by the sun. Silky grey hair shades his jaw, chin, and upper lip. Even in his condition, he's handsome. Dark, nut-brown eyes peer back at me through narrowed slits.

His lips are full and dark from years of smoking.

"*Ven aquí*," he orders.

I take a step closer, and his mouth tilts in a tremulous smile.

"*¿Habla español?*"

"*Un poquito.*"

His lips turn down, and he says proudly, "I taught Camila. Insisted that she speak it at home until she was fluent."

I sit in the chair beside him.

"Would have taught you too."

The rest goes unspoken. If I had grown up with him is what he meant. From what I've heard from Camila and Orenthia, he loved Camila dearly and would have loved me just the same. He didn't know how to care for a woman, not her heart. It took several failings before he got it right with Orenthia.

"I would have liked that . . . I think."

He nods and closes his eyes.

"Did you . . . Did you ever wonder about me?"

He starts coughing, and I'm alarmed, but before I can do anything, he waves me off and then points to the water pitcher. I fill his cup and help him put it to his lips.

I want to be angry at him so badly, but I'm not. I'm curious, confused, and hurt but not angry. We've wasted too many years to be angry at this point.

"I did. I wasn't sure your mamá was pregnant, but I suspected it. Orenthia confirmed it."

"What did you think when she came up missing?"

"I knew. Knew she'd left my sorry ass. Didn't regret it at the time."

He pauses and struggles for breath momentarily, placing the oxygen mask over his face. When he removes it again, he says, "Just regretted Cami got left behind."

"You could have prevented that."

"I know that now. Didn't think so then. I searched for her all over California. I wanted my wife and my child back. I loved your mother more than I ever loved another being. I can't take any of it back, though. After a while, I thought maybe she didn't keep the baby. Didn't want any reminders of me."

"Why didn't you let Camila go with her?"

Mommy had told me this morning when she arrived that he was good friends with the local police and a couple of the social workers at the Department of Family and Children Services, who happened to be married to cops.

He had done an excellent job of painting her as depressed, angry, and suicidal. He'd made people believe she was a danger to herself and their child.

"When she first came up missing, everyone wondered if she'd killed herself, but I told them she didn't."

He takes several puffs of air again before speaking.

"Told them she'd taken her clothes. It was just the baby she left and me."

"People hated her, I bet."

He nods.

The coughing takes over again, and this time, it lasts a bit longer.

"I was an evil man, what with the drinking back then. Didn't do right by your mamá, you, or your sister."

The coughing starts once more, and when it doesn't calm down, bells start ringing on his equipment. I nervously glance around as a nurse comes bustling in and pressing buttons. She checks his oxygen and says, "I think he's had enough company for today. It's time for Mr. Martinez to get his rest."

Her smile is warm and kind, but I want to rage at her. I want to tell her he hasn't had enough company, and we haven't had enough years together, but I don't.

I back out of the room to where Orenthia waits with a worried and sad smile, and Camila hugs herself, biting back her tears. My mother stands beside her, and I can tell they were deep in conversation before I came out.

"Why don't you all go get something to eat and return later," Orenthia suggests.

I look at Camila, who nods and reaches out her hand to me. I take it, noticing how calloused and rough her hand is for a woman. It's the vineyards.

"Mamá," Camila says.

"I'll meet you all. I need to do something first," Mommy says.

"Mamá, we'll be down the street at the café waiting for you."

"Okay," she replies.

I watch as she walks back into my father's hospital room.

Camila and I go to the elevator and don't speak even after the doors close. We stand side-by-side, holding hands.

We're both lost in our thoughts.

☑ ☑ ☑

"You two look like twins."

Mommy beams at Camila and me.

"That's how she was able to pull off her little stunt," Camila says, jerking her thumb at me.

"Mommy and I are often told that we look alike," I reply.

"And yet, you look like your father, Nys. Cami, you look just like me," Mommy says, her eyes tracing Camila's facial features.

Camila's smile is sad and regretful.

"You're beautiful, just like he was," Mommy says, looking at me. "And you're beautiful too, my love," she says, glancing back at Camila.

Camila's smile broadens. "I missed you for so long. It hurt, and I never thought I would see you again."

"I hoped one day that we would," Mommy replies, squeezing Camila's hands across the table.

"It was fate," I interject.

"Are you still angry with me?"

Camila pulls her hands back, wipes her tears, and pulls her hair behind her ears.

"Not anymore, but I was for a long time. I know the anger stemmed from fear and hurt. All I wanted for a long time was you."

"Did he treat you well?" Although she knows the answer, Mommy needs to hear it from Camila.

"He did. He loved and protected me and tried to give me the world."

The smile on Mommy's lips does not meet her eyes. "Good. He always adored you. You were his favorite person in the world, and while I wanted to take you with me, I knew he would hunt me down to the ends of the earth. The punishment for leaving with you would have been more severe than if I'd stayed, and he learned that I was pregnant against his wishes."

"He didn't want you to be pregnant?" I asked.

Shaking her head, she squeezes my hand and places it on her lap. "Not because of his inability to love another child, but because he couldn't take care of us already. He was in jeopardy of losing the vineyard that had been in his family for years. He was a proud man and never wanted help from anyone."

Looking at Camila, she says, "Your father used to love me. He absolutely adored the ground that I stood on. He changed when we were in jeopardy of losing the house and the vineyard and barely putting food on the table. He became mean to me, and I feared for my life. He got worse with time, and he'd already pushed me down the stairs a few times. If I was to survive and if Nys were to survive, I had to leave."

Camila looks like she wants to apologize on his behalf, but Mommy continues.

"From what I've heard from Orenthia, he's a changed man. He's not the same as he was then. She would know."

I don't hear the bitterness in my mom's voice that I would expect from a woman scorned. Her husband beating her and running her from her home and her best friend marrying him three years later was enough to make any woman bitter and angry. Not my mother, though.

"Do you remember anything about those days?" Mommy asks Camila.

"I remember you crying. I remember Daddy shouting. That's all I really remember. And then you would send for Orenthia, and she would come and get me and take me to her house for a few hours. When I returned home, you would smile again, and Daddy would be gone."

I look to Mommy, and I can't help but ask, "Do you think that they were . . . Daddy and Orenthia, I mean, do you think—?"

"No!" she says harshly. "I may not love or trust the man anymore, but he never cheated on me, and Orenthia was a great friend. She wouldn't have even if he wanted to."

I'm unsure how she can be so sure, but I don't want to continue raking over old wounds.

We talk some more, and Mommy and Camila make plans for the holidays as I pull out my phone and continue searching for more news about Nazár.

It's still the same: more rumors about him, and they're starting to spread like wildfire.

"What's wrong?" I hear Camila ask.

I look up to find her and Mommy's eyes on me. Holding my phone up, I wave it around.

"These rumors about Nazár are outrageous. It pisses me off because he's not the man they're painting him to be. He didn't get a good rep over this."

"You said that he didn't care, though, right? He didn't want to address the issue," Camila reminds me.

"I know, but he's a beautiful soul, and I want better for him. He's had enough hurt and pain, even at my hands, that he doesn't deserve to continue getting raked over the coals. He needs a fair break," I point out.

My mother smiles, rubs my shoulders, and angles her head. "Then give it to him."

"What do you mean?"

"You have the platform, Nys. Spread the word. You have just over twenty-five-thousand subscribers on your channel. That's enough to get started. Then you have the articles and your show, which, by the way, aren't you starting to shoot for the fall season soon?"

Sighing, I say, "Yes. In a week, to be exact."

"Use your platform to get the word out," Mommy says.

"Even if it goes against what he wants? He never wanted the attention on him or his resort."

"It's out there now," Camila says. "The only thing you would do is address what's being said. You can do that by sharing a clip from the other sites and then politely calling them out on it."

"You've got a point," I agree.

"Honestly, it's the least that can be done for him," Camila says.

I hear the unspoken part where she's implying after I hurt him the way that I did. I'd finally told Camila everything that happened with Nazár and me. I shared parts with her that I hadn't even shared with Kayla.

I love the closeness she and I have developed, almost falling into the role of siblings like it's always been this way. I was afraid it would be awkward at first, and we wouldn't follow up on promises of calling each other. But we've both upheld our end, and it feels great.

"How long are you two staying here?" Camila asks, changing the subject.

"For as long as you need me, baby," Mommy says.

I squeeze Camila's hand and say, "Yes, and I'm here for you too. As long as I have my computer, camera, and iPad, I can work wherever in the world that I want."

"Must be nice," Camila says, laughing.

Mommy squints and asks, "Do you ever regret being tied down to the vineyard, Cami?"

"No, ma'am. I love it. I've even been able to travel a lot and enjoy my life. Daddy's worked hard to make sure that happens. Things are changing obviously with his declining health. But I am ready to start a family."

"So, you'll hire more staff to take over?" Mommy asks.

"Yes. I've been trying to get a certain someone on board with my marketing team," Camila teases, grinning at me.

"Chile, if you can get that girl to settle down for two minutes, you've done more than I have in a lifetime," Mommy says, laughing.

Camila squeezes my hand, smiles, and says, "It'll come in time."

I bite my bottom lip as my heart squeezes in my chest.

I can only hope her words are an indication of things to come.

Maybe it won't be with Nazár, but one day, I will have my dreams. My mind instantly turns to ways that I can help Nazár, and the sun takes over my heart, blocking out the rain.

29

NAZÁR

"**Y**ou've been grumpy for too long now, Nazár."

"Hasn't that always been your problem with me, Leona?" I bark.

"Not like before. You're different now," she says, walking farther into my office and sitting on the chair across from me.

"I have work to do, Leona. I'm sure that you do too."

"I've done my work, Nazár. Now I'm working on my other work."

"And that would be?"

"You," she says, pointing at me.

I shake my head and say, "I don't have time for the games, Leona. I'm trying to get this meeting back on that Lourdes & Heimer canceled at the last minute. If I don't get this deal pushed through by next week, it will cost another hundred thousand. I have to get this land off my hands."

"And you will, but you'll be better when you deal with your issue. You do an amazing job when you're focused and not stressed."

I grumble, looking at her. "Are you willing to relieve me of my problem? Offering to crawl under my desk on your knees and remove the stress? I thought we'd moved past that, Leona."

"You're an asshole, Nazár. You are an asshole without a woman because you're too proud to forgive the woman. Did you ever give her a chance to explain?"

"I heard her explanation. It didn't make any difference. She lied!"

"She did, but she made a mistake. Trying to help one person out caused her to hurt another one. I'm sure that she didn't mean it. Anyone could see that she genuinely cared about you, Nazár. Just as you were falling for her, she was falling for you. Don't be an ass and be alone for the rest of your life when you don't have to be.

"Shantel called and told me what happened in Switzerland. That woman cleared her schedule for you, and you spent all your free time moping and grumpy about a woman you kicked out of your life! If you were going to have her clear her schedule, the least you could do was give her a good beating and a good fucking!"

"Sounds like you're more interested in what I need than I am."

She holds a hand up and says, "Do. Not. Start!"

I'm sure the sneer that crosses my face is lascivious, but she knows what I'm thinking. I tease Leona often, but I don't want her, and she wouldn't cheat on Gary because she loves him.

She's right, though. The only woman I want is the woman who dared cross me. The only woman I've allowed close to my heart since Bella died.

The only woman I love.

My eyes jolt away from the email I've been scanning, and I stare at Leona.

"What?" Leona asks.

"She didn't do it," I grunt.

"Who didn't do what?"

"Princesa didn't break the NDA."

"How do you know that?"

"Izad has a techie that he works with. The guy, Brian, tracked the anonymous user who made those posts to a specific IP address."

"And?"

"The IP address was *here* at the hotel on one of the computers available for guests to use in the conference room. That part wasn't surprising, but he tracked the date and time the posts were created from the specific computer used. Brian then checked our security cameras and found the person who did it."

"And?"

I turn my monitor to face her so she can see my open file. The picture is clear . . . a color picture of Felice Devereaux.

"But I don't understand. Why would Felice do something like that? She's been a guest for several years now. I know I told you she should be banned, and I didn't trust her, but what was her motive?"

"Princesa."

"You're saying she was jealous of your budding relationship with Ms. Kelley?"

I nod.

"So, she decided to wreak havoc on you? That's far-fetched."

"Not really. Felice and I enjoyed each other's company whenever she visited. We spent many nights together at BoDSMe. She noticed that I was attracted to Princesa. She also saw me taking Princesa to my home, something I'd never done with her. She approached me one night when I was heading home from the resort and asked me about it, and I told her it was none of her business. Then she tried several times after that to get me to go to BoDSMe with her or to her hotel room. I declined the invitation. I've never turned her down before."

"The worst thing you can ever have against you, Nazár, is a woman scorned."

"Obviously. You know what to do, Leona. Get in touch with Carson," I say of my lawyer. "I want them all over her ass for breaking the NDA. Her membership is revoked, and she'll deal with my attorneys in court. If I have it my way, she'll never lay eyes on me again."

"Okay," she says, still sitting in her seat.

"Now that that's addressed, tell me what brought you to my office. You must have wanted something, interrupting me in the middle of the workday."

"You're the grumpiest man I know, Nazár Rivera. But I love you as you are."

I smirk. "Get to business."

"Ms. Marino, the VP of Marketing and Communications for the Hollywood Chamber of Commerce, contacted Carson to confirm the nomination for Bella's Star on the Walk of Fame has been approved."

I nod but keep my thoughts to myself.

"Her parents have been reaching out to you, Nazár. Are you going to take their call?"

Bella's parents were no fonder of me than my parents were of her. When she died, her parents blamed me. Not in the way that others did with the scandalous lies and rumors, but they blamed me for holding her back and not allowing her to rise to the level of stardom she could have achieved. They accused me of wanting her to be a "regular" woman, as if something was wrong with that. But if they'd known their daughter well, they knew there could never be anything "regular" about Bella.

"Nazár?"

"We have nothing to discuss."

"They'll be attending the induction ceremony next year, and they want to ensure that there will be no animosity and to present a united front with you on Bella's behalf."

"I know what they want. I am not their puppet. Now, Leona, if you have nothing else, I need to get back—"

"Deputy Prime Minister Okoye wants to meet with you."

"About?"

"There seems to be an uptick in tourism, and it's being attributed to Belle Baie. Even if people cannot get an invitation to the resort, they want to get as close as possible to where Bella Fouché died, especially since talk about her getting a star on Hollywood's Walk of Fame is going around."

"And what does the DPM think I can do for him?"

"They want us to consider opening the resort for—"

"Hell no!" I thunder, slamming my fist on the desk.

My water bottle shakes slightly, but Leona jumps.

"I'm sorry," I apologize.

She holds her hands up and says, "It's okay. You've been under a lot of stress lately."

As she stands preparing to leave, there's another knock on the door.

"Come in!" I bark.

Jules tentatively pops her head inside, large, round brown eyes staring at me. "Should I come back?"

I smile and shake my head. "Sorry, Jules."

When I'm stressed, I work out of my home office instead of coming to my office at the resort hotel. But today, I wanted to be away from the house because thoughts of Princesa plagued my mind more than ever.

I kept heading to the dungeon to get a whiff of her scent or recall some of the scenes we acted out. It was impossible to get any work done, so I'd packed up and rode over to the hotel instead.

"How can we help, Jules?" Leona asks her sister in a soft tone.

"I thought you might want to see this," she says, shoving her phone at Leona.

Leona takes the phone with a scowl, and then her eyebrows lift. She glances at me momentarily before looking at the phone again.

"What now?" I ask.

"Um, you may want to see this for yourself," she says, walking to my desk.

I see her fingers fiddling with the buttons on the side, turning up the volume. Before she hands me the phone, I recognize Princesa's voice. My anger demands that I kick them out of the office along with the phone, but my need and love for her overrides that anger.

I take the phone in my hands. Her hair is wild and curly, just as I like it, framing her beautiful, cinnamon, heart-shaped face and hanging around her shoulders. A frown mars her forehead, and those lips that bring me pleasure are puckered in disdain.

I turn up the volume a bit more and tune in to what she's saying.

". . . with any scandal. It's the way that people are intrinsically wired. We would rather believe the worst about people than the best about them. I mean, seriously, people, consider what you're saying. How does one supposedly kill their wife and her lover and dispose of her body? No one has heard anything about the lover's body as it relates to a hiding place. No one has been reported missing and never found, nor has any DNA been discovered at his residence. Or what about the supposed male lover that he had? If his wife really found him with a man, and he chased her to stop her, where is this mystery lover who has no name and no one has ever seen or heard of?

"Then there's the fallacy about him chasing after her in his car and forcing her off the road. Worse still, they claim she found that she was pregnant with her lover's child and committed suicide. I mean, these rumors are extreme, horrific, and insensitive. I implore you to use common sense and compassion. How can this be true if, alternatively, the reverse is true? All these things can't be fact.

"And, people, please give credence to the police officials. They thoroughly investigated Bella Fouché's death and ruled it an accident. At what point did you bloggers, gossip columnists, and YouTube reporters become more skilled, talented, or credentialed than the government authorities?

"This year marks the fifth anniversary of her passing. We cite the useless axiom 'rest in peace.' Let's let Bella Fouché do that if we ever really meant that. Let her rest and allow her family peace while they remain on earth. Your desire to see justice served is ill-placed. If justice were truly served, none of you would be spreading malicious lies and gossip.

"How can you serve justice when a wrong hasn't been committed? The only offense here is the lies you spread about this woman and her husband. You refuse to let go of the past and move forward in a brighter future.

"I read somewhere that she will receive a star on Hollywood's Walk of Fame next year. Let that be a time of celebration, love, and fond remembrance of the gift she shared with the world. Not your ill-gotten wishes on her family nor your scandalous need for wicked entertainment that causes you to stir up malice and mischief. You would say anything to get views with your clickbates and other tricks.

"You have tried this man in a court of unpopular opinion, and in your uneducated misguidance, you have found him guilty. Why? Because he won't open his home or resort to ignorance, fallacies, and curiosity of the misdirected? I applaud him for the courage to do that and keep people out who mean him no good. Rather than creating havoc in other people's lives, you foolish, foolish people—live your own life.

"Let's let the fifth anniversary of Bella Fouché-Rivera's death be a celebration of life, a memorial of her gift to the world, and a time to honor her family's sacrifice for loaning her to the world for the short time *that she was on this earth. Let's keep them, her parents, her husband, and the rest of her family, lifted in our prayers. Let's consider how it would feel to be in their place for a minute and then give them what we would want to have. In short, let's treat others how we would want to be treated."*

She blows a kiss at the camera, winks, and I wonder if it's for me before she says, "Signing off."

Her live video ends, and the screen goes to other options for her channel and ones like hers. I stare at the phone until I hear Leona clearing her throat.

When I look up, she's wiggling her fingers, and I hand the phone to her, which she returns to Jules.

"Thanks, Jules."

She beams at me and says, "You're welcome."

I held a virtual staff meeting with my team while in Switzerland. I addressed what I believed happened and strongly discouraged my team from gossiping, addressing, or relating to what occurred in any form.

Although I'd done that, I knew I couldn't stop them from looking Anyssa Kelley up once they had a name. Gary had informed me that most of my staff were now following her YouTube channel, feeling as if they knew her because she'd not only been a guest here but was extremely friendly with everyone.

So, it was no surprise that Jules had seen that video when it went live. Like most others, she probably had the notifications from Princesa's channel turned on.

"It took courage for Jules to do that," Leona says after the door closes.

"I know."

"She was one of the few who knew just how upset you were after that happened."

"I know."

"Not to mention, she should be working and not on her phone," Leona adds.

"I know."

"Glad you know all this. Now, do you also know that you need to take your head out of your ass and do one better and reach out to the woman?"

I slide a scowl her way, but she maintains her smirk.

"You love her."

"I love Bella."

"That's fine too, but you fell in love with Anyssa Kelley. I watched it happen and blossom."

"I fell in love with Camila Martinez."

"No. You fell in love with Anyssa Kelley because *that's* the person that she showed you, no matter what she said her name was. Her soul, her personality, and her heart were authentically Anyssa. Or Princesa, as you like to call her," she says sassily with a twinkle in her eye.

"Maybe it wasn't meant for me to love another, Leona. It's why things didn't work out. It hurts too much," I grunt, raking my fingers through my hair.

"You're being foolish, Nazár. Haven't you heard the old saying, 'Second love is like a bottle of wine . . . It gets better with age'?"

"Or more foolish. With all these issues about Bella, maybe I should leave well enough alone. Things weren't easy, but we loved each other, and I don't want to forget that."

"And you won't. There's one more quote I would like to leave you with, 'You never forget your first love. But after that, it's so much better.'"

Leona pulls the door open, turning her back to me.

"Leona?"

"Yes?"

"Would you please contact Ms. Martinez?"

"You mean Ms. Kelley?"

"No. Ms. Martinez. Find out if Princesa is still visiting her in Sonoma. That's all I need to know."

Leona winks, steps out the door, and closes it behind her.

Dropping my head into my hands, I close my eyes. "Bella, forgive me, love, for not being enough for you. Forgive me for making you feel you weren't enough for me."

Then I reflect on that for a while before whispering a prayer.

"God, if it is meant to be, take me to where Princesa is. May she forgive me for wronging her."

My next phone call is to my parents and then my brothers. I need to make amends with them. They may never accept my choices, but they are my family.

30

NAZÁR

I ride along the road back to the resort and see all the people along the way. These are residents of the island, not tourists.

"Love's Reunion."
"Paradise of Love."
"The Pamela Beatrice Story."
"The Prodigal Daughter."
"Love's Two-Way Street."

Those are just a few of the signs that I see people holding up. They're all titles of Bella's movies. My driver, Errol, slows the car down as I stare out the window. Other signs and placards are being held up.

"Bella will always live in my heart."
"Rest in heaven, Bella."
"Prayers for Bella's family."
"Thank you, Nazár Rivas, for loaning Bella to us."
"God bless you, Nazár."
"We love you, Nazár Rivas."

Confusion blows through my mind, and I dial Leona.

Rose petals litter the street leading up to the secured gates of the resort.

"Leona."

"Hi, Nazár."

"What the hell is going on?"

"Oh, you mean the island residents flanking the mile-long driveway to the resort with their signs and flowers?"

"Yes," I grunt.

"Today's the fifth anniversary of Bella's passing."

"I know that!" I grit out.

I'd just returned from the private cemetery where she's buried and lain flowers on her grave. I'd sat on the ground behind her headstone, resting my head against it. Like I do every year on her birthday, our wedding anniversary, and the day of her death, I return to the cemetery and have an hour-long conversation with her.

"And I know that you know that I know," I bark at Leona.

"Well, sir, it seems that maybe Anyssa's little travel monologue did some good. That video has not only gone viral, but it has *twelve million views*."

"Is that a good thing?"

"It's a *great* thing. It means the message is getting out about you, Bella, the family, and the resort."

"Did you ever get the issue figured out with the website?" I ask, looking at the people lining both sides of the road, waving their hands and shouting affectionately at my car as it passes.

The website for the rum distillery and the vineyard were shut down earlier today.

"Apparently, Simon, our tech guy—"

"I know who Simon is, Leona. Get to the point."

"We received visitors to our websites today with well wishes, condolences, apologies for what you went through, and communicating their love for Bella. So many visitors that it shut down the websites."

I drop my head slightly and squeeze my fingers on both sides of my temples as I close my eyes.

"Sir, are you okay?" Errol asks.

"Yes, Errol. Please proceed."

He nods and opens the gates.

"Nazár?" Leona says on the other end.

"Yes?"

"Have you contacted her yet?"

"No," I say, vowing to change that immediately.

"You should."

"And you should mind your own business, Leona. It's what I pay you to do," I tell her.

"Nazár, you know that I'm right. Just as I've been right about everything since the beginning. Since Anyssa's video about her views on Bella, you, and the island, not only have TV specials and podcasts about you skyrocketed, but so have your sales from the wines produced at the vineyard and the rum distillery sales," Leona points out.

The research that people have done has been extensive regarding the work I do around the world, the properties that I hold, and my investments. Those TV specials have led to people contacting me to do business with them, whether they want me to purchase their properties or want to hire me to buy some for them.

"And I'm grateful for that," I admit.

"As you should be. It wouldn't hurt to express your gratitude to Anyssa, though, would it?"

I blow out a long breath. "People have been genuine in their business dealings with me since then. The morbid curiosity that used to exist seemed to have ceased."

"I think she touched people's hearts, Nazár. Made them see your plight and feel your frustrations."

I pull my hand through my hair and confess, "That video has opened my world and changed the landscape for me. Guests are friendlier."

"And I've done a survey, Nazár. Staff find you more approachable. Generally, you're, overall, a kinder person to everyone you interact with except for me. You're still an ass."

"You wouldn't want anything less from me, would you?"

She giggles, causing me to smile. "You're right, I guess."

"It does seem as if the world is opening up to me more."

"That's because you've become a more open person, embracing the world with open arms. That gruff exterior is still in place but not as harsh as it was. I just think it could be even better if you opened your heart to love the way you've opened it to people in general," Leona shares.

"Maybe," I reluctantly agree, thinking that it might not be a bad idea to call Anyssa and thank her.

I look over my shoulder as we pass through the gate to the resort. Most of those people have lived on this island their entire lives. While the world judged me, the island residents did not.

Seeing the support they're giving me today on what has traditionally been one of the most challenging days of my life is moving. I feel the tears stinging my eyes, but for the first time, these aren't tears of sorrow, regret, or grief. They're tears of appreciation, of humility, of love.

"Leona, I'll see you soon," I say, ending the call without giving her a chance to say goodbye. "Errol, stop the car!" I call out.

"Sir?"

"Stop the car!"

He stops, and I push open the door and step out onto the road. All the people stop shouting and stare in open-mouthed fascination.

I walk to the gate and look at them. "Thank you! Thank you for your support, your prayers, and your love! Thank you all!" I shout.

The cheers and thunderous applause that go up are more than I can handle. I turn back to the car and quickly slip inside.

"Errol, proceed."

I close my eyes and the partition between us so I can have a moment alone—time to reflect on Bella and time to gather my emotions.

☑︎☑︎☑︎

I repeatedly turn the phone over in my hand. I've never called or texted this number since I first got it. It might be what her platform is doing or related to the reflection I did at the cemetery earlier. Whatever the reason, I'm finally ready to deal with things . . . what happened between Anyssa and me, my feelings for her, and I'm ready to release the guilt I feel about Bella's death.

Five years have passed since Bella died, and it's time for me to learn to live again.

The thought of hearing Anyssa's voice again after all this time makes me whole. It's been more than a month since I sent her away.

While I have been open to the world, as Leona pointed out, I haven't been open to the woman responsible for creating a different landscape in my life. It's time for me to let her know that I forgive her. I press the call button and pull the phone to my ear.

"Nazár," she whispers.

Her voice sounds beautiful and hopeful, sending a shock to my groin. When I close my eyes, I see her kneeling, looking up at me, purring my name.

Clearing my throat, I say, "You must have my number saved in your phone."

"No, I don't."

"Then how did you know that it was me?"

"Please don't hang up on me."

"Why would I do that?"

"The phone number that I gave you was specifically for that trip. It was in case something happened, and it landed in the wrong hands so that they wouldn't see all the identifying information in my real phone."

"Oh," I say.

"You're the only one that I gave that phone number to."

I don't know if I should be elated that I'm the only one with the number or angry at how far she was willing to take the game.

"I, uh . . . held onto the phone in hopes that one day you might call me. You haven't answered any of my texts, emails, or calls."

"Oh. Okay."

"So, umm . . . How have you been?" she asks nervously.

"I'm fine. That's why I was calling you."

"Why?"

Inhaling deeply, I exhale slowly. "I wanted to say thank you."

"For?"

"The video that you did on Bella. Me."

"You saw that?"

"You sound surprised?"

"I am. I thought you were a busy man, and I can't imagine you watching my channel."

"I am busy, but let's just say that you've got some fans at the resort who felt it was their duty to keep me informed on what you were doing. The day you went live with that video, it was immediately brought to me."

"Oh."

I know she's thinking about how that was a few weeks ago, and I'm just now calling her.

"There have been a lot of changes in my life since that video."

"Good, I hope."

"Yes. There's been an outpouring of support from the community at large. There have been people reaching out to me from all over the world. Mostly for business, but today, both of our websites were shut down because people flooded it to leave comments about Bella . . . and me."

"Wow! That's amazing," she laughs.

I close my eyes, allowing that sound to pour over me. God, how I miss this woman.

"Yes, it is," I agree. "You didn't have to do that."

"I know. I wanted to, Nazár. After all you'd done for me, it was the least I could do."

"You owe me nothing."

I wonder again what her motives are. The last thing I need is for her to do anything to me out of obligation.

"I know that, Nazár. What I did was wrong. If there were a way that I could turn back the hands of time, I would. But I cannot. All I can do is apologize again and hope we can be friends."

"Friends," I say simply.

"Yes."

"You're right. It seems that things happened between us so fast. Sometimes, I wonder if it was purely sexual."

"It wasn't for me," she says.

"Are you sure? I often wonder if you weren't just enthralled by the idea of me and what I offered. It was a new, different experience for you."

"I know it was. In the weeks since I've been gone, Nazár, all I've thought about is you."

"I've thought about you a lot too, Anyssa. I'm just still trying to get my head settled on right."

"I understand."

"It doesn't mean we can't stay in touch, though. I would love to hear from you."

"I'd like that."

"Well, I just called to thank you for everything you did. It's done more for me than I can express. Not just how people have responded to it, but internally, as well."

"I'm glad to hear that, Nazár. I hope that one day you can know true peace and healing."

"I'm on the road to it."

We both remain silent for a while, unsure of what to say next but not ready to break the tenuous connection.

"Well," I say, being the first to speak up, "I have a meeting in a few minutes. It was good hearing your voice again, Anyssa."

"Yours too," she says softly.

I end the call wondering if I'll hear from her again.

31

NAZÁR

"**W**e know that it's been hard on you these last few years," André Fouché, Bella's father, says.

"And we know we didn't make it easy for you," Danielle Fouché adds.

"No, you didn't."

I refuse to make this easy for them after all the cruel things they said to me and about me right after her passing.

"You must understand that it was also a difficult time for us. Bella was our only child. We knew from a young age that she was destined for greatness," André says.

Danielle nods eagerly. "She was always dressing up and pretending to be someone else. She would mimic our words from the age of two. By the time she was five, she was making up all these names for herself."

"By the time she was ten, she would pretend she was someone else living a different life with different experiences," André says.

"I don't know what it's like to lose your child," I say. "I've never been blessed to have one of my own, so I cannot imagine your pain. The only thing that I know is that you two didn't only lose a child, but I lost my partner, my best friend, my wife . . .

my soul mate. It was hard enough dealing with my emotions, but when the two of you compounded that with your personal issues, it was more than I could take."

"Again, Nazár, we're both sorry for that. Would you please forgive us?" Danielle asks.

"I can and I will because it's what Bella would have wanted. She always wanted us to be close and to get along. It was important to her that I get along with the two of you. It's why I overlooked the innuendoes that I was using her to get new business contracts, or that I didn't love her, or was jealous of her."

"Again, we were grieving," Danielle says.

"With all due respect, Mrs. Fouché, those were the words that you spoke while your daughter was still alive. They don't hold a candle to what you said to me after her passing."

André looks away and grabs his wife's hand while she squirms uncomfortably in her seat.

"You are right, Nazár. We were not happy about your marriage to Bella, and when she passed, it only made it worse."

Looking around the café that's a block from my hotel, Le Bristol Paris, on Rue de Faubourg Saint-Honoré, I ask, "Why did you invite me here today?"

"I called and checked with your assistant about two weeks ago, and she said that you refused to meet with us. I called again last week, and she advised that you would be traveling to Paris this week for business."

"I'm aware of your calls to Leona," I say, thinking of the many times she pestered me to meet with them.

"We hoped that you would meet with us so that we could lay this *désaccord* to rest," Danielle says.

"I no longer have a disagreement with the two of you. When we laid my wife to rest, I laid aside any personal feelings or attachments to you both," I say.

They both look at each other and then back at me with a plea in their eyes.

"The ceremony for Bella receiving a star on Hollywood's Walk of Fame will be next year."

"I am well aware of that."

"We thought that maybe . . ." Danielle pauses.

"Should you be there?" André boldly asks.

Sitting back in my seat, I nod. "Now we're getting to the real reason for the numerous phone calls and emails."

"We would just like our daughter's recognition to not be accompanied by all the rumors and scandalous allegations that come with your presence," André says.

"Do you not think it would be more scandalous if I were *not* there, especially considering things are finally blowing over? I'm receiving more sympathy from the public than ever before. Not that I want or need it, but I say that to say I doubt there will be scandal following my appearance at her ceremony. If anything, my absence will prompt the drama to stir once more," I say, lifting an eyebrow. "Especially if the public gets wind of her parents asking me to stay away."

Danielle inhales and holds her breath until her face almost turns red. Shaking her head, she turns to her husband.

"What is it that you need to keep you away?" André asks.

Leaning forward, I rest my elbows on the table and steeple my fingers. "I don't know if I will be there or not. What I can promise you is that if I do attend, I will stay as far away from you two as possible. I'm no more interested in drama or scandal than either of you. There will be no disputes, discord, or, as you said in French, désaccord, from me. How you carry yourselves is strictly up to you."

I stand and button my suit jacket.

"André, Danielle, it was good seeing you both again," I say, pushing my chair under the table.

I leave them behind and step out into the breezy, sunny evening. That's another chapter of my life that it's time to close. Now, I'm ready for new ventures.

☑ ☑ ☑

I toss my jacket over the back of the couch. Pouring a drink, I head into the bedroom and undress just as the phone rings.

Smiling when I pick it up, I say, "Hi, Anyssa."

"Hello. You know why I'm calling."

Laughing, I reply, "I just returned to my hotel suite."

"Oh, do you want me to call you back?"

"No," I reply, removing my cuff links and unbuttoning my shirt sleeves. "You already know that I was expecting your call."

Since the first call that we had when I called to thank her, I've spoken with Anyssa three times every week. It's been a month since we first began talking again, and I've enjoyed every call.

We spend at least an hour on each call catching up on what's happening in each other's lives. She shares where she's traveling with me, and I tell her about my latest adventure.

Her birthday has passed, and she says she ticked off almost every item on the list except for a few. I have no idea what those are, and she won't share them with me.

"Were you on your best behavior?" she asks now.

"I was."

I sit on the bed, remove my shoes and shirt, and lie back with my whiskey glass in one hand and the phone in the other. I tell Anyssa all about my meeting with Bella's parents and their requests.

"You're kidding me!" Anyssa says.

"I wish I were, but they're still just as full of themselves as they always were. I suspected the only reason they wanted to call a truce was to push me out of anything having to do with Bella."

"You stood your ground, I hope."

"I did."

"Good for you."

"Not sure that I'm going, though."

"Why? Because of them?"

"Not that at all."

"Then why not?"

"I've been honest with myself about many things lately, Anyssa. One of the hardest things I've had to be honest about was the state of my marriage to Bella. I felt guilty about what happened to her, but it wasn't my fault. My wife was unhappy for a long time, and I couldn't do anything about that. We were headed for divorce one way or another. If she were still alive today, I can't say that we would still be married. I can't even say that her career would still be flourishing."

"Because of the drinking?"

"Yes."

"You know that many actors have drug and alcohol problems."

"I know that, but her physical health was declining."

"Oh yes. I forgot you did tell me about the cancer."

"When I consider all that, I don't know if I need or want to be there. But that's next year, so I still have time to figure it out."

"Just don't let anyone bully you out of the opportunity."

Laughing, I ask, "When have I ever allowed anyone to bully me?"

"I don't recall a time."

"How's your family? Mom? Sister? Dad?"

She sighs. "Mommy and Camila are getting along wonderfully. My father's health is declining more each day. I've made my peace with him and forgiven him for what he did. There's no reason not to."

"True. How are you handling the possibility of losing him?"

"Better than I expected. I mean, I just found him, and to turn around and lose him again seems so damn unfair. But then I try to tell myself that he hasn't been here all along anyway, so am I really losing anything?"

"You are. The hope. The possibilities. The opportunity. Don't downplay your feelings over this, Princesa."

I can hear the smile in her voice when she replies, "I won't."

"How are you when things settle down and no one's around?" I ask.

She blows out a breath, "I'm good, I guess."

"You guess?"

"Yes."

"Why do you 'guess' and not know?"

She's silent for several seconds.

"I don't know how to feel, but I think about you a lot."

"And I think about you a lot too. I miss you more than I expected to."

"I know that you needed time. It's just that . . . I wonder if you would ever forgive me."

"I've forgiven you. The one thing that I've come to learn is that we all make mistakes. We all deserve forgiveness. That's the one thing I wish I could have given Bella before she died. I think that's why I felt so guilty for so long because she died thinking that I was angry with her. The blowup that we had was nothing nice. There's no way that you can take things back once they're said.

"That's the same reason that I had to get away from you the day you left Belle Baie. I felt so betrayed, and I was so hurt that

I knew if I stayed around much longer, I might explode. It wasn't easy handling you with care . . . with my words," I add.

"That wasn't an easy day for me," she says softly. "So, I know that it wasn't for you."

"Princesa, I apologize for how I treated your body that day. I was rough with you."

"I handled that much better than I did your words."

"Still, I never meant to hurt you. If I did, please forgive me. I've never been intimate with a woman when I wasn't in control of my emotions."

"Hey," she says. "I'm a big girl. I did something very wrong; you implemented the punishment, and I took it."

"My love, I don't want you ever to equate me punishing you with anger. My form of punishment is meant to teach you a lesson, but it's also a pleasurable experience. I taught you nothing useful that day."

"And yet, still, I forgive you, Nazár."

"I care about you deeply, Anyssa, and I hope to have you in my life. I just—"

"You don't want to rush it this time, and you want to make sure it's genuine."

"Exactly. I want it to feel real this time and not that we've contrived something off what we thought we could have."

"I feel the same way. It doesn't ease the ache of missing and being with you, though."

"Not for me either, Princesa. We will be together again someday soon."

We talk longer, reminiscing on scenes we've enacted in the past, our dinners, and our time at the waterfall.

When I ended our call that night, she left me with plenty of good thoughts.

32

ANYSSA

ANYSSA'S THIRTY—BEFORE—THIRTY LIST

- ☑ Make love in a stairwell
- ☑ Hike the Rocky Mountains
- ☑ Ride an elephant
- ☑ Dance in the rain
- ☑ International road trip
- ☑ Learn an art
- ☑ Ride in a hot air balloon
- ☑ Go backpacking
- ☑ Make love to a stranger
- ☐ Perform on a stage
- ☑ Tattoo on my ass
- ☑ Scale a summit
- ☑ Learn a foreign language
- ☑ Swim at night, where you can see the stars
- ☑ Snorkel
- ☑ Parasail
- ☑ Make love on a train
- ☑ ~~Take a cooking class in a foreign country~~. Get eaten out on a ledge while looking down onto the ocean!!!
- ☑ Learn to ski
- ☑ Stand under a waterfall

☑ Swim with the dolphins
☑ Sing a karaoke duet with a stranger
☑ Ride a gondola in Venice
☑ Travel the world
☑ Send a message in a bottle
☑ View a sunrise from a place where you can see the horizon
☐ Do something along the lines of exhibitionism
☑ Find my father
☑ Try kinky sex
☑ Fall helplessly in love

"**D**id you ever want to do anything else?" my father asks.

Sighing, I smile and say, "No. I always wanted to be a reporter. Mommy always said I would make a good one because I talked too much and told everything."

Laughing, he says, "Cami was just the opposite. She's quiet and holds too much inside."

"You have to have some outlet, or you'll get stressed out," I say.

"Don't I know it," he mumbles before his hacking cough starts up. "So, tell me about Venezuela."

"Of all the places in the world, why that location?" I ask.

"Why not that location?"

I smile and plunge into the details of my two-week vacation in Venezuela last year. He smiles when I describe the architectural beauty of the Minor Basilica of our Lady of the Valley, laughs about the extensive workout I received during my hike through Avila National Park, and stares in awe at my photos of Angel Falls.

"You live a beautiful life," he whispers.

"I live the only life that I know."

"Did your mom travel much?" he asks, reaching for my hand.

I take his in mine and shake my head. "No, she didn't. She was too scared to go anywhere once we settled in Georgia. That's why it was so important to me to travel, see the world, and never settle in one place for long."

"I thought you had a place there."

"I do, but I'm seldom there. I get antsy when I stay in one place for long."

"I'm so sorry," he whispers. "I love you so much, Anyssa. I love you like I've always known you."

"I love you too, Daddy."

He closes his eyes, and tears seep from the sides.

Leaning over him, I kiss his cheek, tasting the saltiness of his tears.

"Don't be sorry. Mommy forgave you, and I forgive you. I just wanted the chance to see you."

"And you have. Nothing too impressive."

"I wouldn't say that. You left a beautiful legacy for my sister."

"And for you."

"No. It's hers. She's worked hard all her life. I have my legacy, and as odd as it may sound, I have you to thank for that too."

Frowning, he asks, "How so?"

"The fear you placed in Mommy taught me never to be afraid."

"I don't know. From what I've heard, it sounds like you're afraid to love."

Smiling, I say, "You've been listening to Cami."

"No. Your mom's been here a few times. She talks about you a lot. She's even shared photos of you as a kid. She tells me that you're scared to love. Says that you claim you want it, but you don't embrace it."

"Daddy, I found someone I love. I lied to him and hurt him, but we're working through it now."

"When you work through it, don't ever stop doing that. Don't ever give up on love, and never give up on someone who loves you completely," he advises.

The hacking starts again but stops after a few minutes.

"Read something to me, baby girl," he says.

"Like what?"

"I don't know. Maybe one of those articles you wrote," he suggests.

Smiling, I pull up the app on my phone for *Travel & Leisure* and go to the dashboard. Scrolling through, I find an article about the best international resort of twenty-twenty-one.

I begin reading the article, smiling as I recall that vacation. I share the photos with him intermittently.

"Daddy, look at this last photo. Isn't it beautiful?" I ask, turning my phone to him again.

"Daddy?"

He doesn't say anything.

I shake him, but he's resting peacefully now.

Camila's out giving tours, and I have no idea where Orenthia is. She went into town about an hour ago but should have been back by now.

I scroll to my contacts and dial a number that I'm familiar with.

It's two in the afternoon on a Sunday in Sonoma, California. It's one in the morning on Monday in Mauritius.

"Hello," he answers groggily.

"My daddy died."

"Where are you?"

"Sonoma."

"I'll be right there, baby."

☑ ☑ ☑

A soft rain falls gently around us, and hushed voices murmur condolences as people reach under small and large umbrellas to embrace. As mourners break apart and return to their cars, I slow down and glance over my shoulder one final time.

My mother remains at the casket with her head bent. I cannot begin to comprehend the level of hurt or pain that she must be feeling now. All her dreams of a beautiful family have washed away. The man laid to rest never had a chance to make up for the wrong that he did, devastating her life and taking so much from her. Not that one could possibly make up for things of a particular nature.

I turn back up the grassy slope, careful not to let my heels sink too deep into the muddy ground. I'm following behind my sister's footsteps. I stop when I hear her voice speaking.

". . . I never went on because I never stopped loving you despite all you did. I always prayed that you would get help, even if I weren't around to see it."

She sniffles, and I start to take another step forward, but her words spill forth, halting me in my tracks.

"I'm so glad that you had a chance to meet Anyssa. She's always been a feisty, free spirit, but she was so gifted and talented. Like you, she can weave people around her finger, pulling them in with her charm. She's a bright ray of sunshine. Camila was more like me; reserved, quiet, polite . . . but you and Nys? You lived life loud and boisterous with no apologies. I love that about her.

"Loved that about you. Those were the hardest years of our lives, and I wanted to stand by your side. But you weren't getting better, only worse. And I don't think you would have gotten help . . . stopped drinking if I had stayed. I think it took for me to leave you to open your eyes.

"I know that Orenthia was there for Cami, and I'm glad she was. Cami says she forgives me, but I pray she truly forgives me one day, and her abandonment issues will go away. God has blessed us with another chance, and I'll take it. I will love her with everything I've got, just as I've done Nys.

"You asked me to forgive you at the hospital, and I said I did. You didn't believe it, but, Chris . . . I forgave you. How can I be forgiven for all my wrongs if I can't forgive you? The only way I can get peace is to let go of the pain you caused me. I choose to remember the man you were before the drinking and celebrate the man you became. The other man . . . was sick. And I know God has forgiven him, and so have I. I just pray that you forgive that man. Thank you for taking care of Cami so well. Goodbye, Chris."

She lays a yellow rose on the casket, lifts her veil, and wipes her eyes before she turns and sees me. A smile lights her face, and I reach my hand out to her.

She takes it, and we walk toward the car, where Camila and Orenthia wait for us.

I will never understand how my father got to where he did or how he allowed the pain and devastation he created to impact his family the way he did. I'm just glad I had a chance to meet him and that we all now have each other.

Mommy wraps her arm around me as we walk to the car together. Orenthia climbs inside, and Mommy places her hand on Camila's shoulder to stop her.

"I hope you find someone to love unconditionally one day. That's how I loved your father," Mommy says to her.

"I hope I find that too, Mommy," she says.

"Most importantly, find someone who loves you unconditionally. Your father tried, but he failed in that area. That's only because he didn't love himself enough."

Camila climbs inside the car, and it's my turn to stop Mommy.

"Mommy, have you forgiven yourself for leaving Camila?"

I know Camila said she forgave her, but I can't help but wonder if Mommy's forgiven herself because it doesn't seem as if she has.

"I'm learning to, baby. One day at a time," she says, smiling brightly at me.

Then Mommy says, "Baby, go ride with your man," nodding to Nazár sitting inside his car behind us.

"I'll be with him soon. He told me to stay with you for now."

We climb inside. I wrap my arms around my sister, and she rests her head on my shoulder.

The drive to Camila's house is made with light chatter and reminiscing between Mommy and Orenthia. Camila and I listen to the stories, both grieving in our own ways. She's grieving what she lost, and I'm grieving what I never had.

☑ ☑ ☑

Camila's five-bedroom, four-bathroom, ranch-style home is overflowing with visitors for the repast. Laughter abounds, and the tantalizing aroma of a southwestern-style meal flows from the kitchen and dining room into the living area.

The wine flows in abundance, and plates are passed around. I'm introduced to people as Chris's baby girl. In the beginning, people were reticent, where my mother was concerned. But that changed in time as a woman named Megan Weatherly came through. She was a talkative, bold woman with a beautiful and charming spirit who wore loud, bright colors that looked striking against her dark skin.

Apparently, she was someone my mother knew in her life with my father, and they were good friends too. When everyone saw her and Megan together, they eventually gravitated toward the two. There were hugs, apologies, and chatter to keep my mother preoccupied.

"You don't have to entertain everyone you know. Why don't you get some rest?"

I've taken a seat on the steps beside Camila. She looks tired, and the dark rings under her eyes grow darker with each passing hour.

"I can't sleep, Nys. Being in this room with all these people makes me feel his spirit is still alive. He would have loved this. He often had large gatherings here in this house."

"How did you come to have this house instead of him and Orenthia?"

"When I was getting ready to move out on my own, he said it made more sense to give it to me since it had been my mother's house. He said that he and Orenthia should be the ones that found a new place."

I see our mother walking in our direction.

"How are you two?"

"We're holding each other up," Camila says, smiling at me.

"Seeing the two of you together is a beautiful dream for me," Mommy says. "I hate that it's under these circumstances."

"Me too," I agree.

"And to believe it all started with a bottle of wine and a pact," Camila says.

We laugh as I push off the stairs.

"I'll let you two talk. Besides, I need to save Nazár from Doralis's grabby hands," I say of one of the neighbors.

Mommy and Camila laugh as I weave my way through the crowd. A few of the men come and surround Nazár, driving Doralis away, and I decide to leave him alone for now. His back is to me, and he doesn't see me anyway, so I won't bother him.

I move along, looking for a quiet place to think. I don't want to head upstairs away from the fray, but I need a moment alone.

Escaping to the back porch is a great idea, and that's what I do. Grabbing the handrails, I look out at the vineyards in the distance, and I'm reminded of another vineyard far away. I close my eyes, reminiscing about his tender touch.

Nazár has been by my side since my father's passing four days ago. Although he's been here, we haven't been intimate, and we haven't even kissed. He's been a supportive friend. I couldn't have asked for more because that's all I needed.

Tears slip from the sides of my closed eyelids, and pain squeezes my heart in a vise grip. Doubling over, my mouth opens as a gasp escapes me, the cry strangled in my throat.

A hand rubs my back in slow, soft circles. Without him saying a word, I know that it's him. He pulls me away from the rail and turns me around. I don't know how I don't detect his scent, but seeing him is like a splash of refreshing cold water in the face.

"How did you find me out here?"

"Did you forget that you belong to me, Princesa? You're mine. I will always find you no matter where you go in this world."

I take his hand, and we walk down the steps.

We talk about my father and my sister for a while before the conversation turns to the inevitable.

We walk for a while, and by the time we stop, we're facing a lake at the edge of Camila's property with a copse of trees behind us. It looks as if we're all alone in the world in this closed-in space.

Nazár looks down at me and cups my chin. He kisses me sweetly, slowly, and gently. When he pulls back, he stares at me.

"What are your plans after this?"

"I have to leave soon. We pushed back the shooting of my show *Romance Abroad* because of what happened with my father. But I know I'll have to be back on location in a few weeks."

"Do you know why I flew all the way here?"

"To support me during my father's passing?"

"That's part of it."

"What's the rest?"

"To bring you home with me."

"Home? With you?"

He nods, and my heart flutters.

"Anyssa, I needed time to heal and time to forgive. I've had that time, and I'm healed, and I've forgiven you for misleading me, and I've forgiven myself for being so damn hard and unreasonable that I didn't give you room to get to know me. Now, I need to be part of your healing."

"I think we both needed time."

"Princesa, I'm in a different space than I was before. I'm ready to open Belle Baie up to the world a little more."

"Really?"

"Yes. I no longer want the secrecy surrounding it or the negativity associated with it. It's all about peace and love. That's what the connotation to Belle Baie was always supposed to be. It changed into something else after Bella's death. I needed to protect my privacy from those who meant me no good, Bella's parents included."

"That's beautiful. But what about the nudist beach and BoDSMe?"

"Nothing changes. People are allowed to embrace it, or if they're not interested, they don't have to accept it. I'll still be discreet in my guest selection process, but I'll be more open about the resort than I have been in the past."

"I'm happy for you, Nazár."

"No, us. I never would have had the change of heart and mind without you."

"I'm glad that I could be a part of that. Besides, the world should be able to enjoy that beautiful place."

"I had this wild and crazy thought that maybe we could spend more time together. I had no idea you were getting ready to start filming, though."

"I know, and I can't get away again. Not right away."

"I have an idea. It might be the perfect way to slowly acclimate people to what Belle Baie is all about."

"What's that?"

"Perhaps we can convince your producer to shoot at the resort. That will keep you close by my side."

My mouth literally drops open, and I laugh. "You are fucking kidding me!"

"Why would I? Your video has renewed interest not only in Mauritius but also in my resort."

"Are you sure, Nazár? You've been such a private man for so long."

"If it brings you back into my corner of the world and allows me more time with you, I'm good with it. Besides, I'm truly ready for people to see the tranquility Belle Baie offers. It would come with restrictions, though."

I tip up on my toes, throw my arms around his neck, and kiss him softly. Nazár bends and lifts me into his arms so I can wrap my legs around his waist. This kiss is hotter and more aggressive than the last.

When we finish, he asks, "When can you leave?"

"Tomorrow morning."

"Perfect. I'll make the arrangements."

His hand reaches under my dress, rolling my panties aside. When his hand smooths across my ass, he growls, "You've been a disobedient little wench."

"What's that supposed to mean?"

"You're wearing panties, Princesa. You know that's against the rules," he says.

I laugh, but his fingers slide inside me, removing all the laughter from my lungs. I bite down on his shoulder as pleasure takes over me.

"I'm going to come, Dominio," I whisper.

"Don't you fucking dare!" he growls.

His fingers slip out of me, and he rolls my dress over my ass as a gentle breeze brushes my bare skin. Nazár sits in the grass, reaches for my hand, and pulls me beside him. He adjusts me so I'm lying over his lap with my ass bared to the sky.

A hard slap to my ass forces my eyes closed and my mouth open. Another slap, this time harder, makes tears come to my eyes. The third smack to my ass produces a deep, throaty moan, which makes Nazár's arousal grow; I can feel it pressing against my belly as I lie across him.

Slowly, his hand smooths over my ass, rubbing away the stinging sensation before he inserts a finger in my ass and then another.

"Ohhh!" I cry out in ecstasy.

He pulls his fingers free and spanks my ass again, but this time in swift repetitions, one after the other, hard and not letting up until I cry, "I'm gonna come!"

"Not yet," he grunts, jerking me upright.

He pulls me forward until I stand over him, and his head is between my legs.

"Go ahead, Princesa. Come for your master," he instructs.

Nazár's mouth opens wide, and his tongue and lips lick and suck at me, begging me to come on his tongue. Why would I deny him what he obviously needs from me and what I desperately want to give him?

With his hands working my ass and his mouth working overtime on my pussy, I let go of the sweetest release of ecstasy.

He moves from underneath me and stands, grabbing the back of my head and kissing me, imploring me to explore my taste on his tongue. I'm delicious, warm, and musky all at once.

I moan into his mouth, and he pulls back and says, "You taste so damn good."

"I do," I purr.

"I love you," he growls.

My eyes widen. "You love me?"

"How could I not, Princesa?"

33

ANYSSA

(EPILOGUE—1 YEAR LATER)

ANYSSA'S THIRTY–BEFORE–THIRTY LIST

☑ Make love in a stairwell
☑ Hike the Rocky Mountains
☑ Ride an elephant
☑ Dance in the rain
☑ International road trip
☑ Learn an art
☑ Ride in a hot air balloon
☑ Go backpacking
☑ Make love to a stranger
☑ Perform on a stage
☑ Tattoo on my ass
☑ Scale a summit
☑ Learn a foreign language
☑ Swim at night, where you can see the stars
☑ Snorkel
☑ Parasail
☑ Make love on a train
☑ ~~Take a cooking class in a foreign country.~~ Get eaten out on a ledge while looking down onto the ocean!!!
☑ Learn to ski
☑ Stand under a waterfall

- ☑ Swim with the dolphins
- ☑ Sing a karaoke duet with a stranger
- ☑ Ride a gondola in Venice
- ☑ Travel the world
- ☑ Send a message in a bottle
- ☑ View a sunrise from a place where you can see the horizon
- ☑ Do something along the lines of exhibitionism
- ☑ Find my father
- ☑ Try kinky sex
- ☑ Fall helplessly in love

ANNY'S ANNALS

Aloha!

Hey, it's me again . . .

A lot has changed since I last wrote to you. When I returned to Belle Baie, Mommy asked if it was okay to lease the home I purchased for her for six months. Of course, I told her that she could. That's turned into a year's lease because she's still with Camila. I'm so glad she and Camila had time together to heal.

Anyhoo, I am back in Mauritius at Belle Baie. We couldn't shoot Romance Abroad *at Belle Baie last season because of all the last-minute changes and expenses that would be required, but they agreed to do it this season. We don't start shooting until a couple of weeks from now, but there's already been a surge in followers and subscribers. We're sure that the ratings will increase one hundredfold as well.*

Everyone wants to see the resort, and the Travel Channel will give the world an up close and personal view. I love Nazár for doing this. I keep checking with him, and he assures me he wants to do it.

Since we returned last year, he has found new and inventive ways to punish me because I'm always acting out. I know that he's figured out that I'm a little brat on purpose just for the excitement and the promise his punishments bring me. During the day, he's the sweetest gentleman, but at night, he tortures my body with pleasure, sexual stimulation, and pain. Then he denies me an orgasm.

Well, in a few hours, I will hit thirty-one, and only two items remain on my list: an act of exhibitionism and performing on a stage. I didn't get to complete them last year, but that's okay. I accomplished the most important one last year. I fell in love before my thirtieth birthday! While I wasn't with him when my birthday came in, I knew I loved him. I just didn't realize that the feeling was reciprocated.

Anyhoo, Mr. Dark and Kinky is waiting for me. He has surprise plans for my birthday. I can't wait to see what it is. I can only hope it includes an orgasm.

Until next time, Anny!

Nys 🧭

There's something so sensual about a woman kneeling before a man, knowing he has the power to dominate her, tame her wildest desires, and unleash her most primal passions.

That's how I feel kneeling before Nazár in this room of mirrors as he walks around me with the flogger in his hand. My nipples ache in the room's coolness, wanting to be sucked, licked, pulled, or some shit.

Bared to him in sacrifice, I know he can hear my nipples crying out, begging to be taken advantage of. If not, then he should be able to detect my scent. This leather crotchless thong is drenched with my juices, and my pussy throbs at the thought of being touched, licked, or, hopefully, fucked.

Nazár walks behind me, cups my chin, gently guides my head, and tells me, "Look into the mirror."

I do as he asks, careful not to meet his gaze.

"Do you like what you see, Princesa?"

Desire threads through me like a spider weaving a fine silk web.

Pushing that to the back of my mind, I concentrate on what's happening.

I'm on my knees with black stilettos, wearing nothing but the crotchless leather thong and the collar around my neck with the bell hanging from it. My curls are pulled up in a high ponytail with just a few tendrils escaping it, thanks to Nazár pulling them free earlier.

My chocolate nipples stand alert, painful as hell. Nazár stands behind me in black dress pants, wearing a white button-down dress shirt opened down to the first three buttons. He's still wearing his suit jacket from a business meeting earlier today, and his long hair is carelessly raked away from his face.

I long to touch the stubble along his jaw, but I know that I'll be punished if I touch him without permission.

We make a sexy pair, though. Me in all my dark beauty with a prideful, haughty, yet submissive spirit. And then there's him. There's *always* him.

"Yes, sir. I like what I see."

Who knew this type of shit would be a turn-on for me? But the evidence of my desire is dripping from the thong.

Nazár drags the flogger over my breasts. Its leather falls tickle my taut nipples.

"Do you know what turns me on, Princesa?"

"No, sir. I don't."

"I'm turned on by pain. Inflicting pain on others arouses me."

A thrill of excitement burns through me, even as fear chases its tail.

"Do you know why?"

"No, sir. I don't."

"Because pain in its finest form is actually pleasure. It allows the person in control to dictate where the play will go and the other person to yield to the controller's passions, desires, and whims. I will never disrespect you. I will always hear you. And I will never do anything you don't want me to."

"I know, sir."

"There's a saying that 'pleasure is at the brink of pain and submission.'"

"I haven't heard of that, sir."

"I can teach you better than I can tell you, Princesa."

A gasp escapes my throat, and I nod. "Teach me, sir."

"Are you sure that you're ready?"

"I am, sir."

Nazár kneels behind me, cupping my chin, and slowly brings his hand down my neck to grasp my collar. He tugs the chain just a little. Unprepared for its pull, I hitch forward slightly.

"Princesa!"

"I'm sorry, sir. I'll be ready next time."

"You should *always* be ready for whatever I bring to you," he corrects as he flicks the flogger against my thigh.

The sting feels nice. This time, though, I remain upright on my knees, staring ahead into one of the many mirrors in this room. I don't see the audience who sits in club chairs all around us in the dark as they each wait their turn to play out a scene.

This wing of BoDSMe is strictly for exhibitionistic scenes.

Nazár still holds the leash to my collar as he moves in front of me and stares down at me.

"So beautiful. A part of me wants to skip all the fun and move to being inside you. But the other part wants to hear you scream my name in pleasure and pain even more."

I inhale deeply, holding my breath and wishing that maybe he would. I want nothing more than to be impaled with his dick, pinned underneath his muscular body. Disappointment soars through me as he says, "But I like the tease and the game almost as much as the act, if not more so."

Nazár reaches a hand out to help me to my feet and leads me to the St. Andrews Cross, where he cuffs me. I wait in anticipation as he removes his tools and returns to me. The tickle of the rose slowly flicks my clit until he turns up the speed.

Nazár didn't secure my waist to the cross. My body unwittingly moves forward, hips thrusting out to feel more of the touch of the rose. Just as quickly as I move without his permission, Nazár spanks me with his crop that has the rubber paddle. It's more intense in impact play than the flogger or his regular crop.

"Ahh!" I hiss.

"Be still, my little wench!" he growls.

Alternating with the flogger and the crop, Nazár spanks my breasts, hips, and thighs until I'm sore. He takes little breaks to pat my pussy with his palm or tickle my clit with the rose until I'm on the verge of an orgasm, which, of course, he denies me. He found me playing a rather frisky game of volleyball on the nude beach without his permission earlier this week. At this point, I haven't had an orgasm in a week.

When he's finished, and I feel I can take no more, he uncuffs me and takes me to a pillow set up in the middle of the stage. Nazár positions me over it so that my ass and pussy are displayed for the entire audience.

Using a stainless-steel metal wand, he plugs up my ass while he uses a bullet on my core. Nazár's attentiveness to my pleasure is simultaneously stimulating and exhausting. I want nothing more than to come as he works over my body.

My flesh still stings in certain places from the impact of the rubber crop against my skin, and that pain only enhances the pleasure I feel as he plays with me. I'm his toy tonight, and there's nothing I like better.

When he's finished with me, Nazár finally unbuckles his pants, kneels behind me, and takes me roughly from behind. Lifting my upper torso from the pillow, he wraps one arm around my midsection, kisses my jaw, and continues pumping.

"You may come now, mi amor," he whispers.

He thrusts harder and pinches my nipple until I cry out in pain, and I release all over his shaft to the sound of an old grandfather clock at the opposite end of the room.

It strikes midnight, and the applause sounds behind us.

"Gracias, Dominio," I whisper.

"*De nada. Feliz cumpleaños*, Princesa."

He just helped me check off the last two items on my list: an act of exhibitionism and performing on a stage. My list is complete, but perhaps the greatest part is that I fell helplessly head over heels in love with this man.

Happy birthday to me!

THE END

ABUSE HOTLINE

According to the National Coalition Against Domestic Violence (NCADV), twenty people per minute are abused by an intimate partner in the United States. One in four women and one in nine men experience severe violence at the hands of an intimate partner.

One in five children is exposed to domestic violence each year, and 90 percent are eyewitnesses.

If you are experiencing domestic violence, please dial the national domestic violence hotline at 1-800-799-7233.

ABOUT THE AUTHOR

Cassie Verano pens romance for readers of all cultures and backgrounds. Her love of romance is borne from the beauty and joy she sees in the relationships around her. She enjoys creating fiction about women discovering true love and women who aren't afraid to explore their sexuality.

As a professional administrator, she dreamed of the day she could toss her paperwork aside and craft stories that inspired love and romance in women's hearts worldwide. As a wife and mother, she enjoys playing quirky games and singing with her family.

This Southern belle is a native Georgia Peach who enjoys reading, writing, and trying different cuisines from around the world. On rainy days, she can be found cuddling under a blanket with a good mystery book or watching a romance movie on Hallmark or LMN.

Cassie is the other half of the dynamic duo podcast *Cozy Sips with C.a.T.* with her cohost Tiye Love. They interview other authors about books, life, love, and sex. Their show airs every other Tuesday at 7:00 p.m. CST/8:00 p.m. EST. Catch it on YouTube (https://www.youtube.com/@C.a.T.cozysips) or Facebook (https://www.facebook.com/CozySips).

Connect with Cassie via email to find out how to join her newsletter. You'll receive news and updates about new releases, upcoming projects, giveaways, teasers, sales, and much more when you join her mailing list:

Email: cassiepensromance@gmail.com
Like: Facebook
Website: http://www.cassieverano.com/

JOIN MY MAILING LIST

Stay connected and get updates on new releases, upcoming projects, giveaways, teasers, sales, and much more when you join my mailing list: **https://dl.bookfunnel.com/xi6niycktl.**

If you haven't read the short story *Elevated Seduction* in the Simply Seductive series, you can grab your free copy by signing up for the newsletter above.

JOIN MY PATREON:

For exclusive access to Patreon-only stories, giveaways, first peeks at upcoming releases, cover reveals, and so much more, join my Patreon page: **https://www.patreon.com/CassieVerano**

JOIN THE DRIP

For monthly author takeovers, games, and chatting about my books, join my Facebook group, The Drip.

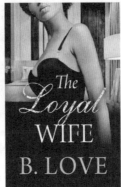

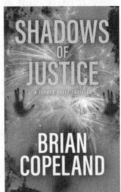
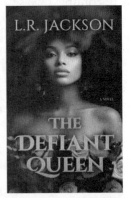

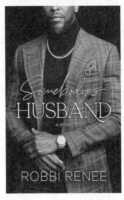